Chemistry

JESSICA SITOMER

Greenlight Publishing
Las Vegas

Chemistry – *Jessica Sitomer*

Chemistry – *Jessica Sitomer*

Chemistry is a work of fiction. Names, characters, businesses, brands, organizations, places, events, and incidents either are the product of the author's imagination or are used fictitiously.
No part of this publication may be reproduced, stored in retrieval system, or transmitted in any form or by any means, electronic, mechanical, photocopying, recording, or otherwise, without written permission of the publisher.
All rights reserved.
©2024 Jessica Sitomer
Cover design by Kathy Hoffman, ©2024
ISBN- 979-8-9917973-1-3

For more information about Jessica Sitomer, please visit:
JessicaSitomer.com

Table of Contents

Dedication 6
Acknowledgments 7
Chapter 1 9
Chapter 2 23
Chapter 3 43
Chapter 4 59
Chapter 5 77
Chapter 6 101
Chapter 7 111
Chapter 8 135
Chapter 9 171
Chapter 10 187
Chapter 11 215
Chapter 12 251
Chapter 13 271
Chapter 14 291
Chapter 15 319
Chapter 16 345
Chapter 17 351
Chapter 18 361

Chapter 19 367
Chapter 20 383
Chapter 21 401
Chapter 22 407
Chapter 23 421
Chapter 24 429
About the Author 431
Book club discussion questions for Chemistry 433

Dedication

To my loving, supportive parents, who have been married for 61 years. Your love story has always been an inspiration, even now, as you lose each other.

Chemistry was a screenplay I wrote in the 1990s. I developed it into a book in 2024, four years into my journey as a caretaker for my parents. Both patients of the Cleveland Clinic, Lou Ruvo Center for Brain Health, watching them lose their memory has been the most painful journey of my life. Waking up to write this book at 6 am every morning before work brought me so much joy.

This book is dedicated to you, the reader, hoping that whatever you are going through in life, it allows you to immerse yourself, if only for a few hours, into a magical world that makes you smile, cry, and laugh.

With so much love,
Jessica

Acknowledgments

Thank you to my very best friend, Kathy Hoffman. I can write a book, but writing the words to thank you for who you are to me is impossible. I'll go with our classic... you are the Frankie to my Grace!

To my sister, who waited for true love... it was worth it!

Thank you to Kathy, Kimberly, Patricia, and Heather for reading and encouraging me along my book journey.

To the actor friends, writing group readers, literary managers, movie producers, and all the people who have loved these characters since they were in screenplay form in the 1990s...

The story is finally told... yippeeeeeeee!

Chemistry – *Jessica Sitomer*

Chapter 1

The cabin on Flight JR718 buzzes with the usual hum of passengers, soft clinks of drink carts, and muffled snores. A young girl and her mother sit in the back of the plane, close to the bathroom. Emela, a 12-year-old cello prodigy with bright eyes reflecting an insatiable curiosity and deep intelligence, is a rare pre-teen who is always humble and kind. Emela's mom, tears forming in her eyes, watches her daughter look out the window at the night sky. She is filled with pride as she pulls her bag out from under the seat, her hand searching. This catches Emela's attention.

"Do you have any gum?" Emela turns to ask when she notices her mom's tears. "Mom, what's wrong?"

"Tears of joy, my Little Monkey." She pulls a small Tiffany box from her bag and hands it to her daughter. "Your father would have been so proud. I know I am."

"Mom." The single word encapsulates, "You can't afford this, but I can't wait to open it." Savoring the moment, Emela slowly opens the box to discover a sterling silver apple charm on a chain.

"It's for the Big Apple," her mom beams, "They didn't have a cello or a music note."

"It's perfect, Mom. I love it."

"Put it on," her mom insists.

"I want my performance at Carnegie Hall to be the first time I wear it," Emela says. Her mom smiles and nods in agreement as Emela hugs her as big as possible with their tight seatbelts. They are interrupted when the plane drops with a sudden jolt. For a heart-stopping moment, Emela's stomach lurches into her throat as gravity seems to abandon her. As quickly as it happened, the plane levels, but now, an uneasy silence has settled over the rows of seats, broken only by the occasional cough or the rustling of a newspaper. The overhead lights flicker, casting an odd, dim glow.

The flight attendants, who had been handing out snacks just minutes ago, are now moving with a controlled urgency, their smiles tight and eyes darting toward the cockpit. One of them, a tall woman with her hair pulled back into a neat bun, grips the armrest of a nearby seat as the plane shudders. It's as if the aircraft has momentarily lost its balance.

Once comforting and warm, the smell of coffee now seems out of place, mingling with the sharper scent of metal and something burnt. A baby in the middle of the cabin wails, piercing the tense quiet. The mother, her face pale, tries to soothe the child, her hands trembling as she fumbles with a pacifier.

The passengers, who had been absorbed in their worlds, are now glancing at each other, seeking reassurance in the eyes of strangers. A businessman in an aisle seat clutches his briefcase a little tighter while the elderly couple in the row ahead hold hands, their knuckles white. The overhead compartments rattle as the plane shivers again, the vibration running through the metal like a nervous tremor.

A low, almost imperceptible whine begins to build, starting somewhere deep within the belly of the plane. It isn't loud but carries a strange, unsettling resonance that seems to pulsate in the passengers' bones. The captain's voice crackles over the intercom, calm but with an edge that suggests this is not just turbulence. "Ladies and gentlemen, we're experiencing some mechanical issues. Please remain seated and keep your seatbelts fastened."

The announcement does little to ease the tension as the cabin starts to tremble violently, the overhead bins rattling as if they might burst open at any moment. Once a steady backdrop, the hum of the engines has turned into a desperate roar.

The flight attendants strap themselves into their jump seats, their faces pale and drawn. A sudden, sharp drop sends a ripple of panic through the cabin. Luggage thuds against the compartments, and a few overhead bins pop open, spewing bags into the aisle. People gasp, some crying out in fear, while others clench their armrests, faces frozen in terror. The plane jerks with a sudden, violent shudder, throwing Emela against her seat. Her breath quickens as she turns to her mother, heart pounding in her chest. The sounds around them, creaking metal, frantic voices, and the high-pitched wind wail fade into the background as their eyes meet.

"Monkey, I—" Her mother's voice breaks, the words caught in her throat.

Emela's hand finds her mom's, fingers trembling but gripping with an unexpected strength. Her skin's warmth and familiar softness feel like an

Chemistry – *Jessica Sitomer*

anchor in the chaos. Emela tightens her hold, her own hands damp with sweat.

"I love you," Emela whispers, her breath shaky but determined. She squeezes her mom's hand, harder this time, as if willing her words to be enough to protect her. Tears brim in her mother's eyes, but Emela smiles, placing her other hand on her mother's chest. She takes a deep breath and encourages her mom to do the same. They breathe deeply in unison, never losing their eye contact.

The low hum of the oxygen masks deploying snaps Emela out of the moment, the cold rubber thumping against her chest. But even as she reaches for it, her eyes never leave her mother's. Emela grabs hers with trembling hands, her gaze locked on her mother's as the plane tilts again.

Then, everything goes quiet.

The sound of servers singing 'Happy Birthday' to a special guest inside Bacchus, the hottest new restaurant in Manhattan, fills the space with joy. The staff maneuvers easily through the bustling crowd, working tirelessly to ensure every guest's experience is exemplary. The ambiance is electric.

In his late thirties, Matt Durand, dressed in an impeccable suit, admires his concept for the restaurant. It is understated and contemporary, using minimalistic elements with subtle nods to wine culture. The main dining area features simple, well-designed furniture with clean lines, such as streamlined tables and comfortable, minimalist chairs in charcoal gray and white. Oversized, frameless windows allow natural light to flood the space, providing a sense of openness.

He walks toward the bar, the focal point with a long, smooth, black marble top. His hand brushes over an empty barstool. The seat is made from authentic cork material, providing a tactile and organic feel. Using natural materials and simple lines, maintain the sleek and modern look while adding a touch of whimsy and wine-inspired elegance. A backlit wine wall showcases a curated selection of bottles and top-shelf alcohol. The bar area is lit by pendant lights revealed through oversized wine glasses hung from their stems. Polished concrete floors, black marble, glass, and metal accents create a sleek and modern atmosphere.

Chemistry – *Jessica Sitomer*

Matt dims the lighting ever so slightly and then catches up to Eli, a server whose passion for life borders the edge of folly. Matt's discerning eye catches a detail that needs correction on a plate Eli is delivering. With a swipe of a napkin, a streak of sauce is removed.

"Is Josh here yet?" Matt asks. Eli says no with a pained expression that propels Matt toward the kitchen.

The kitchen of Bacchus is a storm of activity, but not the controlled, synchronized ballet it usually is. Tonight, it is chaos. The gleaming stainless-steel counters, usually spotless and orderly, are cluttered with half-prepped ingredients, stray utensils, and pots threatening to boil over. The hiss of pans and the clang of metal are louder than usual, underscored by the frantic shouts of the kitchen staff.

The sous-chef tries to keep everything from falling apart, but his face wears a stress mask. He wipes sweat from his brow with the back of his hand, leaving a streak of flour across his forehead. A line cook needs help with three pans at a time. One catches on the edge of the burner and tips, spilling hot butter across the stove and sending up a plume of smoke. Matt takes it all in as the staff realize he's there.

"Let's take a breath and focus!" Matt says, grabbing a towel and quickly wiping up the mess. There's a buttery scent mixed with the acrid smell of something burning nearby. Matt glances over as the pastry Chef frantically tries to salvage the soufflés, but it's too late. The delicate tops collapse, leaving each ramekin a sad, sunken disaster.

"Those are done. Move on," Matt orders, his tone sharp but kind.

The expeditor, ordinarily the storm's calm eye, struggles to keep up with the tickets. They come in faster than she can read, and orders pile up on the counter. Plates that should have been pristine are marred by hasty sauce smudges or garnished incorrectly in the rush to get them out the door. A filet mignon that should have been rare is closer to well-done, and the pasta, meant to be al dente, is limp from overcooking.

Where the hell is Joshua? Matt's thought strikes hard, bitter. The noise of the kitchen feels louder than ever, pots clanging, orders being shouted, the rush of service pulling him in every direction at once. Matt closes his eyes for a brief second, trying to block it out, to focus. But the weight of it all is too much.

"Everyone, stop," Matt says as Eli enters the kitchen. "Eli, tell the guests we'd like to interrupt their meal for a surprise tasting of our Château Margaux." The door swings open, and Joshua walks in. No apology, no explanation, just a smug grin as if he hadn't abandoned them in the middle of a storm.

Matt's fingers curl into fists by his sides. He wants to shout and demand answers but swallows the urge. The staff doesn't care about his drama. They need stable leadership. Keep it together, he tells himself, forcing his feet to stay rooted in place instead of storming over to Joshua. The last thing I need is a scene.

But inside, the anger is clawing at him, threatening to break loose. He's done this too many times. Joshua thinks his charm and charisma can solve every problem, and maybe it works with the customers, but Matt is the one left holding the pieces when things fall apart. Does he even care? Or is this just a game to him?

"Who's giving away three-thousand-dollar bottles of wine?" Joshua jokes. Matt's cocky young chef stands in the kitchen with a stunning groupie on his arm. Joshua was the fifth runner-up on the third season of the reality show Chef's Delight, where he flirted and charmed his way with the judges, past several chefs who outcooked him. His boyish good looks and charismatic personality won him the fan favorite despite his dishes being a delight to the eyes but lacking in flavor.

Servers hover, waiting for their orders, their faces a mix of impatience and concern.

"Where's the damn wine?" Joshua yells, spinning around to see Eli standing paralyzed by the door, "The guests don't want it from him. They want it from me!" Joshua strips the bottle from Eli's hands and exits the kitchen. All eyes are on Matt.

"Okay, let's get it together." Matt says, "The clock is ticking." The orders keep coming. Matt feels the weight of the night pressing down on him, each ticket a reminder that they are in the weeds, deep in it, and there is no easy way out.

He grits his teeth, rallying the team loudly, "Come on! We're not going down tonight!" The team moves with precision, regaining confidence with each passing moment.

Twenty minutes later, Joshua walks back into the kitchen. "Wine has been served, selfies have been taken with the Chef, and guests are enamored." Matt

Chemistry – *Jessica Sitomer*

struggles to hold his tongue as Joshua grabs the spatula from Matt and instructs him to go back to the front of the house, where he belongs. As Matt walks out, he hears Joshua say, "I'm two hours late, and the place falls apart. What's wrong with you people?"

Chop, chop, chop, chop, chop, chop. The rhythm of skilled knife work dicing an heirloom pepper into uniform pieces stops on the wood cutting board. Matt's manicured fingers pluck a piece of pepper and toss it into his mouth. The five o'clock shadow on his dimpled chin accentuates the jawline that chews the vegetable. He nods, eats another piece, then opens the garbage and throws the rest away. Matt stands in his starched white dress shirt, sleeves rolled up, two top buttons undone, takes one last look at his handy work, and closes the garbage disguised as a cabinet.

He makes his way through his upper west side brownstone apartment, picking up dog toys and dropping them in a basket upon arriving in his bedroom. Lola, a 200-pound English Mastiff, pops her head up. Matt scratches her behind the ears, turns on his TV, and goes into the bathroom for a shower. Lola lumbers off the bed and removes almost every toy from the basket.

Matt puts his suit pieces into a dry cleaner bag and enters his shower. For a few moments, he hears nothing but the water, smells only the freshness of the soap, and allows the steaming hot water to pound on his back.

When he's done, he puts his razor back in place, squeegees the glass, and ensures the shampoo and conditioner caps are closed.

Wrapping himself in a towel, he takes a few steps to his sink. From the bedroom, he hears the TV. "Survivors from Flight JR718 are being treated at Ellenville Regional Hospital while more severe cases have been medevacked to Albany Medical Center," an early morning news anchor delivers grim tidings, her voice laden with sorrow, "The plane crashed yesterday at 9:30 pm in a remote area of the Catskill Mountains on its way to JFK. Approximately 160 people, including passengers and crew, were on the aircraft. Around 100 people died on impact, among them, a young cellist on her way to her first performance at Carnegie Hall." On the television, the screen displays the mournful visage of Emela, her promising future cut short.

Matt ignores the TV as he meticulously brushes his teeth. His low-riding pajama bottoms reveal the toned torso of a guy who eats well but doesn't make the time to work out. More disturbing photos flash on his television screen as he glances over, rinses off his toothbrush, places it in its holder, and then takes a shot of mouthwash.

As he swishes from cheek to cheek, he evaluates himself in the mirror, pulling one bloodshot eye down and pushing it back up, checking his hairline to confirm it's not receding, and spits. He grabs a light blue T-shirt from his towel rack, puts it on, and exhales sharply as he leaves. With a sudden stop, he moves one of his high-end grooming products to align with the others, neatly arranged on a silver tray.

The flicker of the television softly illuminates his bedroom as the young cellist's music teacher is interviewed. Photos of the girl as a baby with her first violin turn into a photo montage of her growing up, starting with pictures of her with both mother and father and finishing with a photo of her hugging her mom.

Chemistry – *Jessica Sitomer*

Matt sits on the edge of his luxurious king-size bed, a testament to comfort and design. The crisp, white linens with a thread count that could rival any five-star hotel beckon him as he removes his watch and places it on his nightstand next to a white echo dot that reads 4:38 a.m. The lack of throw pillows gives away his bachelor status as he pulls back the thin grey comforter and slides under the sheets.

The final photo in the montage is from the day's crash, a morbid picture of the smashed cello amongst the charred luggage. Matt sighs heavily, reaches for the remote, and with a firm click, silences the TV. Exhausted and drained, he closes his eyes.

Chapter 2

"Next," a woman's voice calls out in the busy world of Eternity, a place suspended beyond the boundaries of time and space, a vision of unparalleled beauty. The air shimmers with an otherworldly luminescence, casting an ethereal glow upon the landscape. Modern skyscrapers of crystalline glass rise toward the clouds. These towers are not anchored but float gracefully above the enchanted ground, creating a breathtaking cityscape as fluid as it is awe-inspiring.

Amid the city's majestic architecture, enchanting gardens bloom with flora unknown to the mortal realm. Waterfalls of liquid stardust cascade from mid-air rock formations, pouring their effervescent streams into sparkling pools where unknown species resembling fish and other creatures play. At a precise time of day, when the light is just right, diamond-shaped mirrors appear in the falls. Each mirror is a memory of the soul who sees it from their life on Earth.

The largest tower houses Eternity's Hospitality Lobby. The atmosphere resembles that of a luxury resort's check-in area. Its wall-to-wall desk is the focal point, made of a brushed metal base with a thick light green glass countertop comprised of what looks like a NASA control room panel. Busy Greeters dressed in modern powder grey spa attendant uniforms serve the many lines of the "newly deceased." They press buttons and give directions. In the background, a service message plays on a loop. "Welcome to Eternity. Please check in to find your next destination."

An older woman of 92, with a slight hunchback, shuffles toward the check-in desk. "Is this Heaven?" she inquires, looking wide-eyed at the floor-to-ceiling windows, seeing the green rolling hills and unidentifiable, though beautiful trees.

With a hint of amusement, a Greeter responds, "How would you know if it is?"

The older woman chuckles as she looks around, not seeing what she expected: "I'd imagined Heaven as a tropical island with sexy young cabana boys."

The Greeter smiles, presses a few buttons, then points to a row of doors behind her. "Door number five," she says.

The people in line watch as the older woman shuffles to Door 5, opens it and gasps as she steps onto a pristine sandy beach. The smell of salt water and the sounds of ocean waves fill the lobby as the woman disappears into a bright light. The door closes behind her, leaving only the sound of a vacuum seal.

"Next," the Greeter calls with practiced efficiency. Excited after what he just witnessed, an overweight movie producer in his fifties approaches the desk, his eyes gleaming with anticipation.

"Heaven for me is the Playboy Mansion, 1994," he declares.

The Greeter, less enthusiastic this time, responds, "I know, which is why you still have life lessons to learn. See that door that says 'Reincarnation?'"

The producer groans, "Not again!" Two workers each take one of his arms and drag him toward the indicated door.

Emela is watching all the action. She is next to the desk but looks uncertain about taking a step forward. A woman who's had bad plastic surgery from head to toe pushes the young girl aside.

"I've waited long enough," she complains.

The Greeter, unphased, says, "I believe the young lady behind you is first." She smiles at Emela as the irritated woman steps aside in a huff. The Greeter encourages Emela to step forward.

"Ah, young lady, we've been awaiting your arrival!" The Greeter claps her hands, startling Emela and attracting the attention of other Greeters, who whisper to each other as excitement builds behind the desk. Suspicion wells up in the young girl's eyes.

"I know what you're thinking, and no, we had nothing to do with the plane crash," the Greeter reassures her. "But it did happen, and here you are a 'prodigy.'" She squeals.

With confusion, Emela listens as the Greeter continues. "I'm sorry I'm gushing, but you're the first one I've ever checked in. Life prodigies are rare, only coming around every few decades."

"Wait. Am I dead?" Emela asks, growing anxious, "Where's my mom?"

"Not to worry, she and your dad are together, and they are very proud of you." Emela doesn't look relieved, so the Greeter continues, "In fact, in their 'heaven,' you're there with them."

"So, I am dead," Emela confirms, on the verge of freaking out.

"Yes, but these feelings you're experiencing won't last long because you'll be joining us here," the Greeter hands Emela a substantial textbook. "You'll be called Inspiration and working in our Dream Division, which is matchmaking for mortals on Earth. It's our most important department."

Greeters on both sides of her gasp as the excited greeter blushes and looks up and around as if being watched. She leans over the counter towards the young girl and loudly whispers, "But when you meet Mother Nature, don't tell her I said that the Climate Division is equal," she looks up again as if checking for spies, "If not more important." The surrounding greeters nod and go back to their work.

"Gosh," the Greeter says, "I wish I could spend more time with you, show you around, get to know you." The Greeter to her right clears his throat. "Right, well, everything you need to know is in that book, so read up."

Emela looks down at the heavy textbook, her mind racing. She turns and looks at the sea of people, unsure where to go, then back to the Greeter, "What the fu—"

"Oh, you look terrified," the Greeter interrupts, then picks up a megaphone and blares, "I need a tour guide at counter 18." She turns back to Emela, "You'll be reporting to Chemistry. Can't miss her—glasses, tight bun, no-nonsense personality... you get used to her," the Greeter looks beyond Emela, "Next!"

The impatient woman once again pushes the young girl aside and steps up to the Greeter, who points to the reincarnation door without a word. The woman's hands go up as if she can't catch a break.

A tour guide taps the young girl on her shoulder, "Inspiration?" she asks with a high-pitched nasal voice. "Come with me," says the petite middle-aged woman with hair in a French twist and a navy dress that only a flight attendant from the 1950s would wear. The woman's high heels click and clack as her short legs move so fast that Emela must race to keep up.

"Stop! I'm not going anywhere with you! This is a dream! I want my mom!" Emela pinches herself frantically, trying to wake up. The woman pulls out a high-tech walkie and speaks into it.

Chemistry – *Jessica Sitomer*

"Chemistry, your newbie is here. I'm going to need some assistance from Empathy. Can you spare her?" Through the walkie-talkie, a voice says that she's on her way.

Emela walks toward a glass window, looking outside at the waterfalls. She doesn't even realize she's stopped and stares in amazement at the trees and unusual animals when she hears the tour guide shout, "Keep up, Missy."

"This is just a dream," Emela continues to tell herself.

"Excuse me," a voice says from behind her. Emela turns to see a striking woman in her seventies. She has a distinguished presence, with expressive blue eyes and a strong, yet graceful, bone structure. Her hair is long and bright silver. She wears a lab coat with the name Empathy embroidered on it. "You must be Inspiration."

"Emela!" Emela insists.

"Shhhhhhhh!" the tour guide snaps, "We don't use mortal names here!"

"I'm Empathy," the woman shares, "I arrived at 73, and it doesn't matter how old you are. This is just strange, right?" Emela, staring like a stray kitten backed into a corner, nods at the woman.

Chemistry – *Jessica Sitomer*

Empathy waves to a couch a few feet away, "Would you like to sit down and get your bearings?"

The tour guide clears her throat, insisting she speed it up. As if to spite the tour guide, Emela plops down to the couch. Empathy sits next to her. "Eternity is an amazing place. All your mortal emotions, like your fear, will be gone in about," she gently puts her hand on Emela's, who instantly relaxes, "Maybe now?" Emela's state has changed to curiosity. "I've been where you are, Inspiration." There is no back talk, only ethereal understanding. Empathy continues, "Everyone here has. Your most significant work is just beginning. Would it be okay if I returned to work and you continued your tour?"

Inspiration nods as she rises along with Empathy, who encourages her to catch up with the tour guide. Though accepting her current situation, the tour guide still bugs her.

When they enter the first door, Inspiration looks inside and sees people in blue scrubs walking with test tubes and Petri dishes. Above her, a sign reads Epidemiology Division.

"Diseases and cures. Not my favorite division," the tour guide admits as she continues rapidly. Next, on the left door, it reads Holiday Division. "Now that's a fun one."

Chemistry – *Jessica Sitomer*

Another door leads to the Hedonism Division. Inspiration hears a high-pitched gasp and looks in, but before she can see anything, the tour guide pulls her away by the wrist, "Sorry, kid, 21 and over."

Inspiration's eyes widen when the sign next door says "Men in Black Division." The tour guide smiles, "Yep, Aliens are real." This time, Inspiration speeds up ahead.

"Where do I sleep?" Inspiration asks.

"We don't need sleep," the tour guide answers.

"Food?" Inspiration inquires.

"Not necessary, but if a certain meal stimulates your inspirational process, there's an oven that can cook anything on the third floor."

"What if ice cream stimulates me?" Inspiration challenges.

The tour guide stops and turns to Inspiration, who almost walks into her. Her answer is a mixture of irritation and sarcasm, "Well, obviously, if there's a magical oven that cooks anything, it is safe to assume there's a creamery around here somewhere... but as I stated, food is not necessary." She turns on her heels and continues ahead.

Inspiration, feeling overwhelmed, refuses to move and calls to the woman, "What if I need some privacy or to sit somewhere to... I don't know... Read this humongous book. Maybe relax somewhere without sleep... or is there a TV? Or musical instruments, since my cello was probably smashed... somewhere to get away from this weird day-spa music and the insanity that has just become my life!"

"Well, your death, but yes, you have an assigned room custom-designed for you." She returns to Inspiration and pulls a room key from the textbook's jacket. "This will get you into your space on floor 33, room 1111."

"That's my favorite number!" Inspiration rejoices. The tour guide can't help but slip back into her sarcastic persona.

"Yes, dear, that's why it was chosen. And before your mind gets blown, spoiler alert, there's a cello in your room and a poster of Noah Schnap and one of Lola Tung. Apparently, you're the only preteen girl who is not a Swiftie."

"Can you take me there now?" Inspiration begs.

"Nope, because we are here," The tour guide says. She gestures above to the door that reads "Dream Division." Inspiration opens a crack and peeks in.

Chemistry – *Jessica Sitomer*

In Chemistry's office, a modern and spacious domain, Empathy sits amongst fourteen managers in uncomfortable folding chairs in front of a big desk. They wear white lab coats, each embroidered with names like Confidence, Humor, and Sensuality. Large QLED monitors adorn one wall, creating a mosaic of people's dreams. Lust, a 1960s Frat boy, roams from monitor to monitor.

"Erotic dream on monitor 12! No one interrupts me!" Lust ogles the monitor.

The office's steel elevator door opens, and a woman emerges, an uptight and focused chemist. Dressed in a tailored white lab coat that accentuates her figure and immaculate white sneakers, she exudes intellectual precision. Her classic, black-rimmed glasses add an element of seriousness, as does her tight bun with a sharpened pencil, which she pulls out to mark on a clipboard. As indicated by the black embroidered name on her lab coat, Chemistry is an enigmatic, Type A, and by-the-book girl. She beelines for her chair, taking her place behind the desk. She retrieves a file and stamps it "COMPLETE," sliding it into a slot in the wall.

"I had to finish that one myself," Chemistry remarks. "That's terribly inefficient and simply unacceptable." Chemistry notices Lust as he continues to gawk at the dream. "We're having a staff meeting, Lust. Care to join us?"

Lust reluctantly tears himself away as he puts on his lab coat and takes a seat.

Chemistry turns her attention back to her files.

"So, what's done?" she inquires, directing her gaze at Humor.

"The Adams and Jones match," Humor, a neurotic Catskills comedian, responds. "What a disaster. Kidding! Done. Tough crowd..."

Confidence, a petite cheerleader with big metal braces and uneven pigtails, can't hide her excitement.

"Chemistry, I was great! You should have seen Rothman when I matched her. She just glowed!"

"I don't need to know details, Confidence, just that it's done," Chemistry replies. "Anyone else?" The managers squirm in their seats.

From the safety of the doorway, Inspiration realizes that Chemistry is more intimidating than described. She slowly pushes the heavy door open, stepping in as a chute above Chemistry's desk opens, and a pile of files drops into a bin. Empathy gives Inspiration a small wave. Inspiration returns the wave and smiles.

Chemistry – *Jessica Sitomer*

"Good thing I've hired a new manager to increase productivity," Chemistry says. All eyes turn to Inspiration as she enters the room.

"Everyone, this is Inspiration," Chemistry motions and points for her to take a seat. "She will be heading up section 19. I believe a little inspiration is just what this division needs."

Lust can't resist making a suggestive comment. "Little is right—but cute."

"And young," adds Humor, "Kidding! Wait... no, I'm not."

"Okay, everyone back to work," Chemistry instructs. Her staff jump up, leaving Inspiration behind. The young girl waits for instruction, but none comes. Chemistry is engrossed in another file.

"Excuse me," Inspiration says, "did you say I'm heading up a section?"

Chemistry, startled by the young girl's presence, looks up. "Yes, 19, go go go," she waves her off.

"I don't..." Inspiration chooses her words, "Shouldn't I get some sort of orientation or something?"

Chemistry sighs. "Didn't you get briefed?"

"I don't think so," Inspiration says. "I mean, they told me my name is now Inspiration, gave me this ginormous textbook, and walked me down the hall. I thought I saw Marie Curie in scrubs."

"You did. She took over the Disease Division in 1934. Whenever I want to scream because we are so far behind, I think of how overwhelmed poor Marie is." Chemistry shakes her head. "Speaking of overwhelm," she grabs the textbook from Inspiration, "You don't have time to read this. I need you to work now. Follow me." Chemistry picks up a folder marked Matt Durand and heads back to the elevator. "Come on," Chemistry insists as Inspiration, two steps behind her, slips in before the doors close.

When the elevator door opens Chemistry and Inspiration see Matt in an empty stairwell, the echo of his racing heart pounds in his ears. An unseen adversary pursues him, his bare feet banging on the steps like a drumbeat of impending doom. One flight, two flights, three flights. He keeps climbing, each step a testament to his determination, sweat pouring from his forehead and staining the armpits of the light blue t-shirt that now clings to his body like a second skin.

As he sees the Exit sign on the 14th floor, he lunges at the door, slamming his hand on the exit bar, only to find the door locked. Panic surges within him as he looks out a window, revealing a dirty alley 14 stories below with cracked cement and broken bottles, overflowing garbage bins, and rats the size of a watermelon that are ironically eating a watermelon. Matt turns away from the window, his back against the wall, realizing there is no escape. Fear grips him as he keeps his eyes fixed on the stairs, waiting for the unknown pursuer to catch up.

At the bottom of the stairwell, Chemistry checks her watch and mutters to herself, then glances around the stairs with exasperation.

"Where is she?" Chemistry wonders aloud.

"Where is who?" Inspiration asks.

"Style, she's the lead on this case." With an imperious wave of Chemistry's hand, a pack of ferocious Dobermans ascend the stairs.

"Whoa!" Inspiration jumps, "Where did they come from?"

"Follow me," Chemistry drones, "We'll cut her off at the next spot.

Chemistry – *Jessica Sitomer*

Still evaluating the situation, Matt decides he is no longer in danger. Just as he is about to retreat down the stairs, he hears the dogs' barking and panting grow closer. Within moments, their snarling jaws are in Matt's sights. Fear grips him once again, and he has no choice but to open the window and jump.

Matt plummets toward the unforgiving pavement, his mouth and eyes wide open in sheer terror, yet his throat unable to release a scream. He braces himself for what is sure to be a life-ending crash when he bounces upon impact, landing on his feet.

Bewildered and shaken, he glances back up at the window where the dogs continue to bark, their mouths foaming. Matt doesn't understand what has just happened, but unfamiliar with his surroundings, he looks for a safe place to regain his composure.

Matt sees a sliver of light through the darkness, where a door is barely propped open. With newfound determination, he bursts into what turns out to be a culinary school, disrupting a class in progress. Students in aprons beat eggs as Matt sees the ominous words "Surprise Quiz- Souffle" written on the blackboard. The startled cooks turn their attention toward him. Matt's eyes widen in embarrassment as he realizes he is completely naked. His jaw drops as he stands full frontal, wondering if he is being pranked.

Another woman wearing a lab coat materializes in the culinary kitchen. Her name is embroidered on her coat pocket in fuchsia stitching: STYLE.

Style is a gorgeous, full-figured woman with a penchant for high-end fashion. She wears her hair braided, covered in a wide-brimmed statement hat, chunky bold-colored jewelry, a Gucci belt that sinches her lab coat at her 40-inch waist, and her nails are adorned with rhinestones that add a touch of glamour and luxury. Her Gucci sneakers juxtapose the white sneakers Chemistry had been wearing earlier. She spots Matt immediately.

"There you are." Style walks to him, but Matt and everyone else in the classroom don't appear to see her. Chemistry, concealed by a door, scribbles something on her clipboard. Inspiration stays hidden behind her. Style pulls Matt toward an unassuming, mousy Chef who is engrossed in her lecture on souffles, utterly oblivious to what her students see. Style maneuvers Matt and the culinary teacher into an awkward face-off. The shocked woman tilts her head, gives Matt a once-over, and then smiles as Style produces a Louis Vuitton clutch. Chemistry, still hidden, clears her throat, startling Style.

"Chemistry! What are you doing here?" Style asks defensively. Inspiration stays behind the door, watching.

"Let's just get this done," replies Chemistry. She takes a small bottle from her pocket and applies its contents to Matt's hand, causing green beads of sweat to rise from his palms.

Style reaches into her clutch and retrieves a small jar containing a single plastic butterfly. As she opens it, a swarm of turquoise-winged butterflies magically emerge, flutter, and disappear into the culinary teacher's stomach. Inspiration's eyes widen both at the magic and seeing her first naked man.

Style wipes her hands with satisfaction and smiles at Chemistry, but Chemistry remains focused on her clipboard.

"It took you six minutes to find the classroom, and you hadn't even found Mr. Durand yet," Chemistry said, glancing at Matt, holding her clipboard in front of his privates. With a shudder, she says, "I hate it when they're naked."

Chemistry – *Jessica Sitomer*

Style waves her hand, and a pair of boxer shorts appear on Matt, bearing the words 'Lucky You.' Style can't help but notice Chemistry's attempt to hide a smile.

"Let's go. His alarm is about to wake him up," Chemistry instructs.

"How do you know?" Style asks.

Chemistry raises an eyebrow, and just as she does, a blaring alarm echoes through the room. Everything around them vanishes, leaving Chemistry, Style, and Inspiration standing alone in a white space, facing a massive steel elevator door.

Style resigns as she presses the elevator button going down." Because you know everything," then startled as she turns back, "Who's she?"

"Inspiration," the young girl answers with a new sense of purpose.

"She'll be heading up section 19, which you would have known if you were at the meeting."

Inspiration tries to break the tension, "Will we be seeing more naked guys?"

"This just happened?" Style asks Chemistry, who nods yes, "And you were how old?" she asks Inspiration.

"Twelve," Inspiration says.

"You have no sense of fashion," Style says, looking at the girl.

"Oo! You're quoting Devil Wears Prada!" Inspiration cheers.

"No, they quoted me," Style retorts as the elevator door opens and Inspiration follows the two women out.

Chapter 3

Bacchus is fully booked this Saturday night, but Matt's face twists with displeasure. Eli stops in front of him with two plates of the evening special.

"Everything okay, Boss?"

"Are you delivering those to Josh?" Matt asks as he stares at the window table where Joshua is dining with a young woman.

"Yup, she came in for the special," Eli replies, "I'm sure it will be great for her blog. She always says the nicest things about us."

A stunning model sashays by, bearing a striking resemblance to the culinary teacher from Matt's dream. She mouths a friendly "hi" to Matt and subtly touches her stomach to quell the butterflies she's feeling. But Matt focuses on Eli's plates as he rearranges a rosemary sprig, oblivious to her presence. Disheartened, the model continues to the bar.

Eli seizes the moment to impart some wisdom, "We are too busy to see what's in front of us, and then too soon, it's gone, though not the ache that it leaves behind," he quotes.

"You're overusing that one, Eli. Don't tell me," Matt searches his memory, "Ana de Gournay."

"Correct!" Eli replies. "Repetition is the mother of learning, Zig Ziglar."

Matt glances back toward the model, but she has disappeared into the crowd. "She must've been pretty if you're quoting a 17th-century poet," Matt remarks.

"Gorgeous, Boss," Eli confirms.

"Next time," Matt says, his thoughts drifting briefly.

"Time is a companion that goes with us on a journey," Eli continues, "It reminds us to cherish each moment because it will never come again." Matt has no idea, "Patrick Stewart, Star Trek: Generations."

"I never saw it," Matt says. "Better get the plates to the table before they get cold." Eli nods and starts to move on. "Eli, wait." Eli does as he's told.

"When you drop them, ask Joshua what inspired the dish."

"Sure thing, Boss."

Chemistry – *Jessica Sitomer*

"Wait!" Eli stops again. "Don't ask that," Matt says. Confused by nature, Eli is completely confused as he approaches Joshua's table.

Joshua stands as Eli approaches and takes the plate, presenting it to the woman he's dining with. As he does, he addresses the crowded restaurant. "Ladies, Gentlemen," he places the plate before the woman. "This is the remarkable Fiona from @FeastWithFiona, the Food Influencer and Blogger. She's here specifically to try my latest special, Savory Sagebrush Chicken." The crowd cheers and watches as Fiona takes her first bite.

"Euphoric!" Fiona says, "You have to tell us how you came up with the concept."

Matt moves closer to the table, making eye contact with Joshua and challenging him. The patrons sit anticipatory as Joshua sees a server about to present an appetizer to a young couple.

"Allow me," the patrons' focus follows Joshua as he removes the smoke-filled glass cover from a cutting board to reveal a beautifully presented steak tartare. The couple gasps with delight as the Chef tells them to enjoy it. Then, the wife pulls out her cell phone to take a picture with him. Fiona waves him off to work the room as more requests for selfies are made, and Eli is left holding Joshua's plate, unsure if he should take it or leave it.

After making his way through the crowd and smiling for a few more selfies, Joshua steps away to look for Matt, who looks glum as Joshua approaches him.

Joshua sizes Matt up, "I don't like that face. Tell me we've got an investor meeting next week."

Matt can't feign disappointment any longer and responds, with a sly smile, "Friday. Happy hour."

Joshua can't contain his excitement and offers a high-five to Matt. Then, he pulls him over to meet Fiona. "Matt, Fiona." They each nod at each other having been introduced every time she'd been in. "You think this place is fabulous?" Joshua boasts, "My partner and I are going to be the hottest restaurateurs in Manhattan."

Matt flinches when Joshua uses the word partner, knowing what he is forfeiting to expand. Then he smiles with a sense of pride, fully aware that Bacchus is not just a restaurant but a dream he has had for a long time, a testament to his hard work and vision. He knew chefs tended to get all the glory for a successful restaurant, and he left plenty of room for Joshua's ego. But Bacchus was his baby even if Joshua forgets to mention that Matt created the menu, the décor, and the ambiance. Moving forward with Joshua is a risk Matt will take to see all his unique concepts come to life in Manhattan and beyond.

Chemistry opens the door to her lab and waves Inspiration in. The young girl gasps. The laboratory walls are painted in the most enchanting shades of lavender and baby blue, making it feel like a fairy-tale world come to life—the colors shift and shimmer, like a hummingbird's wings, as if the walls are bewitched.

    The crystal-clear beakers on the lab tables catch her attention. They're not like any she'd seen in science class. Each beaker has a different color, and they glow like tiny fireflies. As she approaches, she can hear them ringing like the tinkling of wind chimes in a gentle breeze.

    Her eyes widen when she sees a chemist working on a row of Bunsen burners. Instead of ordinary blue flames, they cast flames that dance in slow, graceful swirls of deep blue and silver. One flame becomes a ballet performance, putting on a

Chemistry – *Jessica Sitomer*

mesmerizing show for her. Within the beaker above it, the liquid forms into a plastic ballerina. The chemist removes the toy with tweezers and drops it in a glass jar.

Chemistry pulls Inspiration along as they navigate the vast laboratory alive with colorful explosions and mystical items. Inspiration can't help but stop again when she sees a massive white wall with metal shelves and thousands of glass jars holding a treasure trove of tiny wonders. She sees teddy bears that wave at her, carousel horses that seem ready to give her a ride, and stars that twinkle like they're telling her secrets.

Chemistry, oblivious to Inspiration's awe, observes the workstations, making notes on her clipboard. She occasionally stops to issue orders and ensure everyone is in their assigned place. Chemistry halts at an empty station and reaches for a futuristic walkie-talkie.

She instructs, "Empty stool in section four." Within moments, a scientist rushes back to his chair, acknowledging the command.

Inspiration asks, "What do you do here?"

"Our department is responsible for creating chemical love connections down on Earth," Chemistry explains.

Chemistry – *Jessica Sitomer*

Inspiration probes further. "What do you mean?"

"Have you ever heard of Anthony and Cleopatra? Sampson and Delilah? Bogie and Bacall?" Chemistry asked.

"You do realize I'm twelve," Inspiration responds.

"Taylor Swift and Travis Kelce?" Chemistry offers.

"Ah, they're cute." Inspiration acknowledges.

"We'll see how long they last," Chemistry replies.

"That doesn't sound very promising."

"Our job is to get them to meet. What they do after that is up to them," Chemistry clarifies.

Inspiration mutters under her breath, "Very uninspiring."

Chemistry moves on, leading Inspiration to another scientist. She observes his work, checks his file, grabs some bottles filled with colored liquid, twirls and mixes them like a skilled bartender, pours the mixture into a squeeze bottle, grabs the file, and motions to Inspiration to follow her.

Chemistry walks to the shelves of glass jars.

Chemistry – *Jessica Sitomer*

"Which one should I pair with this?" Chemistry shakes the squeeze bottle, and the mixture swirls like a liquid sandstorm.

Inspiration studies the wall enchanted by the tiny toys in their jars. She points to one with a tiny swan making circles in the water. Chemistry checks her file, then picks up the jar with a stagnant plastic goose next to it.

"Close, but unless it's the perfect formula, they'll miss each other."

"Who?" Inspiration asks, disappointed by Chemistry's choice of the dull goose. Chemistry motions Inspiration to follow her into an open elevator door. It closes.

It reopens, and they enter a graduation ceremony under a perfect blue sky. A professor speaks on stage, and Chemistry and Inspiration sit in the audience.

Whispering, Inspiration asks, "Where are we?"

Chemistry opens the file and points to a photo of a young man. "We're in his dream," she says. And you don't have to whisper. They can't hear, see, or touch you."

Inspiration questions, "Then what's the point of being here?"

Chemistry – *Jessica Sitomer*

Chemistry directs her attention to the stage where the professor has just called up the young man from the file. The sound of his heart pounding and his steps echoing in slow motion causes Inspiration to cover her ears.

When the young man reaches the podium, there is complete silence. Chemistry motions for Inspiration to follow her, and they walk onto the stage.

As Inspiration looks around at the crowd, Chemistry waves her hand in front of the young man's face. He gasps for air, struggling to find his voice.

"He can't remember his speech, can he?" Inspiration asks, "I had a recurring dream about being on stage and forgetting how to play."

"Then you're the perfect one to help him." She hands Inspiration the squeeze bottle and instructs her, "Aim for his eyes."

Inspiration is puzzled, follows the command, and squeezes the water concoction into the young man's eyes. When it comes out, it is dry sand, which immediately irritates and blinds him.

Inspiration cries, "Oh my gosh! What did you make me do to him?"

Chemistry – *Jessica Sitomer*

Chemistry opens the tiny jar, and the plastic goose becomes real and flies off the stage and up the sleeve of a girl in the front row. The young man rubs his eyes, and when his vision clears, he looks straight at the girl, smoothing the goosebumps on her arm. She smiles at him, and he smiles back and begins his speech.

"Today, we begin an incredible adventure," he declares. Inspiration marvels at the outcome.

"Wow! What was that?"

Chemistry smiles, "Poof."

"Poof?" Inspiration asks.

"Poof. Chemistry. That's how it's done."

Inspiration still doesn't fully grasp it, but she beams with pride, knowing she is a part of something important.

Back in Chemistry's office, the elevator door opens, and Chemistry, followed by Inspiration, walks to a table next to the elevators. She grabs a wooden block, dabs it in purple ink, and stamps the file "COMPLETE." Then, she walks to her desk and slides it into the slot in the wall.

Suddenly, a single blue file slides out of the chute and lands on top of a box filled with manila files. The room falls into a hush in anticipation. Chemistry picks up the blue file and examines it.

Confidence is jumping in place. Lust looks at the blue file as if it were a sexy lingerie model. Style taps her acrylic nails on her desk, dabbing her forehead with a Gucci scarf. Humor giggles with nervous anticipation.

Chemistry asks Inspiration, "Are you ready?"

"For what?" Inspiration asks.

"To execute your first match."

"I have to kill them?" Inspiration gasps.

"What? No!" Chemistry rebukes.

Empathy steps in, "Give her a break, Chemistry. She's brand new."

Chemistry hands Inspiration the blue file, and disappointed groans fill the room as the other managers disperse. Inspiration thrown by their reaction looks to Chemistry for an explanation, but she's already handing out manilla folders to the others.

Confidence walks over to Inspiration, "Blue files are for soulmates. They are rare, so everyone wants them. Congratulations, you!"

Feeling the task's weight ahead, Inspiration worries aloud, "Soulmates? This is my first one. What if I mess it up?"

Chemistry – *Jessica Sitomer*

Without even looking back, Chemistry reassures her, "You can't. Just follow my equation. It always works."

Empathy approaches Inspiration, "Don't worry, we're all going to help you." She turns to the group, "Right?"

They all grumble and nod.

Chemistry hands Empathy a manilla folder, "Then get to it."

"But—"Inspiration says.

Chemistry insists, "It always works." Empathy smiles at Chemistry, who immediately softens and then walks away.

The chute opens again, and a big red file with an "UNSUCCESSFUL" stamp lands in the box. Murmurs of confusion fill the room as Confidence picks it up.

Inspiration asks excitedly, "Who are the red files for?"

As she examines the file, Confidence soberly calls, "Uh, Chemistry? You have a problem."

Chemistry – *Jessica Sitomer*

Chemistry walks down a hall with green arrows that slowly turn from white sterile walls to more of an ethereal forest. She approaches a door, a massive slab of reclaimed wood, exuding an aura of rustic elegance nestled in jasmine vines. Chemistry yanks open the door and burst into Mother Nature's suite. With the red folder bearing Matt Durand's name, she proclaims, "We have a problem!"

The bedroom is a sanctuary of tranquility. A king-sized bed with a live-edge wooden headboard is adorned with soft, organic linens in earthy tones. A living green wall serves as the backdrop, a vertical garden that breathes life into the room. The ceiling is designed with a retractable skylight, allowing one to fall asleep under a star-studded night sky or wake up to the gentle warmth of the sun's rays. Mother Nature, still groggy from sleep, isn't alarmed.

"Yes... I was asleep, now I'm not."

Chemistry thrusts the folder under Mother Nature's nose, demanding her attention. Mother Nature examines it briefly. A hummingbird flies over and takes a sip from a ring on her finger. "Well, darling, I don't see how 'we' have a problem," she responds.

"What?!? They completely missed each other!" Chemistry argues, "I mean, I know sometimes the connection only lasts a few seconds before they talk themselves out of it, but—"

Mother Nature, putting on a bamboo thread robe, interrupts, reminiscing, "I remember when you treated each connection like they were meant for each other. And now I listen to you, writing off a match that lasts a few seconds as if it was expected. Such a pity."

She walks onto her private terrace, where a heated infinity pool blends seamlessly with the forest below. Wooden loungers with plush cushions soak in the sun, surrounded by hanging gardens and flowering vines. A gentle waterfall feature provides a soothing backdrop, and the air is filled with the fragrance of blooming flowers and the soft sounds of birdsong. Mother Nature walks to a nest of tables covered with hundreds of snow globes. She picks one up. Inside is a tiny city in Japan. She shakes it. The action makes cherry blossoms gently swirl around the globe. "At least it's a lovely day in Kyoto."

Chemistry pulls the globe from Mother Nature's hand and places it back in its spot, "This is my first red file! I've had a perfect record for 428 years."

"You used to care more about the..." looking at the file, "Matt Durands of the world than a perfect record. That's how you achieved it," Mother Nature reminded her.

In a moment of panic, Chemistry admits, "I'm going to get fired."

But Mother Nature had a different perspective. "Maybe it's a good thing you failed—"

"Failed? I rechecked the math. My algorithm is correct. It should have worked," Chemistry debates.

Mother Nature delivers the harsh truth, "Chemistry! He is not an algorithm. You've been in this position longer than anyone... ever. After a couple of thousand matches, we thought you'd want to retire and find someone special to settle down with through Door Ninety-Two. Perhaps it's time for you to move on."

"No! This is all I know. All I want to do. I would never want to love someone again. You've got to help me."

Mother Nature, unyielding, responds, "Sorry, Sweetie. If you need a tidal wave, come to me. A hurricane? I'm your gal. But matchmaking? You're on your own." With that, Mother Nature reclines on a lounger and dismisses Chemistry with a wave. Refusing to go, a swarm of bees make their way toward her. She runs back inside, out the door, down the hall until she's surrounded by white walls again. As she checks to be sure no bees have followed, she slides down the wall to the floor, alone, to grapple with the consequences of her failure. She opens the red file and looks for anything that can help her. It had to have been Style's fault. She was late. It could've made her sloppy. She closes the file. Nope, I can't blame anyone else. I must go in there and fix it myself. She gets up and heads down the hall toward her lab.

Chapter 4

Fatigue has finally caught up with him, as Matt leans back in his office chair, the exhaustion washes over him. He knows he must stay sharp for a little longer. Once Joshua is done in the kitchen, they will discuss the new investors meeting. This brings a trace of a smile to his face. He opens his top desk drawer and pulls out a short list written by hand: Rye on First (if we get the 1st Avenue space), Reserve Bar & Restaurant, Demeter. As he debates the list in his head, there's a knock at the door, and before he can say, come in, it flies open, and in walks Joshua, clearly drunk.

"Can we do an after-hours party tonight?" Joshua asks in a casual tone. He does not even remember his commitment to their meeting.

Chemistry – *Jessica Sitomer*

Matt furrows his brow, his patience waning. "I thought you were helping me plan for the investor meeting."

Joshua, ever the hedonist, shrugs off Matt's concerns. "Right. I was. But it turns out tonight's not a good night. I have some people to entertain."

"People," Matt states matter-of-factly, his weariness evident in his voice. "Josh, I need to know you're taking this seriously."

"Come on, of course, I am," Joshua flashes a mischievous grin, his carefree attitude unapologetic. "But someone's gotta capitalize on our success." Unable to charm Matt, he sobers for a moment, "Look, Man, don't make this about our history. We are doing well, and nothing can stop this... us... we're a sensation."

"I'm right here in the present, Josh. Where are you?"

"Ah, my friend," Joshua pats Matt on the back in a friendly, if somewhat condescending, manner, "This is the present." There's knocking on the door, "And the present is calling."

Left alone in the quiet office, Matt can't help but shake his head in exasperation. He grabs a pen and adds to the list: Ghost Restaurant.

Chemistry – *Jessica Sitomer*

He shakes his head in aggravation, then stops and examines his writing. Ghost Restaurant. This trend started in 2020. Ghost kitchens, AKA virtual brands, are restaurants without storefronts, no front-of-house staff, no dining room furniture, and no outdoor signage, just an online presence. Mobile ordering made it simple. He could even look for a spot near Central Park so patrons could pick up and picnic. The concept tended to gear toward less expensive food, but what if he did the first refined dining version, maybe even raw cuisine, so that the temperature wouldn't be an issue for delivery? He starts to sketch plates and ideas for dishes. He crosses off 'raw' and writes Vegan Inspired. He's been following a cruise ship with a vegan restaurant offering non-vegan options, like a typical menu that would provide vegan options. He wanted to tie in his passion for wine. He turned to a fresh page on his pad and made a list:

Vine & Veg
Greens & Grapes
Plant & Pour
Vino Verde
Vegan Vineyard
Leaf & Grape

Chemistry – *Jessica Sitomer*

The Green Cork
Veggie Vines
Wine & Herb Bistro
Vegan Vintages

He couldn't write as quickly as the names were coming. This is a social media dream. It could be huge! His expression quickly turns from excitement to dread. He grabs his phone and clicks on Bacchus' Instagram. Food. Food. Wine. Joshua. Joshua. Food. Joshua. Wine. Joshua is the face of Bacchus. He is the draw. How could Matt create the hype and branding needed without Joshua? Not to mention the backlash of Joshua's wrath if Matt told him he wanted to go out alone. No, he had made a deal with a despotic. Deflated, he puts the list and notes back in his drawer, pushing it closed more forcefully than necessary.

The lab becomes a playground of creativity and camaraderie when Chemistry is away. The rigid order imposed by her presence melts away, replaced by a light-hearted buzz. The techs, usually tense and silent, now laugh and chat as they work. Even the flames on the Bunsen burners seem to flicker in time with the laughter, as if the lab relaxes in her absence.

Beyond the techs, in a separate lab area, is a boardroom where the managers collaborate. Inspiration watches as they read through their files. Lust wears a swaggy smile as he closes his file, "I like my guy, I reeeeally like my guy." Humor pulls the file from him, looks, and whistles as he writes notes. "Aw, come on, man!" Lust complains as Humor pushes the file over to Confidence, who, after a quick read, reaches into her Pound Puppies pencil case and marks up the file with a pink pencil. Lust protests, "Seriously? What he lacks in confidence, he makes up for in girth."

Inspiration opens her file, where she sees a picture and bio of a 32-year-old woman. She lifts the page and sees a picture and bio of a 34-year-old man. Empathy points at the man, "He's your guy. The woman is 'the match'. Inspiration turns the page and sees a strange formula with letters and percentages. Empathy continues, "That's Chemistry's equation. See the 'I' at the top?" Inspiration nods. "That means that to get these two to connect, what she needs most is to be inspired. Which is why the file was given to you."

Confidence leans in and points to the 'C,' "That's me," she says, writing a few notes with a turquoise pencil.

Inspiration re-reads the equation, looking up at her counterparts. "There's no L," Inspiration notes.

Humor laughs, "That's because they're soulmates."

Lust imitates him like a snarky kid, "That's because they're soulmates."

Empathy explains, "All of us make up the chemical attraction between soulmates, except," She looks at Lust, "No offense."

Lust pouts, "Offense taken!"

Style pulls the folder toward her and reads, "Nice looking couple, don't need much from me." She signs off and pushes it to Humor.

Empathy continues, "Once we're all done, you decide the best method of transferring the formula to each of them in his dream. These two know each other, and if you look here," she points to a timeline at the bottom of his page, "It shows how often he dreams about her, so getting them together in the dream will be easy."

"The fun part," Confidence interrupts, "Is giving the formula to a lab tech and watching them concoct the recipe into something cool!"

Empathy reaches over and turns to the first page, "See the snowflake symbol?" Inspiration nods, "I'll show you where the snowflake jars are. You grab one, and when you open it in the dream, a flurry of snowflakes will swirl down her back."

Confidence springs up her arms in a straight V for victory, "The next time they see each other, she will get chills up her spine, and he'll get... whatever you decide, and they'll fall madly in love!"

Inspirations worries, "Seems pretty complicated,"

"Love is complicated," Lust agrees, "But in time, you'll get it."

Inspiration watches her colleagues swap folders, make notes, and debate decisions. There is an easy rhythm to it. She interrupts the rhythm, asking, "How long have you each been here?"

Confidence jumps in, "Since 1986, I was hit by a drunk driver."

"1978," Style says, "I...I'll just leave it at Studio 54."

Chemistry – *Jessica Sitomer*

Lust stands announcing, "1964, heart attack, doing what I loved best." He raises an eyebrow at Inspiration, "If ya know what I mean."

"I don't," Inspiration confesses.

Humor distracts her, "I got stung by a bee in the Catskills during my show. I started talking funny because my throat was closing, and the audience laughed and laughed, thinking it was part of my act." Humor reminisces, "Ah, the Borscht Belt in the summer of 1952... was my best show... went out with a bang!"

"You went out with a bee allergy," Lust argues.

"Why do bees have sticky hair?" Humor asks, "Because they use honeycombs."

Inspiration laughs, then turns to Empathy, "What about you?"

Empathy looks down at her folder and says, "I was a nun... during the Civil War."

Inspiration nods her head, "Makes sense that you're here. My mom explained the difference between sympathy and empathy to me after my dad died."

Empathy smiles at her, "Trust the process. It will all come to you innately."

Inspiration nods, though she doesn't know what innately means and has no internet to look it up.

Chemistry – *Jessica Sitomer*

When the team gets up to leave the board room, she follows.

The dimly lit lab in Eternity is quiet. The staff galivant through dreams after hours. The ritual was in place long before Chemistry arrived, though she never wanted to partake and never understood the appeal. The otherwise bright room is shrouded in shadows, save for a single station at the center. Chemistry, partially obscured by the billowing haze of her experiment, wears protective goggles as colorful mixtures boil.

Through a magnifying glass that emerges before her with a wave of her hand, Chemistry scrutinizes her work with unwavering focus. The room is heavy with the scent of chemicals, and the formula in her round-bottom flask emits tendrils of smoke, hopping like supernatural frogs.

Unbeknownst to Chemistry, Inspiration saunters into the room with an air of nonchalance. In her hand, she holds a banana.

Inspiration queries, her voice breaking the room's silence, "What am I doing here?"

Chemistry – *Jessica Sitomer*

Startled, Chemistry tears her gaze away from her arcane experiment, turning to face the intruder. "Interrupting my work," Chemistry replies.

Inspiration persists, her curiosity unquenched. "No, I mean here.... in this place?"

Chemistry, already exasperated with her formula, decides to take a break. She turns to look at Inspiration straight on.

"Everyone in my department has something to contribute to what determines attraction. A little Knowledge, a sprinkle of Humor, a dash of Style, a boost of Confidence, and too often, Lust," Chemistry explains, her words measured. "I calculate how much on a case-by-case basis and give assignments to whoever dominates the formula."

Inspiration remains perplexed, "I get all that. But why me?"

Turning back to her bubbling concoction, Chemistry ponders the question. Her eyes, concealed behind the goggles, betray a hint of hesitation.

"You were chosen for your inspirational gifts and the pure goodness you personified," Chemistry responds.

Chemistry – *Jessica Sitomer*

Inspiration laughs, "Uh... inspirational gifts? Goodness? Are you sure you got the right girl?"

Chemistry, eager to return to her work, remains resolute. "Everyone is perfectly selected, okay? Now scoot!"

With a nod of acquiescence, Inspiration turns her attention back to Chemistry's experiment. She takes a bite of the banana, and her lips smack as she chews, a counterpoint to the delicate alchemy before her.

"Whatcha doin'?" Inspiration inquires, mouth still full of banana.

"Working on a problematic case," Chemistry replies, her focus wavering.

Seeking to learn from the master, Inspiration asks, "Can I watch? I mean, who better to learn from than you?"

After a brief internal struggle, Chemistry concedes. "Fine. If you stay quiet and don't tell a soul."

Inspiration nods and takes another bite of her banana.

Chemistry rethinking her altruistic decision, "That's an ingredient for formulas. We don't have to eat here."

Chemistry – *Jessica Sitomer*

"I know," Inspiration muses as she observes, "But it reminds me of home. My mom used to call me her little monkey, and—"

Chemistry's disapproving look prompts Inspiration to zip her lips again, her eyes fixed on the experiment's mesmerizing dance. Chemistry extends her hand, and Inspiration stuffs the rest of the snack in her mouth and reluctantly hands over the banana peel. Chemistry tucks it away in her pocket. Inspiration's eyes widen as the chemicals form a green mass that continues to morph until...

"So, cool!" admires Inspiration, "How do you get that to look like a frog?"

Chemistry sighs heavily and rechecks her math. "Something's missing. It's supposed to be the green beads like last time, but it keeps coagulating."

"Maybe you need to capture the liquid in the bottle faster."

"I can't," Chemistry says, "the only way to analyze what went wrong last time is to examine it."

"The frog is a removable device at the lower end of the bow stick that secures the hair and regulates its tension," Inspiration says thoughtfully. Chemistry looks at her with utter confusion. "Well, I don't know, I'm looking for some Cello inspiration," the young girl explains.

Chemistry – *Jessica Sitomer*

"Inspiration, this has nothing to do with you playing the Cello, and you are not helping."

"Okay, okay… my mom always told me to simplify. It would be best to have green beads, but you're getting a frog. A frog was once a tadpole, a green bead with a tail. See? Capture it in the bottle before it grows a tail."

Chemistry tilts her head a moment, considering. She starts over and quickly captures the liquid as it beads. "Now that, young lady, was inspired."

Inspiration does a happy dance as Chemistry walks to the elevator, then inspired again asks, "Can I come?"

Chemistry enters the elevator and looks at Inspiration, "Absolutely not." The doors close. Inspiration stomps her foot momentarily, then smiles and skips out of the lab.

In the heart of dense woods, the moonlight struggles to pierce the thick canopy of trees. Sounds of metal clashing on metal reverberate in the air. Chemistry forges her way through the underbrush, her lab coat protecting her from the thorny brush, but her hair getting tangled in the branches slows her down. Frustration growing, she finally sees the light of day when she enters an arena.

There, chained to a crude stake, is a woman, the same culinary teacher from Matt Durand's dream that Style had somehow failed. The woman cries out for mercy but not for herself. She is crying out for her husband. The crowd chants in the Roman arena as Chemistry retrieves the rejected red file from her bag. She examines it before reaching for a glass jar containing a tiny turquoise butterfly. As she twists open the jar, a swirling swarm of butterflies cascades down the woman's tattered dress. Chemistry's gaze momentarily shifts as she sees two warriors in battle.

One heavily armed fighter battles his way toward the chained woman, slaying one warrior after another. With each victory, a larger opponent is released, and a new battle begins and ends. Chemistry impatient sees an opening as another Gladiator is slain. She approaches the iron-clad soldier as the crowd demands blood. Reaching into her pocket, Chemistry is disgusted as she pulls out the slimy banana peel. She throws it on the ground and wipes her hand on her coat. Back-to-back with the Gladiator, she reaches in again and pulls out the greenish liquid-filled spray bottle. Turning to face him, she confirms it's Matt as his jaw drops, the perfect opportunity for Chemistry to spray down his throat. Beyond Chemistry, Matt sees a giant charging toward him. She sprays him in the face. Nearly blinded and coughing, he grabs Chemistry, pulling her from harm's way.

Shocked, Chemistry slips on the banana peel. Matt catches her just before she hits the ground. He tries to speak, but no sound comes out. Suddenly, a mace crashes on Matt's armor, creating a resonating sound that becomes the sound of an alarm clock.

Everything in the dream disappears. Chemistry, alone in the white room, no longer held up by Matt, falls to the ground. She doesn't move.

He did not see me. He did not touch me. That could not happen!

Chemistry charges out of the elevator toward her desk.

"That was weird," a voice says, startling Chemistry, who trips and barely catches herself as she falls into her chair and whips around to find Inspiration standing by the monitors.

"Why are you in my office?" Chemistry demands.

Chemistry – *Jessica Sitomer*

As if hearing nothing, Inspiration continues in the same tone, "It almost looked like he saw you."

"He didn't see me."

"But he caught you."

"He didn't catch me! He can't see me!" Chemistry stammers," You, you, you... read your manual. You have no grasp on the rules here!"

"I don't need a manual to tell me what I saw on that monitor, and it was pretty hot."

"Hot? Hot?" Chemistry lurches from her chair, crouches in front of Inspiration, and grabs her by the shoulders, "There was nothing hot happening. I successfully applied the chemicals to both subjects."

"If it was so successful, why are you hurting me?"

Chemistry releases Inspiration from her tight grasp. She straightens Inspiration's lab coat and lets out a big sigh.

"I'm sorry. I overreacted. I'm not used to staff..." Chemistry searches for a word, "Interacting with me."

"No one talks to you?"

"No one questions me," Chemistry corrects, "Because I've never been wrong. Inspiration, we are prodigies. You have to trust the process."

"But I know what I saw."

Chemistry – *Jessica Sitomer*

"It was a dream. Dreams don't make sense."

Inspiration opens her mouth to contest, but Chemistry stands and cuts her off, "If you were watching closely, you'd recall that the only weird thing that happened in that dream is I found your slimy banana peel in my pocket. We don't need to eat here. The sooner you learn and follow the rules, the better your chance of being an asset to this department."

Looking down at her toes, Inspiration nods and shuffles her way out of Chemistry's office.

Chemistry falls back into her chair, eyes closed, relieved to have put out that fire. Then, her eyes flash back to what happened in the dream. She bites her lip. It was kind of hot. Her chin falls into her hand, braced by her elbow propped up on her desk, which slips a few inches under the weight of her head, snapping her back into reality. He saw her. He touched her. Chemistry can't hide her alarm.

Chemistry – *Jessica Sitomer*

Chapter 5

The alarm pulls Matt from his dream. He grabs his phone, turns off the alarm, and then sits up in a sweat. His hand rests on his throat as he recounts the dream before it leaves him.

Matt does not exude his typical air of composure as he emerges from his apartment. His hair looks unbrushed, his tie is crooked, and he has clearly lost something as he walks through his neighbor's wide-open door.

Sitting on her couch beside Lola is Misty, a young woman whose outfit and jewelry are a mixture of hippie meets gypsy. When Matt enters her apartment, she is tying her wild, curly brown hair with home-done highlights into a messy bun.

"You're up! We were worried about you," Misty rejoices, her demeanor resembling an overexcited puppy. She turns to the massive dog, "Lola, go give your daddy a hug."

Chemistry – *Jessica Sitomer*

Lola lumbers off the couch and stretches up, placing her front paws on Matt's shoulders. She is eye-to-eye with him when she's on her hind legs.

"Sorry," he says, "I overslept. I'm running late."

"That explains why Lola came over for breakfast."

Matt pulls two crisp hundred dollar bills out of his pants pocket and hands them to Misty, "I may be late tonight."

"Matt, this is too much," she insists, immediately depositing the cash in a ceramic piggy bank on her coffee table.

Misty's apartment is an eclectic mix of thrift store collections. Shelves of old toasters, ice cream scoops, and MacDonald's glasses from the seventies are surrounded by Mandala Bohemian fabrics and hanging rows of beads. Her globe collection is so extensive that it looks like wallpaper. The furniture is all secondhand that she turned into DIY projects, most still unfinished.

When Matt kisses Lola goodbye on her head, the empathic and ever-observant Misty can't help but notice something unusual about his appearance.

Misty, her concern evident, asks, "Do you realize you're wearing two different shoes?"

"Damn it," Matt mutters.

Chemistry – *Jessica Sitomer*

Amusement dances in Misty's eyes as she spontaneously takes charge of the situation. "Lola, fetch," she commands.

With an enthusiastic wag of her tail, Lola trots into Matt's apartment, eager to assist. She emerges a moment later, and a matching shoe clutched delicately in her massive jaws.

Matt sighs in relief, his gratitude evident as he pats the dog's massive head, "Good Girl." He takes off one shoe and puts on the match. He puts the extra shoe in Lola's mouth. Her sturdy body walks out of the apartment back to Matt's with an extreme wiggle.

Misty comments, "You never oversleep." Matt blushes, and a shy smile plays on his lips. "Wait! What is that smile?" Misty demands.

"It's nothing," Matt insists. Misty looks at him, disbelieving. "It's silly," Matt redirects, but Misty bounces on her couch with a knowing that forces Matt to ask, "Have you ever dreamt about someone you don't know and found yourself unable to stop thinking about them?"

Misty's eyes widen with curiosity. "You dreamt about a woman?"

Matt nods, confusion evident in his expression. "But I don't know her."

Chemistry – *Jessica Sitomer*

Misty's optimism is infectious. "Matt, this is incredible! You must've seen her in the neighborhood, and your subconscious has picked up on her presence."

"The only thing my subconscious picks up on is flaws in produce."

"That would be your conscious mind," Misty redirects, "Matt, she's out there somewhere." A thought occurs to her, "We have to find her!"

Matt, however, remains skeptical. "Oh, sure. I'll pencil 'find imaginary dream woman' into my calendar between meeting with investors and ordering octopus."

"Octopus? That's specific and phallic."

"It's this week's special, and what's phallic about an-- oh, I see it now. And now I can't unsee it. I've got to change the special."

"You've got to change your aura, make it more inviting-- Wait!" Misty insists as she opens an old trunk filled with tarot decks. She closes her eyes, begins to hum, and moves her hands over the decks.

"Misty, I'm late," Matt reminds her.

"Shhh!" She holds up a deck, quickly shuffles it, pulls The Lovers card, and shrieks excitedly!

Matt turns to leave, "I'm going to work."

Chemistry – *Jessica Sitomer*

Misty's determination is undeniable. "Don't you see? You can escape your life into work, but fate has its way of intervening. Yesterday, I was so occupied with walking the dogs that I forgot to eat. When I returned home, a pizza was waiting for me on the counter."

Matt dismissed it with a chuckle. "That wasn't fate, it was Eli."

Misty looked puzzled. "Who's Eli?"

"The guy I hired from that Community Program you kept on me about?" Misty shows no recollection, "You've met him a hundred times." Off her blank expression, "Never mind. I have to get to work."

"No! You have to find her! She obviously lives on the Upper West Side since you never go anywhere else," Misty watches him, torn between trepidation and determination, as he waves her off and walks down the hallway.

She calls after him, "Keep your eyes peeled. She could anywhere- oooo, she could be a homeless woman and you can save her from the streets!"

Matt stops and looks back at her with an expression of 'Really?' as she nods yes in excitement. He walks out, shaking his head. Misty kneels where Lola sits, "Your daddy is such a good man," she has a new thought and gasps, "maybe she's a hooker like Pretty Woman." Lola drops her head. "You're right, no hookers on the Upper West Side. Come on, it's time for your acupuncture. We need to clear your chakras if we're gonna solve this mystery." Lola follows Misty inside.

Chemistry examines folders determined to ensure they are all perfect. Her tight bun has pieces of hair falling over her eyes. She blows them away, grabbing at papers and wheeling her chair back to a blackboard filled with equations that look as if a mad scientist has written them. She stands and erases a corner, re-filling it with more shapes and numbers.

Style and Confidence enter her office reluctantly with an unspoken urgency. Their footsteps are as quiet as their anxiety is loud until Style halts abruptly and flicks off imaginary lint, trying to maintain composure. Confidence, mid-step, collides with her, bracing herself on the taller woman with a muffled curse.

They hold their breath, expecting Chemistry to turn and scold them. When Chemistry doesn't notice the intrusion, Style walks backward in slow motion, careful that her heels don't make a sound. Confidence adjusts her posture, tries to assert authority, and braces herself against the more prominent and robust woman, pushing her forward.

Straining, Confidence says, "Style, you've got to show her."

"No, I don't."

"You do."

"Don't."

"Do."

Chemistry's voice chimes in, "Do what?"

With a few furtive gestures and nudges from Confidence, Style extracts a red file from her Chanel tote and places it on Chemistry's desk. The two women wordlessly retreat, leaving the conspicuous file.

"Wait," orders Chemistry. She approaches the file and reads its label: DURAND. What is happening?!" Her eyes lock on Style, "Did you go back in?"

"No! You didn't give me the assignment."

Chemistry – *Jessica Sitomer*

Breaking the tension, Confidence states the obvious, "Well, someone went in, and something went wrong."

Style rolls her eyes, "Thank you for the insight, Nancy Drew."

"Oooo, I love Nancy Drew! We can solve this with--"

"Research," Chemistry interrupts.

"Research?" Style questions as she walks to the elevator, "I'm gonna go visit my friends at Vogue," she pushes the down button, "and research me some new Jimmy Choos. Then I'm gonna research my way to Dior," she steps into the elevator and as the doors close adds, "and research my ass off."

As Chemistry watches Style go, Confidence holds her breath, bursting to speak. Chemistry gives her the nod to proceed.

"Iiiiiiiiiiiiiieeeeeeeeyyy don't know what to research, but I'm here to help. Tell me what to do, Boss."

Chemistry thinks momentarily, "Why don't you research what we should research?"

"Oh, my... that's why you're the boss," Confidence heads out the door. " Research what we should research. It's so brilliant!" Chemistry hears Confidence yell from the hallway, "I'm on it!"

Chemistry – *Jessica Sitomer*

With a pained expression, Chemistry looks down at the file and opens it. Her eyes scan the single page. What do you research when everything's correct?

In the heart of Eternity's vast and labyrinthine library, every written book fills endless rows of bound volumes. Chemistry sits in a secluded corner, where she has gathered a substantial pile. With furrowed brows and a sense of desperation, she peruses the pages of her chosen texts. Her eyes scan the words intently, her fingers gently tracing the weathered pages as if they held the universe's secrets and her fate.

Unbeknownst to her, a peculiar and youthful presence observes her from the meticulous stacks. His oversized lab coat is unbuttoned to display his fifties-style tweed suit and bowtie. The lab coat pocket reads Knowledge. A spindly figure of merely seven years, Coke bottle glasses perch precariously on his nose, his appearance heightened by the charming marks of his youth, with two missing front teeth contributing to a prominent lisp in his speech. As he watches Chemistry engrossed in her studies, his wide eyes register a moment of horror when a book suddenly leaves her grasp as she tosses it across the room.

Knowledge rushes to the scene without hesitation, cradling the thrown book with utmost care as if rescuing a fragile relic. His eyes plead with Chemistry for understanding as he holds the book close, a surrogate guardian for its precious contents.

"Do you mind!" Knowledge's voice, a blend of irritation and innocence, implores Chemistry.

Still absorbed in her literary pursuit, Chemistry does not tear her gaze away from the pages before her as she replies, "Not at all. I'm done with it."

With an indignant huff, Knowledge returns the dismissal and walks away, clutching the rescued book. But Chemistry's voice, laden with curiosity and longing for answers, halts his retreat.

Chemistry hesitates, eyes narrowing on the page before her, then glances up. "Knowledge? Have... peculiar things ever happened in dreams? You know, things that shouldn't happen?" Chemistry's voice is higher pitched and less confident than usual.

From a distance, Knowledge considers the question, his brilliant mind sifting through the vast vocabulary he has absorbed from the library's contents. "Peculiar? As in abnormal, bizarre..."

"Yes," Chemistry nods, her interest apparent.

"Odd or fishy?" Knowledge ventures, eager to assist.

"Uh huh," Chemistry confirms with an eager nod.

"Fantastic, grotesque, atypical?"

Chemistry cuts him off. "Yes! Yes! Any of that!"

Knowledge responds with assurance. "No."

The revelation extinguishes the flicker of hope that had briefly illuminated Chemistry's expression. "No one's ever... found themselves lost within a dream? Or struggled to escape one? Or I don't know, perhaps... been touched by a mortal?"

Knowledge's reply is swift and decisive, his voice firm, "Touched! Never! Such an event has never occurred!"

The weight of uncertainty hangs heavily in the air as Chemistry considers the implications of Knowledge's response.

"Are you certain? Could such occurrences have transpired before your time? There are a lot of books in here," Chemistry points out.

Insulted, Knowledge gets in her face, "I've read every book, every record in this library eighteen times—except Pleades' 'On Dreams and Understanding,' which I've read nineteen times."

The sheer thoroughness of Knowledge's understanding leaves Chemistry momentarily silent.

"Perhaps," she muses carefully, "no one ever reported it?"

Knowledge's brow furrows as he considers this possibility, his mind working through the particulars of the matter.

"I've examined the intricacies, the complexities, and the labyrinthine depths, comparing the accuracies and authenticity of what perplexed me. I pondered if it was plausible, then concluded that it was both spurious and dubious."

Chemistry requests, "In simpler terms?"

"In simpler terms," Knowledge obliged suspiciously, "it's never happened."

Chemistry's shoulders slump, but she quickly rebounds, under Knowledge's watchful eyes, "You're right. Of course, it didn't... couldn't, hasn't... never..."

Knowledge observes Chemistry with more suspicion as she rises from her corner, straightens her lab coat, and gives him an awkward smile. She quickly leaves the library, disregarding the mess of books piled and scattered in the corner. Knowledge, grumpy from the experience, waves his hand, and the books magically lift from the ground, going their separate ways back to their given space on the shelves.

In the tranquil silence of a bedroom, the moonlight filters through the curtains, casting a gentle glow. Chemistry slowly and cautiously cracks open the closet door where she's hidden. As the door creaks open, she peers out into the room. Her ears pick up faint, breathy sounds that disperse in the air. With trepidation, she widens the gap in the door just enough to reveal what lies beyond.

The sight that greets her brings an exasperated sigh to her lips. A couple occupy the bed, their entwined limbs and soft murmurs painting an intimate tableau.

"Blech," Chemistry murmurs as the man lifts himself, holding one of the woman's legs up by his ear.

Well, gosh, sex sure has changed. Okay, she's flexible, he's... wow, I don't even know what he's doing. Chemistry grabs for the file. This makes no sense. Lust isn't even in the equation. This guy isn't even interested... he hasn't had sex in... whoa, okay, that explains why it's manifesting in his dream, I guess. Now, I need to confirm that's... she opens the file and looks at the picture of the culinary teacher.

Chemistry makes her way out of the closet toward the bed. Matt and the woman keep changing positions, and neither comes up for air. Chemistry tries to tap the woman. Nothing. She slaps her arm. "Oh, right," she whispers, relieved that her expectation of catastrophe was ridiculous. She reprimands herself, "Invisible." As the reinforcement sinks in, her voice grows louder and more arrogant, "Can't see me, can't hear me, can't feel me. Good."

Matt lifts his head and stares at Chemistry. A small cry of fear escapes her, and her hand instinctively covers her mouth, stifling any future sounds. She stiffens as his muscles flex. Her face contorts with embarrassment. The two stare at each other like a human and a gorilla in a zoo, trying to figure each other out between a pane of glass. Her breath quickens. This can't be happening. This is bad bad bad, I'm going to get fired bad, no no no! He cannot see me. It breaks every rule. Breathe Chemistry, deliver the formula, and go. You're entirely misreading this situation. She closes her eyes, taking a deep breath to control herself. Upon opening them, Matt rolls off the woman in his bed and, in doing so, reveals a startling revelation—the woman in his dream was none other than Chemistry herself.

Chemistry's words catch in her throat as her eyes lock onto the captivating image of herself that Matt has conjured in his dream, "Oh, holy Sh...akespeare —" Her hair cascades in long, flowing locks, her face adorned with makeup, and her glasses are nowhere to be seen. She is utterly stunning. Yet, before she can retreat into the closet, a voice, like a whisper from the shadows, reaches her ears.

"What is he doing to her?" Inspiration asks from the tight closet space.

Chemistry jumps, her heart racing, as she turns to confront the unexpected presence. "What are you doing here?!?"

Matt answers her, "I think it's pretty obvious."

"Not you! Stop talking!" What is happening here?! Chemistry charges for the closet, pointing at Inspiration. "You!" Chemistry demands

With a disarming nonchalance, Inspiration responded, "Trying to learn—"

Chemistry – *Jessica Sitomer*

Before Inspiration could finish her explanation, Matt lets out an exclamation of amazement. Chemistry barges into the closet. Desperate to divert Inspiration's attention from this intensely personal exposé, Chemistry instinctively grabs Inspiration and covers her eyes.

Inspiration's interest is immediately triggered as she eagerly questions, "What? What happened? Let me see! I won't tell anyone!" Inspiration pleads to catch a glimpse of the dream. "Please let me look! Please!"

"Shhhh!" Chemistry hushes her, unable to tear her gaze away from the mesmerizing image Matt has created of her as it slowly disappears.

Now alone in his bed, Matt says, "It's okay. Come back," waving Chemistry over like a timid animal.

Determined to end this surreal situation, Chemistry declares, "We're out of here."

She hits the elevator button, determined to distance herself from this perplexing dream scenario. *I am in so much trouble!* She presses the button continuously, hoping to move faster.

Moments later, Chemistry, her composure distressed, rushes out of the elevator into the

Chemistry – *Jessica Sitomer*

bustling central floor lab. Inspiration follows closely behind, undeterred by the unusual events of the evening.

Chemistry approaches a panel next to the door and presses it, causing an "OUT OF ORDER" sign to pop up. The monitor above the door flickers into an indistinct blur.

Inspiration fires questions at her, "It's broken? Can you fix it? Can we go back tomorrow? Can I go in alone?"

Chemistry sighs, her frustration evident. "Absolutely not! This is a problem case! It's now confidential."

Inspiration's voice rises with anxiety as she tries to explain her intent, "I'm just trying to learn so I can do a good job. I don't understand any of this! I've never been in love. I only had one boyfriend, and he was jealous of my cello!"

Get yourself together, Chemistry. She needs you! Chemistry kneels to the young girl, her tone softer now, and attempts to impart a valuable lesson. "And what did you learn from that?"

With a hint of humor, Inspiration responds, "That my next boyfriend better play the tuba."

Chemistry's eyes sparkle with pride as she imparts wisdom to her young apprentice. "Exactly.

Chemistry – *Jessica Sitomer*

Every match isn't designed to be permanent, but both people learn something from the experience. That way, when they meet their soulmate, they're ready for it." As soon as the words leave her mouth, the anxiety returns, "There! You learned something!"

The scientists observing this exchange silently returned to their work, eager to avoid Chemistry's searching gaze. Determined to put this matter behind her, Chemistry takes off again, her steps guided by determination. Inspiration, like a curious companion, follows her closely, refusing to be dismissed.

As she stays in step with Chemistry, Inspiration asks, "Do people have a lot of lessons to learn before they meet their soulmate?"

Chemistry considers the question as they walk, her knowledge of the intricate dance of love etched into her very being. "Some have only one lesson. It just takes a lot of matches before they learn it."

Inspiration's curiosity leads her to another question. "How many lessons did you learn before finding your soulmate?"

Chemistry stops just before the lab's exit, her eyes distant as she recalls a past love that still haunts her. "None. I was ready." Chemistry steps out of the lab, leaving her questions and doubts behind.

Chemistry has cornered Lust in the hall in a dimly lit Eternity corridor.

"And then he was doing this thing where he kinda twisted her," she tries to act it out.

"The helicopter."

"From there, he pulled her onto his--"

Lust, over-eager, blurts, "Reverse Cowgirl, Superman, The Rowboat."

Chemistry pleads, "None of that means anything to me!"

Lust circles her, inspecting her from head to toe. Chemistry squirms. They both freeze as three managers from the Epidemiology Division walk by, noses down, discussing a file. Lust hides his face until they are out of sight.

"Greatest gift this place gave me... no more STIs, all gone," Lusts says.

"That's the greatest gift? Not adding a little fire to a potential match or mixing in a.. rowboat?"

"You are paying attention," Lust recognizes, "But why? Since when have you been curious about my work?"

Chemistry – *Jessica Sitomer*

"That's just it, you weren't in the equation at all, and I've never seen anything like... I mean, what I want to understand is if she's doing something wrong. She went, kinda down there..." She points toward his 'privates.'

Lust thrusts his tongue out, salivating, "Nothing wrong with that."

With an ick in her tone, Chemistry asks, "But what was that?"

Lust's eyes light up, and he's about to answer when he freezes and abruptly leaves the conversation, taking off down the hall.

A voice, gentle yet commanding, "Chemistry? A word."

Reluctant to turn around, Chemistry lets out a resigned sigh before spinning to face Mother Nature.

"Oh, hi. Were you looking for..."

"Follow me," Mother Nature insists.

Minutes later, they find themselves within the confines of the Weather Wing, where glass doors lead to different climates. Each step down this seemingly endless hallway is like a transition between seasons. As they walk, a door flies open with a thunderous clap, releasing a flurry of snow and ushering out a man wrapped in a pristine white parka.

"There's been a lot of talk around here about this," Mother Nature remarks, her gaze unwavering as she holds up Matt's conspicuous red file.

Chemistry, resentful, her voice is tinged with a mix of conspiracy and exasperation. "How did you get that?"

They round a corner, entering a lush, vibrant greenhouse teeming with employees who tend to exotic flora. The air is heavy with the scent of blooming flowers and the faint rustling of leaves as the plants seem to respond to an unspoken rhythm. Seeds are planted and almost instantaneously begin to grow, producing fruits and vegetables that defy nature's laws.

With the file still clutched tightly in Mother Nature's grip, she probs further. "Were you seen?"

Chemistry's response is confident, bordering on defiant. "That would be impossible."

But Mother Nature isn't so easily swayed. She sternly reminds Chemistry, "That would be grounds for termination."

Chemistry – *Jessica Sitomer*

Reluctantly, Chemistry attempts to clarify her position. "No. Of course, I wasn't."

However, Mother Nature remains undeterred, her voice carrying a mixture of concern and compassion. "Chemistry, it's not nice to fool Mother Nature."

With an underlying tension current between them, Chemistry exhales slowly and finally admits her dilemma. "You don't understand the pressure I'm under."

Mother Nature regards her with a blend of sympathy and skepticism. "Really? I guess you haven't seen Al Gore's documentary on climate change."

The exchange between the two women intensifies as Chemistry weighs the consequences of her actions. She poses a hypothetical question, her voice tinged with desperation. "What if I was seen, which I wasn't, but what if I was? What would you do in my position?"

A heavy silence hangs in the air before Mother Nature responds, her voice somber yet resolute. "I'd quit. Go back to... What is it you did? Poetry?"

Chemistry dismisses the idea, her determination overriding any thoughts of quitting. "Quit! Forget it. No. I will solve this case, even if it means..." She pauses, her brows furrowing in deep thought as she considers the gravity of her decision.

"Means what?!" Mother Nature prompts with concern.

Chemistry makes up her mind, her face contorting with determination as she declares her intentions. "I've got to go down there."

But Mother Nature hesitates, cautious of the implications of such a decision. "It's too soon."

Chemistry can't hide her impatience, her voice tinged with exasperation. "Too soon? It's been 428 years, not to mention it's a completely different continent."

As the weight of the situation settles upon them, Mother Nature poses one final question, searching Chemistry's eyes for the truth. "Do you really think you're ready?"

With unwavering conviction, Chemistry responds, "Ready or not, it's better than writing poetry for eternity through door number twelve."

Mother Nature, despite her initial reluctance, can't help but empathize. "They are a bit pretentious there."

Chemistry, her purpose solidified, sums up her determination with a simple statement of vulnerability, "This job is all I have."

Chemistry – *Jessica Sitomer*

Recognizing Chemistry's unwavering resolve, Mother Nature offers her blessing and encouragement: "Then go down there and save it."

As they continue their conversation, a miniature volcano on a three-dimensional map of Hawaii draws Mother Nature's attention. She waves her hand over it with a sense of resignation, causing the simulated volcano to erupt in a brilliant display. Chemistry's face changes from contemplation to sheer determination. She is ready for the challenges that lie ahead.

Chapter 6

The 'challenge' is an understatement as Chemistry's managers gather around a blackboard in her office, adorned with a meticulously plotted timeline. A photograph of Matt Durand, along with images of his brownstone and restaurant, are meticulously scrutinized. With unwavering resolve, Chemistry holds a red laser pointer, her expression a mix of determination and trepidation.

Chemistry begins. "This is Matt Durand," her voice carrying the weight of an extraordinary situation. "He has an unprecedented case, so I am forced to do something unprecedented. I'm going down to Earth," Ignoring the guttural gasps of her entire team, she continues, "and will start here—"

With a deft motion, she points to the initial part of the timeline, which marks the path leading to Bacchus.

"I will watch him in his work environment, looking for clues to decipher his problem,"

Chemistry asserts, her gaze unwavering as she scans her team for any signs of doubt.

Confidence, ever the beacon of encouragement, chimes in with an enthusiastic affirmation. "That's right! You've got this!!!"

However, when Lust presses Chemistry for more specific details, "Clues? Like what?" Chemistry's response is candid, revealing her uncertainty.

"If I knew that, I wouldn't have to go. I need insight into this guy I don't have access to in his dreams."

The room remains momentarily contemplatively silent as the implications of Chemistry's mission hang in the air. Knowledge voices the question at the forefront of everyone's minds: "Under what guise will you be there?"

With her resolve unwavering, Chemistry outlines her plan. "I will be going as a patron in his restaurant, so if I need to return on multiple occasions, it won't appear strange."

Humor can't resist injecting a note of levity. "How about going as a health inspector? That'll freak him out!"

Chemistry is not in the mood for jokes, "I don't want to freak him out, Humor. I want him to trust me so I can convince him to meet his match." Chemistry takes an old briefcase out of her desk drawer. "I don't know what I'm in for down there. So much has changed in 400 years, and dreams can be telling but also misleading." She waits for her staff to offer reassurances, but when no one responds, she says, "I'm going to need your help packing."

Now her staff understands what she wasn't saying, and all get into purpose mode. Style is the first step up. She throws the relic briefcase in the garbage and replaces it with a Chanel Graffiti Printed Canvas Street Tote Bag. Chemistry removes the briefcase from the trash and throws out the tote. Style shrieks, grabs the tote, and scolds Chemistry.

"This is an iconic 2019 Chanel!" she cries, wiping it down with a satin cloth. She glares at Chemistry, "You said you need our help, and you sure do! I will not let you go down there with some disgusting-looking, old Indiana Jones briefcase."

"Fine, but I am not carrying that," Chemistry points at the Chanel. Style cradles the bag as if Chemistry called her 'child' ugly.

"Fine!" Style retorts, "Compromise." She materializes a large black Saffiano Leather Handbag.

Chemistry looks over the bag, "I guess it's okay. Do you have anything without the big name on the front?" Style lunges at Chemistry, but Lust and Confidence hold her back.

Through gritted teeth, Style seethes, "You will carry Prada with pride. Nod if you understand me."

Wide-eyed, Chemistry nods as Lust whispers to Style to cool off. As Style goes, Lust swats her on the behind like he would a player leaving the field. She turns and slaps him across the face with crazed eyes. Lust responds with a delighted look. Style regains her composure and says with resentment, "I have an entire wardrobe to reimagine." Then, she slams the door as she leaves.

Humor approaches the bag and drops in a rubber band.

"That's it?" asks Chemistry.

"I'll have you know that that rubber band belonged to Buddy Hackett," off Chemistry's blank expression, "And having no understanding of the comedy world," he murmurs to the crowd of managers, "or any trace of a sense of humor," he turns back to Chemistry, "I suggest you accept my gift of joy and laughter with grace."

"Fine. Rubber band. Whatever." Chemistry looks to the managers to see what else they have for her.

Chemistry – *Jessica Sitomer*

Dejected, Humor walks toward his chair muttering under his breath doing his best Buddy Hackett impression, "No orda for her!"

"Knowledge, I'm going to need high-tech communication," Chemistry requests.

Knowledge stands up and produces an iPhoneXXX, a marvel of technology. "This has 3-D mapping, a Siri who actually knows answers to your questions, your calendar, contacts, files, best camera ever—"

He continues to list its features, much to Chemistry's chagrin. "Knowledge!" She gestures for him to hand it over.

"Wait!" Knowledge insists as he points out more essential features. "This app makes your phone a walkie-talkie to contact us." Chemistry looks wholly lost. "Or just text," he suggests, which only seems to baffle her more, so he starts to show Chemistry how as Lust grabs it from him and types...

Within seconds, Lust exclaims, "Yes! 3-D Por—"

Knowledge grabs it back, "You are a disgrace to humanity."

"Oh, stop!" Lust gushes, "You flatter me."

Knowledge rolls his eyes in contempt and hands the phone to Chemistry. She puts it in her bag.

"You'll also need a city map," Lust offers. "Just ignore the red dots unless, of course, you want a beer... or a prostitute."

Chemistry looks at the map. There's a giant beer stain and thousands of red dots.

"Don't be ridiculous," Knowledge insists, "she has Google Maps."

"I have what now?" Chemistry asks, the concept of earthly navigation foreign to her, as she nervously secures the top button of her collar. The transformation she would undergo for her mission weighs heavily on her mind.

Back in the room, Style swats her hand away before the button is through the hole. "That MIT look is not going to work down there. Here." Style pulls over a rack and folds a garment bag into Chemistry's bag. She looks Chemistry over and rethinks, grabbing all the clothing from the rack and dropping the entire wardrobe into the magical bag with one fell swoop. "Now you have choices," Style snarks.

"Thank you," Chemistry smiles at her, "I know I'm a disaster in your area."

Feeling Chemistry's sincere attempt at an apology, Style unstiffens. She takes Chemistry by the wrist and pulls her behind a dressing curtain.

Seconds later, Chemistry emerges in trendy jeans, a t-shirt that reads, 'but first, coffee,' and a pair of black leather Prada sneakers. Style points at the sneakers, "to go with the bag." Chemistry doesn't make the connection. Style again looks hopelessly at her colleagues, "I thought it was a teachable moment."

As her dedicated staff continues to pack her belongings, Chemistry ventures to the other side of her office to close out some files. The atmosphere is charged with anticipation, but Inspiration can't help but voice her surprise at the sudden development.

Vexed, she inquires, "We can go down there?"

With a touch of amusement in his voice, Lust addressed her concern. "Of course. You don't think she'd break a rule, do you?"

But Inspiration can't ignore the unease she senses in Chemistry. "Why is this the first I'm hearing of it?"

Confidence steps in to provide a reassuring explanation. "You haven't been gone long enough to go. Someone could recognize you."

Yet Inspiration remains uncertain, her gaze fixed on Chemistry. "She doesn't look pleased about it."

Knowledge, the perennial voice of reason, adds his perspective. "She's never been back to Earth. Never wanted to go."

Seeking further clarification, Inspiration asks, "So why now? What can she do down there that she can't do up here?"

Chemistry calls from behind her computer screen to reveal her mission. "Here, I only have access to his subconscious." She hits a button and comes back to her staff. "I need to get into his conscious mind."

Inspiration mouths "twelve years old," indicating her limited understanding.

"I can get to know him, find out why he's so resistant to learning his lesson so I can show him the errors of his ways, getting him matched and closing this case," Chemistry reiterates, her tone patient and understanding, though her grip on the red file indicates otherwise.

Inspiration has one final concern to address. "Will you lose your superpowers?"

For the first time, maybe ever, Chemistry breaks into laughter, the sound filling the room and causing a shocked reaction from the managers, who laugh with her, recognizing how they must appear to the earthly experience young Inspiration still carries. A sense of camaraderie and shared purpose bonds them to Chemistry in a way she's never let them in before. "You really are twelve. Unfortunately, the only power I'll lose is the power to be invisible."

Humor interjects, "I think the rubber band is working."

As the meeting concludes, Confidence affirms Chemistry's readiness for the mission. "You're ready!"

With the travel bag in Lust's capable hands, Chemistry is ushered toward the elevator, her journey to Earth imminent.

"I will be down there for the duration of this case," Chemistry declares. "I don't expect to need your assistance, but be ready just the same. I do expect each of you to maintain your department's workload and pick up any slack my absence may cause."

Her team nods in sincere agreement as the elevator doors open and Chemistry steps inside. As the doors close, her managers wave her off, their expressions filled with support and relief.

Lust announces, "Party in Chelsea Handler's dream!" All but Inspiration follow him into an elevator.

Chemistry – *Jessica Sitomer*

Chapter 7

Chemistry walks out of the elevator, her first step back on Earth, and into the lobby of the historic Plaza Hotel. She is immediately enveloped in an aura of timeless elegance and grandeur. The expansive space is adorned with intricate marble floors, polished to a mirror-like sheen, reflecting the luxury around her. Tall, majestic columns rise to meet the coffered ceiling, each detail meticulously crafted and gilded with gold leaf, adding a touch of regal splendor. Chandeliers of dazzling crystal hang gracefully from above, casting a warm, inviting glow that dances off the furnishings' rich, sumptuous fabrics and deep wood tones. Plush, velvety sofas and chairs are arranged in intimate clusters, inviting guests to relax and enjoy a luxury ambiance. The scent of fresh flowers from lavish arrangements permeates the air, adding a hint of nature's beauty to the sophisticated surroundings.

In the corner, a live pianist plays melodies on a grand piano, enhancing the refined atmosphere. The impeccably dressed staff move with an air of effortless grace and professionalism, ensuring that every guest feels like royalty from the moment they arrive. Chemistry is no exception as the concierge approaches her and asks if she can help.

Chemistry explains, "I'd like to go to Bacchus. It's a restaurant."

"Of course," says the concierge, "Everyone knows Bacchus. Excellent choice. Five minutes by cab. Shall I call over a reservation for you?"

"That's not necessary," Chemistry says.

"Oh, but it is. You'll never get in on Friday on your own, but as our guest, the owner will make room."

"I'll take my chances," Chemistry insists.

"Okay," the concierge warns, "At least have the Doorman get you one of our cars. If they see you pull up in it--"

"Thank you, I'll be fine." Chemistry says.

Determined to proceed with her mission without the help of anyone, Chemistry presses onward, making her way toward the hotel's entrance. The doorman, a courteous and wise figure, holds the door open for Chemistry as she emerges into the dazzling New York City day. She can't help but marvel at the unexpected beauty of the cityscape.

"First time in New York?" the doorman inquires, his tone friendly and welcoming.

Chemistry nods in affirmation, enamored by the unexpected excitement she suddenly feels.

"Business or pleasure?" he continues, curious about her presence.

With a hint of reluctance, she replies, "Business. Can you tell me where this address is?" She points to her iPhone.

"Whoa! What model is that?"

Chemistry immediately conceals it in her pocket, "It's not out. I'm a… product tester."

Unfazed by Chemistry's mysterious demeanor, the doorman provides helpful directions. "Go west 'til you hit Broadway, then north. It's not far. About 30 minutes if you walk. Mother Nature gave us a beautiful day."

"I don't think she had us in mind when she planned today's weather, but you're right. I will walk."

Happy to be of service, he tips his hat to her.

Chemistry – *Jessica Sitomer*

The streets of New York are busy as usual. Still, Chemistry takes her time experiencing the sounds of the car horns and people speaking into their Bluetooth, the smells of the hot dogs and pretzel carts, the beauty of Central Park, and the intimidating traffic lights. At first, she doesn't trust the walk sign and waits for a few light changes to determine the pattern. Then, she finally walks across the street.

At the next corner, as she waits alongside a crowd of impatient New Yorkers, she notices the young man from the graduation dream right in front of her. Leaning in close, she offers him a whispered blessing.

"Good luck," she says softly into his ear.

As the traffic light changes, the startled young man walks into the crowd of people crossing the street and inadvertently bumps into the girl from the graduation dream. As their eyes meet, he rubs his itchy eyes, and she soothes the goosebumps on her arms.

Car horns blare around them as the light changes again, yet they remain rooted to the spot, their eyes locked in a magnetic gaze. Chemistry can't help but smile at the encounter before her. Her expression reveals the pride she feels seeing her work in real life.

Chemistry finds herself at the Columbus Circle Shops. Looking at the beautiful window dressing, she stops when she sees her t-shirt on a very chic mannequin. Feeling stylish, she gets a spring in her step, but as she turns, she collides with a gentleman wearing a suit.

"I'm so sorry," he says, "please excuse me." He helps her regain her balance.

Chemistry freezes mid-step, thunderstruck. Her arm tingled where his hand steadied her. Actual human contact for the first time in centuries. She rubs the spot as if testing whether it is real. Flesh. Warm. Strange. Chemistry flinches, not out of shock but because of the rush of memories it stirs. His hand's warmth and simple, human contact weren't foreign. It was familiar. Painfully familiar. Her body remembers what it felt like to be alive, the warmth, pressure, texture. She hadn't realized she missed the sensation of touch until that very moment.

Chemistry – *Jessica Sitomer*

The man looks at her with concern, "Are you okay?"

Her mind buzzes with the weight of memory. The touch stirred a deep ache within her, not just in her skin but in her soul. She'd felt this a thousand times, and now it hit her all at once. I remember this…her thoughts whisper. I used to feel this way.

The air around her thickens, and for a moment, she is overwhelmed by how tangible everything feels, too tangible. Every nerve in her body seems to hum with the memory of a life lived long ago. I haven't felt this in so long… her breath catches in her throat. It's been centuries, she realizes, but it feels like only yesterday. Being down here isn't just work. It's a return to the pain, the joy, the love, and the heartbreak that came with it. She'd known it once, and now, standing here, it's all rushing back.

She continues up Broadway, startled and unsteady, until finally, she has to stop and support herself on a bodega fruit basket. The owner checks on her.

"Come inside. I have coffee," he offers.

"No, thank you. I don't--"

He cuts her off, pointing at her t-shirt. "'First coffee' I sell you coffee."

"Ah, no, it's just a saying. It's fashion."

Chemistry – *Jessica Sitomer*

"You try strawberry, very fresh." He gives her a strawberry. As she bites into the sweet berry, her eyes light up, "You like? Okay. I fill a bag." He fills a plastic bag and hands it to her.

"Thank you," she smiles and starts to walk away, bag in hand.

"Lady! You pay!" he demands.

"Oh, oh. Of course, of course. Ah..." she searches his face.

"Ten dollars."

"Ten dollars," she agrees, "I need money." A Prada wallet pokes out of her bag as she says the word. "Yes, money." She opens the wallet, pulls a hundred-dollar bill, and hands it to the bodega owner.

"Too big. Can't break."

Chemistry looks in the wallet. It is filled with hundred-dollar bills. "I don't have anything smaller. These berries are so good. Keep the change."

He smiles from ear to ear, "Yes? Okay, you wait." He grabs a large paper bag and fills it with blueberries, blackberries, heirloom tomatoes."

"That's fine," Chemistry insists. He shrugs and hands her the bag.

A woman approaches the bodega, ready to shop. Chemistry hands her the bag, "Will you please take this? The owner is so generous, but I'm allergic... to everything in there." The woman appreciates it as Chemistry walks away with only the strawberries.

A big orange sign catches her eye. It reads Zabar's, and then just a bit farther, she sees the sign she was looking for: BACCHUS.

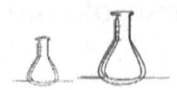

Inside of Bacchus, the restaurant looks impeccable. Everyone is at the top of their game. Servers are handing out complimentary tasting glasses of the specialty wine of the night. The mood is festive, and the kitchen door is propped open, so the delectable smells fill the air.

Matt walks up to Rusty, his bartender, and gives him a once-over.

"You ready for this?" he asks Rusty.

"Hundred percent," Rusty replies, "Where's Joshua?"

"He'll be here," Matt says, looking around the restaurant with pride. The servers are excited and eager to please as they go about their business.

The three investors arrive, and Matt greets them warmly, leading them to the bar. With practiced ease, Rusty pours five shots and sets them before the men, reserving one for himself.

The first investor expresses his admiration, remarking, "The place couldn't look better, Matt."

The next chimes in, "If the reviewer is kind tonight, we could be looking to expand."

"Where's Joshua?" the third one asks.

"He'll be here," assures Matt as he raises his shot in a toast, declaring, "Gentlemen, to a great review tonight."

Rusty and the three investors throw back their shots in unison, savoring the camaraderie of the moment. Matt is poised to do the same, but his actions come to an abrupt halt as his gaze is drawn to a striking figure entering the restaurant – Chemistry.

Unable to tear his eyes away, Matt unconsciously lowers his shot glass. A sudden lump forms in his throat as Chemistry stops to converse with the hostess, who then directs her toward the bar. Matt clears his throat, his eyes still locked on her.

Desperate for his shot, he reaches for it, but it's gone. He counts the empty shot glasses left by Rusty and his guests... four. As he continues to cough and choke, Chemistry steadily approaches.

Chemistry – *Jessica Sitomer*

Matt, losing his typically calm demeanor, implores, "Rusty, where's my shot?"

Rusty, seemingly unfazed by Matt's discomfort, responds, "I put it on the bar, Matt."

Matt grumbles, "Well, it isn't here."

As Chemistry draws nearer, Matt attempts to speak, but his voice fails him. When Chemistry arrives at the bar, she slips on the polished floor, careening into Eli, carrying an enormous food tray. Although Matt manages to catch Chemistry before she hits the ground, a domino effect has already started.

Eli tumbles to the floor. Food goes airborne, and chairs and patrons topple over, increasing the chain reaction. Servers stumble, more food soars through the air, and the calamity climaxes when a steaming cup of coffee spills onto a man's arm. In his pain, he inadvertently flings his metal briefcase hurtling directly toward Rusty, striking him square in the forehead and rendering him unconscious.

Eli, picking himself up, usually the cause of restaurant mishaps, promptly disassociates himself from the situation, "I didn't do it."

Covered in food, the investors hastily reach for napkins, while an older woman who had been on her way out lets out a colorful expletive when she sees the massive stain on her designer dress. With a calm demeanor, Matt addresses the situation.

"I'm so sorry, Mrs. Capo. Please bring me the dry-cleaning bill. Your next meal is on the house." He surveys the chaotic scene, frustration mounting.

"Rusty, I could really use my shot," Matt pleads, realizing the seemingly small request was his anchor in this storm.

Eli, popping up from behind the bar, delivers the unwelcome news, stating, "Rusty is out cold."

As Matt runs his fingers through his hair to regain his composure, Chemistry steps forward, her keen eyes trained on him.

"It's in your pocket," she informs him matter-of-factly. Matt, baffled, prompts her to elaborate. "Your shot," she clarifies, gesturing to the puddle on the floor, "that's why I slipped."

Matt's confusion washes over him as he looks down at his jacket pocket. The stain is undeniable, and he retrieves the shot glass and places it on the bar.

Joshua finally arrives, prepared for his grand entrance, and when he sees the disarray, he asks, "What happened?"

The hostess points at Chemistry, "Her."

Chemistry – *Jessica Sitomer*

The first investor tells Matt that the three will get out of his way and be in touch. They approach the door as Eli calls out, "Is there a doctor in the house?"

The well-trained staff is in excellent form, cleaning, charming guests, and bringing everything back to its state before the setback. Rusty is awake, but the three doctors behind the bar, tending to him, agree he is concussed. Eli calls Rusty's girlfriend to pick him up, then taps Matt on his shoulder, urging him, "You need to get a replacement in here, pronto."

"I'm already on it," Matt says, pulling out his phone as he walks through the restaurant, thanking guests and comping meals until he reaches his office. After one final look, confident his staff is back in their groove, he closes his door.

"He's never going to find a bartender this late on a Friday," one server laments.

Chemistry, however, has a twinkle in her eye as she surveys the bar, a plan forming in her mind. A smile creeps across her lips as she contemplates her next move.

Chemistry – *Jessica Sitomer*

Inside Bacchus's dimly lit back office, Matt sits at his desk, a list of twelve names and numbers before him. The list's first eleven names are marked with a conspicuous red line.

"Siri, call Mitch R." Matt listens to Siri confirm that she is calling Mitch R, a sense of resignation evident in his expression. He can't help but sigh in frustration as he hits speakerphone.

Matt is not surprised when Mitch offers apologies. With the call concluded, his shoulders slumped in defeat, Eli opens the office door, and sounds of raucous cheering and excited chatter shift Matt's attention.

"We don't have a TV, so why does it sound like someone put a game on?" Matt asks, puzzled by the sudden burst of enthusiasm.

"You've got to see this!" Eli beams. Intrigued, Matt follows Eli out of his office and into the central area of Bacchus.

The bar is a hub of activity, with a sizeable crowd gathered around. Matt pushes his way through the crowd. Amid the vibrant scene, he spots Chemistry skillfully twirling bottles and crafting cocktails in a dazzling array of colors. Arranged behind her on the bar are numerous squeeze bottles, each filled with a different hue, drawn from her scientific laboratory.

"You're still here?" Matt inquires, his tone a mixture of surprise and amusement.

Chemistry responds with a casual flip of a bottle, her movements as fluid and graceful as those of a seasoned bartender. She meets Matt's gaze, her expression tinged with playful defiance.

"Want me to go?" she challenges, her eyes sparkling with fun. Matt ponders her presence as he observes the lively crowd in his establishment.

"I haven't decided." His eyes glance over her collection of colorful squeeze bottles, interest gleaming in them. "What are those?" he inquires, his curiosity getting the better of him.

Chemistry offers him a drink, a faint smile playing on her lips. Matt accepts the drink and takes a sip, his expression thoughtful. "Not bad," he admits, acknowledging her mixology skills.

She divulges her secret, "Food coloring. I carry it wherever I go." Matt raises an eyebrow, bemused by her eccentricity, before outlining a challenge.

"That's... odd, but let's see what you've got. See that older guy at the end of the bar there," Matt gestures toward a surly older patron. Chemistry follows his gaze, her eyes settling on the cranky older man. "He's been here for hours milking that one drink," Matt explains. "I believe he's reviewing us. Impress him."

Chemistry glances at the man with clinical precision. "He's not reviewing you. He's lonely," she declares as if diagnosing a patient.

Matt insists, "How about you indulge me on this one?"

"Fine. But I do have a bit of expertise in this area." Accepting the challenge, Chemistry mixes a lavender-hued drink and approaches the older man. She confidently swaps his original drink for the concoction she has prepared. "You'll do better with this one," she assures him with a friendly smile.

The older man raises a curious eyebrow but tries the new drink. Chemistry's actions soon draw the attention of two young women nearby.

"Hey, what's that?" one of them asks.

The other young woman chimes in, "Can I try it?"

In a gesture of goodwill, the older man hands the drink to the first young woman, who takes a sip. Her reaction is immediate and positive, marked by an enthusiastic "Yummm." She then passes the drink to her friend, who follows suit.

Chemistry – *Jessica Sitomer*

Witnessing the transformation in the patron's demeanor, Chemistry can't help but feel a sense of accomplishment. She nods at him, conveying her silent understanding and well-wishes.

Seeking validation from Matt, she inquires, "Indulged?"

With an enigmatic smile, Matt responds, "Hm. What's your name?"

Chemistry stammers, her tongue seemingly tied by the unfamiliarity of an alias. "Chemm... meee—"

Suspicious, Matt carries on, "Well, good job... Chemmie. Keep it up."

With a nod of acknowledgment, Chemistry turns her attention back to her bartending duties, seamlessly mixing another drink to serve.

As the night continues, Bacchus's bar remains bustling with patrons. It has transformed into a haven for socializing singles, where lively conversations flow freely, and selfies are taken and shared on social media. Chemistry continues to serve colorful concoctions, each garnished with her unique touch.

"This place is great!" an awkward woman gushes, "I wasn't even going to go out tonight, but I just felt compelled."

Chemistry – *Jessica Sitomer*

"I know," Chemistry smiles as she hands her a cherry-red drink. "Here. Pass this to the guy behind you."

The awkward woman turns to hand the drink to the stuffy guy behind her when she is bumped, spilling the drink down his white shirt. "I'm so sorry! I was pushed and—"

Their eyes lock, and she lets out a hideous giggle while he breaks out in a flush. Chemistry nods knowingly, "Okay. Who's next?"

Misty, determined to join the festivities, maneuvers her way through the crowd and settles herself right before Chemistry. Chemistry, in response, places a vibrant lime green drink in front of her.

"Ooo. Pretty!" Misty exclaims, her eyes lighting up with intrigue. Eli approaches the bar, balancing a tray empty glasses. When he sets eyes on Misty, he suddenly loses his composure, stumbling and spilling the tray's contents all over himself. Chemistry swiftly rushes to his aid, her concern evident.

"Are you okay?" she inquires, extending a helping hand to assist Eli.

Eli, flustered by Misty's presence, struggles to articulate himself coherently. Instead, he offers an awkward quote, clearly influenced by his infatuation.

"Confucius says, 'Our greatest glory is not in never falling, but in rising every time we fall,'" he recites, emphasizing the proverb's wisdom. In a hushed tone, he adds to Chemistry, "She loves me," sporting a somewhat awkward smile before hastily exiting.

Chemistry returns her attention to Misty, who has completely ignored the exchange. I doubt that. Chemistry notices Misty looking for someone, pining. Chemistry clears her throat to break Misty's daze. Misty turns to Chemistry and seizes the opportunity to engage her in conversation. "You're new, so before you try and charge me 18 bucks for this concoction, let me just tell you--"

Matt appears behind the bar, interjecting smoothly, "Misty drinks for free."

Misty, caught off guard but quick on her feet, readily concurs, "Right, that's exactly what I was going to say."

Confused by the exchange, Chemistry enters detective mode: "Because she's your girlfriend?"

Misty lets out a honking laugh that brings the entire restaurant to a momentary silence as everyone looks in Misty's direction. "She thought I

Chemistry – *Jessica Sitomer*

was Matt's girlfriend," Misty announces. The staff and regulars laugh, too. The rest of the crowd gets back to their conversations. "I'm his neighbor," Misty assures her, "I mean, look at him. Not. My. Type." Matt strikes a pose so Chemistry can assess for herself. Chemistry's eyes sweep over Matt, from his newly polished shoes to his confident smirk. Step by step, she moves closer until they stand inches apart. She pauses at his eyes—searching, calculating, as if the answer to her puzzle might be hidden there.

Matt trips back, recovers, and smiles at Chemistry, "You've got paying patrons to attend to." Her facial features soften as she notes a vulnerability in his demeanor. She can't pull her eyes away, as if he will reveal the clue to unlock her case any second.

Misty breaks the trance, "Hello? Barkeep? Lots of customers vying for your attention." Chemistry breaks her stare, suddenly aware of all the eyes on her. "You're right. He is not your type," Chemistry excuses herself and sets about catering to the lively crowd.

Misty leans over the bar and taps Matt on the shoulder as he watches, entranced as Chemistry returns to work. "Matt!" he whirls around to face her and regain his composure, "I thought you didn't hire female bartenders after Joshua's lawsuit."

Matt offers a casual response, "I was in a bind. It's just tonight."

Misty persists with her observations, "She's pretty."

Matt adopts an air of nonchalance, replying with a hint of feigned indifference, "Is she?"

A waiter, counting his tips, approaches the conversation. His enthusiasm is palpable. "This is my best night ever!" he declares.

Matt cautions the waiter, "Don't get used to it," he quips. "I have no intention of turning this place into a meat market."

The singles continue to mingle while Chemistry spends the night multi-tasking. She expertly serves drink after drink while noting Matt's every move. He's charming but in the sincerest way. Pouring a neon yellow drink into a martini glass and pushing it toward an elegant woman, she watches as Matt easily walks through the restaurant. She also notices every woman swooning as he takes a moment to acknowledge them and thank them for coming. He treats the male customers similarly, with a practiced masculine charm that makes each feel like a

Chemistry – *Jessica Sitomer*

celebrity. Maybe it's medical, she thinks, then quickly types in her phone, 'Have Curie check his testosterone levels.' When she looks up Matt and Misty are looking at her. He mouths "no phones at work."

"She has been watching you all night... like a hawk," Misty adds.

"I know. I feel like I'm under a microscope." He checks his watch, "Two more hours." He looks back at the lonely man surrounded by women with lavender drinks and empty plates that Eli is clearing. "I think he enjoyed it." Matt smiles, confident that this is the beginning of something great.

At the end of the night, Misty exits Bacchus, venturing onto the bustling street to hail a cab. Chemistry emerges from the restaurant with a wad of cash. A homeless man shuffles by, muttering about the one who had slipped away. Chemistry extends her hand, offering him the money. The man's eyes fill with tears as Misty, observing from the curb, tries to make out what Chemistry is saying. Chemistry hugs him before she lets him go, and as he walks away with his shoulders back and head held high, Chemistry calls to him, "I believe in you!" Almost like a spell, she watches him walk a little taller.

The compassionate gesture touches Misty, and she shouts to Chemistry. "You gave him everything you made?"

Chemistry shrugs, her gaze still fixed on the homeless man as he continues down the street. "I don't need it," she explains. "Besides, there's someone he's still longing for. Maybe he'll use it to clean up, get a haircut, make things right."

Misty considers Chemistry's response, a warm smile forming on her lips. She decides to forego the cab that had pulled over for her and approaches Chemistry instead.

"That's the sweetest thing I ever heard," Misty remarks. "Which way do you live? We can share a cab."

"I don't live here. I'm just in town for a short time."

"Oh, that's too bad," Misty pouts, "I had already claimed you as my best friend... in my head. Which hotel are you staying in?"

"I hadn't given that any thought," she admits, looking lost. "Any suggestions?"

Misty, ever resourceful, gives a four-finger whistle, summoning a cab that pulls over. She gestures toward the open door with a spirited grin. Chemistry climbs in as Misty follows and closes the door.

Chemistry – *Jessica Sitomer*

Chapter 8

Misty unlocks the front door to the brownstone and then locks it behind them. She walks toward her place, but Chemistry stands at the entrance, confused by the floor plan. Within this quaint yet characterful space, five doors, two on either side, are slightly ajar, and at the far end of the corridor, the fifth door is wide open. The open door is the one Misty walks into. Chemistry examines her file as she cautiously takes a step forward. This doesn't seem right. It feels like someone's dream. She pinches herself as Misty pokes her head out and tells her to come in. Chemistry's eyes dart from the document to the surroundings as she comprehends the unusual setting.

"Is this floor all yours?" Chemistry asks, noticing a guy in a robe through the crack of the first door she passes.

"I wish," Misty says.

Chemistry – *Jessica Sitomer*

"All the doors are open," Chemistry says, "Are you sure it's okay that I'm here?"

Unfazed by the unorthodox atmosphere, Misty reassures her. "Of course. The neighbors are used to me bringing home strays. You're good as long as you remember to lock the front door."

Misty meets Chemistry halfway to coax her to her apartment. "Two years ago, the plumbing burst and the whole floor was flooded, so the doors warped. Our landlady is 97. She couldn't understand our calls about what was happening, so Matt paid for the plumbing to be fixed, and we all live harmoniously with our doors open." In a whisper," She's never raised our rent, so we don't want to call any attention to us."

Lola emerges from Misty's apartment. Chemistry freezes.

"That's a big dog," Chemistry observes with a hint of apprehension. "A massive dog."

"Don't be afraid," Misty reassures her. "She's Matt's. Come here, Lola." Misty calls Lola over with an inviting tone. The dog responds by approaching Misty and nuzzling her affectionately. Chemistry watches with a mix of curiosity and unease.

Her tone knowing as she closes her file and inquires, "So, Matt from the restaurant lives here?"

Misty points to the last door to her left, "Right there. He's a great neighbor. Kinda looks out for all of us when he's not busy with the restaurant." Chemistry pulls a pen from her bag and makes notes on Matt's file. "And I have the privilege of looking after Lola while he's at work." They reach Matt's door, "But now it's time to go home, big girl, go to bed." Lola nudges the door open obediently, returning to Matt's apartment. Chemistry attempts to catch a glimpse of his living space as Misty pulls his door as closed as it will go and then, with grandeur, presents hers, "Ta-da!"

Chemistry's eyes widened with surprise as she steps inside. After seeing so many in the dream world, this apartment is not what she expected. It looks like a junk collector's version of Chemistry's labs with piles of magazines and displays of collectibles. It's hard to tell where functionality ends and pure chaos begins. Appliances, trinkets, and... is that a toaster doubling as a vase?

Yet Chemistry immediately feels comfortable, as if Misty's love for choosing every item emanates from them, raising the vibration of the small space. The only area that feels cold to Chemistry is the wall displaying framed magazine covers and articles chronicling Joshua's achievements.

Chemistry – *Jessica Sitomer*

A pack of quirky dogs enthusiastically greet Chemistry, darting through Misty's legs with uncontainable excitement.

"Hello, babies," Misty greets the dogs. "Look who I brought home. We have a new friend. Yes, we do."

Chemistry, initially hesitating in the doorway, steps into Misty's place. Her eyes dart around the room, taking in the astonishing collection of oddities that populate every corner.

"If you don't mind me asking, what do you do for work?"

"I don't mind at all," Misty beams, "I am a certified dog aromatherapist, acupuncturist, and proud 5-star sitter and dog-walker on Rover."

"Wow, you're the first celebrity I've met. Speaking of... what's with all the pictures of Matt's chef?" Chemistry asks.

Misty can't help but gush, "Joshua? Isn't he to die for?"

"He is something," Chemistry says as she turns in place, taking it all in. "When will Matt be home?" she asks, then realizes Misty has left the room.

"Not for a while," Misty calls back. He's never home before 2 a.m."

Chemistry identifies a potential issue. There's the problem. All work and no play. She retrieves

Matt's file and jots down more notes, determined to address Matt's situation effectively. Let's fix him once and for all.

As Chemistry makes her way to the couch, she is surrounded by Misty's eclectic pack of dogs. She navigates them cautiously, as her attention is drawn to the window with the slightest peek of Central Park. Suddenly, she steps on a squeaky toy, causing the dogs to go wild and her to jump in surprise. She quickly recovers her composure and reaches for her iPhoneXXX. With a sense of urgency, she types a message: "NEED YOU IN THE AM."

The message was sent, and Chemistry settles onto the couch, awaiting Misty's return and formulating the best plan for closing Matt's file tomorrow.

From behind a pile of sheets, blankets, and pillows, Misty makes her way to the couch and tells Chemistry to scootch as she makes up Chemistry's bed for the night. Misty, now dressed in all black like a cat burglar, informs her, "I saw a cot on 85th and Central Park West. Rich people always throw out top-quality stuff. I will grab it for you if no one got it already."

Chemistry – *Jessica Sitomer*

"Wait, Misty," Misty halts but shuffles from side to side, eager to go after her find, "I'm going to be leaving tomorrow, so there's no need."

"Leaving! You just got here. I'll get the cot. If I build it, you will stay."

Chemistry opens her mouth to speak, but Misty is gone. One of the dogs jumps on the couch and plants his butt on her pillow. Chemistry swats him away, "You're lucky I don't need to sleep." She tosses the pillow to a chair, pulls out the file, and works on Matt's formula.

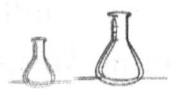

Morning sunlight filters through the curtains, casting a warm glow in Misty's cluttered apartment. In all her enormity, Lola pads into the living room, stopping to stare at Chemistry, who is fast asleep on the couch. A cot, neatly folded beside her, hints at an uncomfortable night. Chemistry's nose wrinkles in her sleep as Lola's heavy panting fills the room.

Lola, ever eager for attention, takes matters into her paws. She leans in, licking Chemistry's face with slobbery enthusiasm. Chemistry's eyes snap open to find the giant dog inches from her face. Panic reflects in her gaze as she realizes her state of undress—boy shorts and a bra. She bolts upright, trips over the cot in her scramble toward the bathroom, and flushes a bright red, even though no one can witness her embarrassment.

Moments later, Misty emerges from her bedroom, clutching the morning newspaper under her arm. She greets Lola with a warm smile. "Good morning, Lola. Where's Chemmie? Where's your daddy?"

Clad in casual morning attire, Matt enters the apartment, beating scrambled eggs into whipped cream.

"Did you read it?" Matt asks, his eyes on the newspaper, his whipping more aggressive.

Misty grins at Lola before addressing Matt with a teasing tone. "Of course, I read it! 'Bacchus is the best singles spot this reviewer's ever seen!'"

Matt frowns. "Singles spot! I want to be known for the menu and the ambiance."

Misty takes the bowl and whisk from Matt, setting them down before pressing acupuncture spots on his hand. Matt tries to pull away, but Misty's grip is firm.

"Relax!" she insists, "take the win."

"It didn't feel like a win for Djokovic when Federer pulled out of the ATP finals because of a back injury."

"I'm sure that.. guy who won.. was happy to have the medal."

"Trophy, and clearly, you know nothing about competing."

"This is not a sport, Matt, but if it were, you won the review."

Matt grabs the bowl and mashes the whisk into the fallen concoction. "The restaurant business is as competitive as any pro sport. Last night, I was aiming for Yankee fame, and instead, I got Banana Ball."

Misty laughs, yanking at the bowl as they enter a playful tug-of-war. "You know what's bananas? Your reaction!" Misty says, "The review says, 'Come for the bar scene, stay for the food.' The food, Matt! Your food!" He seems to concede when she continues, "You've got to admit that bar scene was awesome!"

"And therein lies my problem," Matt laments. He lets go of the bowl before Misty can regain her grip. It falls to the soft kitchen mat, and before he can apologize, the dogs move in to clean up the mess. Misty pulls him to the couch, trying to understand.

His head is crestfallen, and she hugs her friend. Matt explains, "They will show up tonight eagerly anticipating Chemmie and her food coloring, but I have no idea where to find her." Lola barks deeply at the bathroom door.

Misty begins, "Actually--"

Matt cuts her off, "Lola! Leave the other dogs alone."

Suddenly, a SHHH! Comes from behind the bathroom door. Matt's eyes narrow as he slowly rolls up the newspaper.

Matt whispers, "There's someone in your bathroom." He raises the paper over his head like a makeshift weapon.

"Matt, no!" Misty warns, but it's too late. With increasing force, Matt yanks on the doorknob until Chemistry, flustered and disoriented, tumbles out. She grabs the newspaper from Matt's hand and fashions a makeshift towel around herself.

Lola nuzzles Chemistry, her tail wagging wildly as Misty claps her hands together. "Look who I found!"

Still processing the surprising turn of events, Matt takes a moment to assess Chemistry's appearance. His expression displays a mix of curiosity and intrigue.

Chemistry – *Jessica Sitomer*

"About time you brought home a stray who doesn't need her shots..." Matt says, his eyes scanning Chemistry. "Or a groomer."

Not sure if he's complimenting or insulting her, Chemistry grasps for a retort. What would Humor say? What would Humor say? Wishing she had the rubber band.

Misty, eager to diffuse the tension, chimes in. "Didn't you want to thank Chemmie for her help last night?"

Matt crosses his arms. "Thank is a strong word for turning my bar scene upside down, but I'm grateful that you filled in last night," Matt says to Chemistry.

"It's not a problem," she replies. I have exceptional skills, and you desperately needed me."

Matt raises an eyebrow. "Desperate is a bit of an exaggeration."

"Oh, so you had someone lined up if I didn't pass your quality test?"

"I never said you passed my quality test. Neon drinks and fine dining don't exactly go together."

Misty interjects with a grin, "That's exactly what the review says they do."

Chemistry – *Jessica Sitomer*

Matt frowns, recalling the review. "That reviewer was probably seduced by a couple of Gen Zs and a lavender cocktail."

Chemistry walks over to Misty and peruses the article. A smile creeps over her face, then a laugh. Matt grabs the paper. "What's funny?"

"Only that the writer's name is Sue, sooooo not an old guy," Chemistry retorts.

Matt opens his mouth to protest but then smirks, unwilling to admit his mistake. "Ever heard Johnny Cash's A Boy Named Sue?"

Misty and the dog's heads watch the banter like a pickleball volley. They continue to argue back and forth.

"I don't need your thanks or songs. In a few hours, my job will be done here, and I will never have to see you again. Poof!"

Matt, recognizing his predicament, finally blurts, "Or... you could work for me."

"I already have a job that's all work, no play. Last night was fun and loose," she idealizes, "You're all work and," she looks him over, "Stiff."

"I can be fun and loose!" Matt insists, though even he seems doubtful of his own words.

"Really? What time did you get home last night?" he opens his mouth to answer, but she continues, "When's the last time you took a vacation—a day off? Had a good belly laugh?"

Misty and the dogs look expectantly at Matt, waiting for his answer.

Matt pivots, desperate to seal the deal. "Did I mention I pay really well?"

Chemistry stares him down and then offers a poetic reflection. "Nothing does the soul so sweet than walking down a tree-lined street." She whistles for Lola, "Want to go for a walk in the park?"

Lola hears 'walk' and instantly stands at attention. Chemistry grabs her bag, drops the newspaper towel, and gracefully returns to the bathroom. Moments later, she emerges fully dressed and confidently clicks her tongue for Lola to follow, leaving Matt clouded with more questions than answers.

The sun peeks up in the morning sky, casting dappled shadows across the winding paths of Central Park. Lust perches on a weathered bench, his eyes darting back and forth as he watches a parade of jogging women pass.

Chemistry – *Jessica Sitomer*

"Fake... fake... fake..." he mutters under his breath, his head bobbing in time with his observations. Then, as if struck by lightning, he exclaimed, "Real!" His gaze lands on a woman who, in his estimation, is the genuine article, only to realize, "Ew!" It's Chemistry.

"What?" questions Chemistry asks as she approaches him. Lola clambers up Lust's leg, attempting a rather unconventional form of affection.

Lust pushes Lola off, "Down, girl! You're not my type." Lola, the gentle giant, flops onto the grass with a groan. Lust turns back to Chemistry. "I've been keeping watch, but no sign of her. How do you know she'll show?"

Chemistry, ever enigmatic, smiles knowingly. "Because I know everything."

Lust raises an eyebrow, leaning back with a smirk. "No way your boy's missing this one." He gestures toward the jogging path.

Sure enough, in the distance, Matt's dream girl—the model from the bar—appears, her graceful stride catching the morning light. Lust nods approvingly. "Not bad. He won't be able to resist."

As Chemistry prepares to leave, Lust adds, "Gotta hand it to you, Chemistry. You've got a talent for planning these moments."

Chemistry doesn't reply, her gaze fixed on the approaching woman, and then she searches for Matt.

Inside Misty's cozy apartment, three dogs sit with military precision, eyes glued to Matt, who is staring anxiously at his wristwatch. The tension in the room feels thick, like the calm before a storm.

"Okay, go!" Misty suddenly exclaims, breaking the silence.

Matt's head jerks up. "You really think so? I don't want her to think I'm chasing her."

Misty rolls her eyes. "You are chasing her."

Matt sighs, rubbing the back of his neck. "I don't want her to think I'm desperate."

Misty snorts. "You are desperate."

Matt's anxiety seems to ramp up as he rechecks his watch. "What's the plan again?"

Misty grins mischievously. "You're offering her a job, not asking her for a date. It's simple."

He doesn't look convinced. "You sure?"

Misty nods enthusiastically. "Positive. Unless, of course, you'd rather ask her out..."

Chemistry – *Jessica Sitomer*

Matt shoots her an impatient look, which quickly becomes a wry smile. "Sure, I'll fit her in between menu changes, finding a new prep chef, and inventory... Don't even get me started on that. How are we out of basil? Along with keeping the accursed kitchen from going down in flames, literally and figuratively, and of course, everything else that Joshua isn't doing--"

Misty cuts off his diatribe, "Perfect!"

Matt shakes his head and looks back at his watch, "I think now."

Misty chuckles, her gaze shifting to the dogs. One lets out an unexpected burp, adding a touch of levity to the tense atmosphere. Misty giggles, and Matt even cracks a smile despite his nerves. He waves to them as he leaves, heading for the park.

Chemistry strides purposefully along the grassy hills lining the jogging path. She can't help but notice happy couples lying on blankets, reading books, or listening to music. People play frisbee and fetch with their dogs while others scoff up breakfast or sip coffee. Style and Confidence follow behind her. Style stops, checks that no one is watching, and changes her heels into sneakers. Confidence skips to keep up, waving at a toddler who falls after a few steps. She gives him the thumbs up.

With an edge of impatience in her voice, Style remarks, "We've been waiting for twenty minutes."

Confidence skips along, unbothered. "He'll be here, I'm sure!"

Chemistry stops, her gaze fixed on the path ahead as she counts down in a hushed voice, "Three... two... one--"

But there is no sign of Matt. A perplexed expression creeps across Chemistry's face until, like a mirage, he appears across the street, dressed impeccably in a suit.

Confidence can't contain her excitement. "Ooo! Ooo! There he is."

Chemistry glances at her watch again, bewildered. Matt sees Chemistry and skillfully maneuvers his way across the path, narrowly avoiding a rollerblader but not escaping an accidental collision with "the match." As they trip over each other, Matt manages to catch her so she doesn't hit her head, causing him to land hard on his side.

Lust, observing from a distance, chimes in with a sly grin. "That's gonna leave a mark."

Chemistry – *Jessica Sitomer*

Lola dashes over to Matt as he's back on his feet. He dusts himself off and extends a hand to help "the match" up. Chemistry is pleased that the quirky teacher from Matt's dream has finally made eye contact and admires her work as "the match" swoons over Matt, her free hand clutching her stomach. What? Incomprehensible to Chemistry, Matt pulls his hand away with a nod of apology and casually takes hold of Lola's leash and newspaper. Then, without a second thought, he continues toward Chemistry, leaving "the match" to brush herself off.

"Did you see that?! Nothing," Chemistry criticizes.

Lust observes with a mischievous glint, "I wouldn't say nothing. A large A cup can still fill a palm."

Chemistry sighs, shaking her head. "No connection. This doesn't calculate."

Matt, now approaching Chemistry, calls out, "Chemmie!"

Lust mumbles to her, "Chemmie? That's the best you could do?"

Too frustrated to deal with Lust, she turns and walks briskly away, her loyal companions, Style and

Confidence, following her lead. Lust remains behind, keeping a close watch on "the match."

"Chemmie!" Matt calls out again, determined to catch up to her.

The three women came to an abrupt halt. Matt walks up to them, and Confidence can't help but gasp in admiration.

"Wow!" she exclaims.

Style nods in agreement. "I told you he was hot."

Chemistry shoots a warning look at her employees. "Ladies, he can hear you."

"Hi!" Confidence greets Matt with a friendly smile. Matt returns the gesture with a warm smile of his own. Chemistry discreetly nudges Style, urging her to make her exit.

"Bye," Style says, pulling a reluctant Confidence away.

As they depart, Confidence calls to Chemistry, "Going back up. Call if you need me! You got this! But I'm happy to help-" Style pulls her along, leaving Chemistry and Matt to continue their conversation.

Matt baits a conversation, "Interesting friends."

"Not my friends." Chemistry's tone is a mixture of amusement and caution, "Following me, Mr. Durand? There are laws regarding that--"

Chemistry – *Jessica Sitomer*

Matt interrupts with an offer, "I'll pay you whatever you want. It'll be fun and loose, and..." But Matt's words are cut short as he stops, sniffing the air, checking for Lola, who is off sunbathing. He glances down and bursts into laughter.

"What's so funny?" Chemistry asked, perplexed.

Matt can't contain his amusement. "You're standing in dog..."

Chemistry looked down, her expression quickly shifting from confusion to disgust. She has stepped in a pile of--

"Crap!" she yells, trying to wipe her shoe on the grass as Matt laughs. "Oh, disgusting!" This only makes Matt laugh harder.

"It's not funny," Chemistry complains.

"I'm sorry. But it is a little funny," Matt admits between chuckles. He laughs even harder, struggling to regain his composure. He unravels his paper, "I can't have you working in my restaurant like this," he finally manages to say.

He squats down, carefully removing her shoe, and armed with the newspaper, cleans it. Chemistry, despite her initial irritation, leans on his shoulder.

"Willing to clean the doo off a shoe. How chivalrous," she remarks. "Why aren't you off the market yet?"

Matt pauses momentarily, his gaze softening as he continues working on her shoe. "Because I'm not on the market," he says. "Besides, I wouldn't wipe the doo from just any shoe."

Chemistry arches an eyebrow, intrigued. "Is that so? Please give me an idea then. Is it the designer shoe that gets you, or a running shoe, perhaps? You don't seem like the sensible shoe type of guy. Maybe a--"

"Not interested," Matt interjects, his tone firm.

"But if you were? Indulge me," Chemistry presses, calling back to their moment at the bar.

Matt considers her question for a moment, then relents. "All right. Here it is. I like a sexy shoe, you know... tall, skinny heel that accentuates the calf. I like a color that catches your eye but doesn't scream for attention. But that's all packaging. The most important thing about a shoe, which most shoes lack, I must stress, is comfort."

Chemistry can't help but chuckle. "So, you don't find a lot of comfortable shoes out there?"

Matt nods, a hint of amusement in his eyes. "Turns out when the heels get that high, they're awfully painful to wear."

"You sound like you're speaking from experience," Chemistry says.

Matt finishes cleaning her shoe and carefully slips it back onto her foot. Standing up, he takes her hand, ready to lead her away. "She was a stiletto," he admits with a smile.

"Ouch," Chemistry plays along, "But that would've been a long time ago. You don't seem outwardly damaged. Surely, you've gone shoe shopping since then?"

Matt takes a deep breath, wanting so badly to change the subject. "How about no more questions? We walk to the other side of the street, you watch your step, and when we get to the corner, you tell me if you will accept my job offer."

"Can I ask you more questions if I do?"

"Already breaking the rules."

"That's me... a rule breaker," she says, sounding like the geekiest possible version of a rule breaker. She tries to recover, sounding tough, "You must know who you're hiring if I decide to say yes." Matt shakes his head, "And my yes is contingent on me being able to ask all the questions I want."

Chemistry – *Jessica Sitomer*

Matt throws his arms up in surrender as they leave the park.

When Chemistry returns to Misty's apartment, a new bejeweled divider curtain is by the window. The dogs bark as Chemistry walks in and looks at the aesthetic blight. "Ta-da!" Misty draws the curtain, startling Chemistry. The cot is made up with bright blankets and mismatched pillows. A secondhand night table is placed next to it, with an old alarm clock and fresh flowers in a short vase. The decoupaged dresser is what's most distressing to the eyes.

Chemistry attempts to sound light, "What is all this?"

"Matt told me you took the job, so we're gonna be roomies!" Misty can't contain her excitement. "I'm so glad I grabbed the cot! And this..." she presents the dresser like a game show host, "I made myself and want you to have it. Will you have your things shipped? I can take you shopping in the meantime."

Chemistry – *Jessica Sitomer*

Chemistry stares, eyes wide, mouth agape, accessing the situation as quickly as possible. On the one hand, this living situation is way too much for her, but on the other hand, she is here to do a job and go back. This proximity to Matt is ideal. If she has her way, she'll be gone in 48 hours. You can do anything for 48 hours, she tells herself.

"It's great, Misty. Thank you for your hospitality."

"Of course! Let's go shopping!"

"I prefer to shop alone," Chemistry says. Misty's face drops. "I find it more fun to pick out outfits and then surprise my friend with a fashion show." The word 'friend' instantly brightens Misty's entire demeanor.

"Fun!" Misty agrees. "Okay, go to Columbus Avenue. You'll have a blast. Then you can come back and model...Oh! I'll go down to the garment district and get some red remnants so you can walk the red carpet."

Chemistry smiles, having no idea what she is referencing, but at least Misty's happy again.

Columbus Avenue encapsulates the essence of Upper West Side fashion: a sophisticated blend of timeless elegance, contemporary trends, and a touch of eclectic charm. Whether hunting for the latest runway-inspired looks, unique vintage pieces, or stylish activewear, Columbus Avenue offers a diverse and dynamic shopping experience that caters to every fashion sensibility.

    This is lost on Chemistry, who avoids the task ahead of her, admiring the tree-lined streets, charming brownstones, and inviting cafes. It's a picturesque backdrop that makes shopping here a leisurely and enjoyable activity and, for Chemistry, a necessary one. The stores are small, and Chemistry wants to disappear, so she chooses Bloomingdale's as her first stop because of its large size. Immediately, she is approached by a saleswoman, who looks Chemistry over disapprovingly and winces when she realizes the strange odor in the air is coming from the stains on her shoe. The avid professional chooses to focus on them being Prada, and the matching Prada bag she also assesses with her keen eye is authentic. Knockoffs in this city are a problem, but a seasoned professional can spot them in seconds.

    "May I help you?" she asks Chemistry warmly.

    "Thanks. I need black jeans and black T-shirts."

    "Oh, surely you need more than that," she pulls Chemistry by the arm. "As a start, you need new shoes. We do have Prada, or perhaps you'd be interested in Jimmy Choo's Embellished Knit Low Top? Black or ash mixed? There's a new shipment of sundresses you'll love. They're great for showing off your figure."

Chemistry pulls her arm away and swings herself in the opposite direction, right out the door. Briskly walking, unsure if she'll be followed, she decides on a new approach. Chemistry stops at the first store with a mannequin clothed in jeans, and as she window shops, she takes a photo of the jeans and the store logo. She continues down the street, snapping pictures of store names like Theory and Rag & Bones, Anthropologie and Free People, and, on final inspection, Lululemon.

Chemistry peeks into Misty's apartment. No Misty, no dogs. Relieved, Chemistry puts her Prada on the table and pulls out paper bags, branded by the names of the stores she photographed, filled with clothes that only Style's touch could curate. She searches for tonight's wardrobe and finds the black jeans and t-shirts in the Rag & Bones bag. "Black shoes?" she asks into the bag, then pulls out a Steve Madden box with gorgeous but chunky heeled shoes inside. She looks, then drops it back in,

Chemistry – *Jessica Sitomer*

"Comfortable black shoes." A bag handle pops up, and Chemistry pulls out an ECCO bag. She places the rest around the living room for appearances and steps into the bathroom to get changed. She hurries, intent on leaving before Misty returns expecting a fashion show.

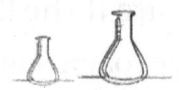

The lighting casts a warm, golden glow inside Bacchus. Chemistry works deftly behind the bar, mixing a drink with practiced ease. Matt observes her with a pensive stare. She looks over at him and smiles, then turns to add a little flare to her mix to tease him. Matt shakes his head with a slight roll of eyes, clearly not wanting the antics of the night before, yet wanting the magic she brings. He's about to walk away when she says, "You have to be willing to break them in." Her voice conveys wisdom, "You know, the shoes."

Realizing she's referring to their earlier conversation rather than her bartending skills, Matt leans on the bar, offering a playful retort. "I'd rather go barefoot."

Chemistry – *Jessica Sitomer*

Chemistry counters with a knowing smile. "Somewhere out there, there's a shoe that fits."

Matt's lips curl into a faint grin. "I'm beginning to hope so." They stare at each other, neither willing to turn away first, until Matt, with a bottle of champagne in hand, remembers he's working. "Come with me."

He waves his hand, gesturing Chemistry to follow. With a hint of intrigue, she does. They go to a table occupied by an elderly couple, Mr. and Mrs. Topel. The pair wear matching outfits and savor basic grilled cheese sandwiches with a side of curly fries.

"Chemmie, I'd like to introduce you to Mr. and Mrs. Topel. They are celebrating their sixty-fifth wedding anniversary tonight," Matt announces.

Chemistry's eyes light up with genuine admiration. "Wow! Congratulations."

Mr. Topel graciously acknowledges the praise. "She's the one to congratulate for putting up with my mess, my inventions, and my lady chasing all these years."

"'Lady chasing!' Don't pay him any mind. He's been a dream," Mrs. Topel chimes in with a fond smile.

Chemistry – *Jessica Sitomer*

Matt can't resist a playful jab. "I don't know about that. I've seen his table manners."

The Topels laugh. Their affection for each other is evident in their shared glances. Mr. Topel leans closer to Chemistry, his voice filled with reminiscence. "No, she's right. After all, everything started in a dream..."

Chemistry's interest piqued, she leans into the conversation, listening intently.

"My mother had been retelling stories of the depression, and I wasn't sleeping well, but that night, I fell into a deep sleep, and there she was," Mr. Topel began, taking Mrs. Topel's hand in his. "I was lost in a dark alley, and I was--" he continues, his eyes locked with Chemistry's.

"Hungry," she interjects, remembering the story.

"Yes!" Mr. Topel exclaims. "And she came out with bushels of food, but suddenly all of these strangers filled the alley and stole her food, then ran off. She had nothing to give me but her hand. I reached for it, and I felt--" Mr. Topel pauses, his eyes shimmering with emotion.

Chemistry whispers under her breath, her eyes well up, "Electricity."

"I woke up and couldn't shake the feeling. A few days later, I was applying for a job. I didn't get it, but the owner's daughter sauntered in as I was leaving. As we walked by each other, she touched me and gave me such a shock--"

Mrs. Topel interrupts with a practical explanation. "It was from the carpet."

"Carpet, nothing!" Mr. Topel insists. "I recognized her immediately. Love at first sight."

Matt seizes the moment to pour champagne into their glasses, proposing a toast. "To 'love at first sight.'"

The Topels clink their glasses and share a tender kiss. Their connection is as strong as it had been sixty-five years ago. Matt leaves them to their celebration and escorts Chemistry back to the bar.

Wanting to shake off the moment's spell, she says, "I don't remember seeing grilled cheese and curly fries on your menu."

"This used to be their diner. They came every Saturday for grilled cheese sandwiches and curly fries. 'Not steak fries, not skinny fries,'" Matt imitates Mr. Topel, "When we opened, they kept coming. Josh knows to have those American cheese slices and frozen fries ready every Saturday. Creatures of habit," Matt explains, a sense of admiration in his voice.

Chemistry – *Jessica Sitomer*

Chemistry can't help but inquire, "Why did you want me to meet them?"

Matt pours himself a drink, his eyes locking onto Chemistry's. "Do you believe in soulmates?"

The question catches Chemistry off guard, and her stomach flutters in response. She averts her gaze and starts mixing a drink. She answers, "Without a doubt. Do you?"

Matt quickly covers his tracks. "No. But I figure girls like that kind of stuff, and I'm trying to make work fun and light for you, and the Topels are... special."

Chemistry nods and hands him a drink, "Give this to the woman at the end of the bar."

Matt dutifully walks over to the woman at the end of the bar. She turns on her bar stool to meet his practiced work smile as he presents his "match" with her drink.

"You," the woman lights up. "We've got to stop meeting this way... unless it's fate. We wouldn't want to mess with fate, right?" she flirts.

"Have me met?" Matt asks, confused.

"I was here twice before, as were you, and then the park?" Matt has no recollection, "You knocked me over this morning while I was running."

Chemistry – *Jessica Sitomer*

"Oh, of course. Are you alright?" Matt asks, concerned.

"I'm fine," she laughs. "My ego's a little bruised that you don't recognize me."

"Are you a model or something?" Matt offers.

"Well, yes, but I thought you'd recognize me because we've bumped into each other four times now, and I—" Her tone is a balance of embarrassment and insecurity, "I usually leave quite an impression on men."

"I'm sorry I don't remember you." He adds gently, "I meet a lot of people."

"Really?" her voice grows desperate, "You don't remember me at all? Because I can't seem to forget you. And since you've been here when I've been here, I thought I'd give it a shot, come by, try and catch you, introduce myself." She extends a hand. Matt shakes it professionally.

"I own the place, so I hate to upset your fate theory, but..."

Chemistry watches intently as the woman holds her stomach, swooning, but when she looks at Matt, there is no spark to be seen.

Matt looks uncomfortable. "Anyway, drinks on me tonight for tripping you. Again, my apologies," he says, pointing to Chemistry to make sure the woman is cared for. Chemistry glares at him but nods her head in understanding. He shakes the woman's hand again. "I do have to get back to work."

The model is stunned and disappointed as Matt disappears into the bar crowd, which has grown considerably in the last thirty minutes. She leaves her drink and the restaurant. Chemistry wants to scream in frustration but keeps it together, smiling at patrons shouting drink orders at her.

Later, Matt goes behind the bar to check on Eli as he replenishes the garnishes and empty bottles.

Eli grins, "Want me to place a rush order on all the empty bottles? We are going through the alcohol tonight, Boss."

Matt gives him a thumbs up and is about to walk away when Chemistry, unable to contain her annoyance, steps between Eli and Matt, putting her finger in Matt's chest. "You mean to tell me that you felt nothing when you looked at that gorgeous woman?" Chemistry vents.

Surprised, Matt questions, "What are you talking about?

The conversation volume sparks the interest of the people on the barstools. "That supermodel? The one I asked you to give the drink to? You felt nothing?"

Matt thinks back, shaking his head. "What did you want me to feel?"

Chemistry's irritation grows as she paints a vivid picture. "Oh, I don't know-- a combination of you going speechless as butterflies flutter in her stomach."

Matt muses, "That's strangely specific and would be something, but no. Sorry. Why are you so fixated on my attraction to women?"

"I'm... I'm not, but... What was wrong with her? She's perfect. Do you realize that all you do is work?" Chemistry argues passionately.

Matt, somewhat taken aback, counters her argument. "How do you know? You just met me!"

Eli mumbles out the side of his mouth, "She's not wrong."

Chemistry, unyielding, insists, "I know your type, and one day you are going to wake up alone and arrive at your successful restaurant and wonder, 'Is this all there is?'"

Matt remains composed. "Don't worry. I'll meet someone eventually."

A man in his sixties dressed like he's in his thirties interjects with a dose of reality, lifting his left hand to reveal its emptiness. "I said the same thing when I was your age."

Chemistry, defenses up, retorts to the man, "Yeah, well, you had your chance!"

The man recoils, and a young woman chimes in, trying to offer guidance. "I'm a Certified Life Coach, and if you want to be successful, you need to find balance--"

Matt attempts to cut her off, unwilling to engage. "Excuse me, but I'm perfectly fine the way I am. Thanks for your concern, everyone."

Chemistry, however, won't let him off the hook so quickly. "No, you're not! Trust me."

Matt's face gets red, and the Life Coach jumps in again, this time addressing Chemistry, "You could show a little compassion for him. What are you, a man hater? Take my card. I can help." She puts her card on the bar and pushes it towards Chemistry.

Matt is done with the conversation. He excuses himself, "I have to get back to work."

"Fine! Go back to work. Your zealous mistress, who will strangle your heart until it is smothered forever, awaits you."

"That was beautiful," Eli responds.

Chemistry – *Jessica Sitomer*

Chemistry walks away exasperated and makes a few more drinks. Bothered, she ducks under the bar and into her briefcase. It is no surprise when she finds a red file in there. She pulls off the blue sticky note on which Confidence wrote, 'If anyone can fix this, you can!' What am I missing?

Chemistry – *Jessica Sitomer*

Chemistry walks away exasperated and makes a few more drinks, gathering. She ducks under the bar and into her briefcase. It'll be no surprise when she finds love again there. She pulls off the blue sticky note with Confidence wrote, 'If anyone can fix this, you can! What am I missing?'

Chapter 9

Chemistry, who worked until 2 a.m., is awoken by a blender. Startled, she sits up in the cot, pushes the curtain aside, and finds Misty blending a green concoction. Chemistry watches her add more ingredients and blend, turning it into a purple tone. Once more, she adds a few more ingredients and blends it until it's brown. Misty reaches for a water bottle.

"What is that?" Chemistry asks concerned.

Misty jumps, almost spilling the drink. "Yikes! I didn't know you were awake, or I would've made enough for two."

"Well, the blender kind of--"

"Oops, sorry. Still getting used to having a roomie," she sings.

"Usually, I don't sleep. But here, it feels pretty good."

Misty examines Chemistry's face from a few yards away, then moves toward her, scrunching her

Chemistry – *Jessica Sitomer*

eyes for a closer look. Then, she puts her finger on Chemistry's frown line right in the middle of her brows. "Then what's this?" She steps behind Chemistry and puts her hands on her traps, "Chemmie, why are you so tense?"

"I'm not."

Misty reaches for her shoulders and pulls away abruptly with a pained cry, "Then why did your aura just bite me?"

"My, what did what, now?"

Misty grabs and lights a large sage bundle from her living room table, "Stand!" Chemistry does as she's told, unsure if she's in Earthly danger. "Arms at a T, legs spread, hips width apart," Misty orders. Chemistry complies. Misty hums a mystical chant as she dances around Chemistry, brandishing the sage around her front, then her back, up over her head, and back down to the floor, where she stubs out the remaining embers on the worn wood. Chemistry tries to speak, but Misty shooshes her and flicks the air around her like she is shooing away mosquitos. Then she stands before Chemistry and declares, "You are coming with me."

"Where?"

"We are going to open your channels, heal whatever's going on here," Using her pointer finger,

Chemistry – *Jessica Sitomer*

she makes a circular motion around Chemistry's head, "and here!" She makes a circle around Chemistry's heart. "You've got to get some binary beats into your chakras stat, or you might not make it! Put on your Lulus," Misty orders, then pours the bulk of the brown drink into another water bottle. She sticks a straw through the hole in the top and turns to see Chemistry fully dressed, which startles her. She forces the BPA-free plastic bottle into Chemistry's hand. "Here, drink this. You need it more than me. Let's go." Misty pulls Chemistry out the door as the dogs put their heads down, knowing she's in trouble.

Forty minutes later, Chemistry finds herself in a Happy Baby yoga pose on a mat next to Misty. On a raised platform, the teacher sits cross-legged on a furry blanket before a giant gong while incense burns in every corner. Trios of electric candles are placed in front of each mat. The teacher instructs the class to let their inner babies play. Chemistry looks to her right and left, watching the other women sway from side to side. Chemistry is

Chemistry – *Jessica Sitomer*

completely lost and extremely uncomfortable for at least the tenth time in the last half hour.

"Don't turn your neck in this position," the instructor barks, as Chemistry realizes she is standing directly behind her. "Play babies play," the instructor coos. The woman behind Chemistry loudly passes gas. "Wonderful, Poppy," the instructor says, "let out sound." Chemistry cringes and holds her breath until the smell dissipates.

"Is this almost over?" she whispers to Misty. Before Misty can respond, the teacher instructs them to go into shoulder stand, reminding "the class" not to move their neck in this position. Chemistry sits on her elbows as she attempts to identify the new position she is supposed to get into when she notices a fit woman in the front row, stretching one leg over her head until her toe touches the floor. At the same time, the other remains straight up in the air. Chemistry gasps, then in a whispered exclamation, "Is that? Is that the helicopter?"

Misty shooshes and whispers to her to breathe, but Chemistry, shocked, whispers, "Before the rowboat pose--"

Misty corrects, "Boat pose."

Chemistry – *Jessica Sitomer*

"Now the helicopter pose!" Chemistry grits her teeth," did you take me to a sex class?"

"What? No!" Misty insists, "Yoga is for your mind."

The woman in front of them goes from Shoulder Stand to Plow, then says from between her legs, "But the flexibility certainly improves your sex life."

"Class, please, silence," The instructor insists. "And now... Shavasana."

Chemistry is about to protest when Misty tells her to lie back and close her eyes, "This is the best part... and it's almost over." Chemistry resigns herself to lie down, but the moment she closes her eyes, she can only think about that red file. Her eyes pop open as she stares at the ceiling fan, thinking. Is this it? Am I just a big failure now? She sits up, rounding her body over her stomach like a lactose-intolerant person who ate an entire cheesecake. She moans in agony. This sucks! Great, I'm not even poetic anymore. I'm a pathetic, untalented trainwreck! The yoga instructor sits behind Chemistry and wraps her body around her, swaying Chemistry back and forth. Abruptly, the teacher stands and, without touching Chemistry, purges unseen energy with flicks of her fingers and shaking off her hands.

With one eye closed in Shavasana and the other open, watching the treatment, Misty whispers, "Oooo, Reiki, you're so lucky."

Chemistry can only muster some weak sarcasm, "Yeah, I feel so lucky."

That night at the bar, Chemistry comes prepared. Observing is getting her nowhere. It's time for an interrogation. Eli and Rusty prep the bar as Matt walks out of his office toward them. Chemistry sees him coming and pulls out a list of questions, which she slams on the bar. Matt picks it up and reads. After a few, "What is this?"

"You said if I took the job, I could ask you as many questions as I want."

Matt turns the paper over, "Chemmie, there are 104 questions here."

"Precisely, so we'd better get started."

"Ask him number 17," Rusty calls from under the bar, holding back his laughter as he stands with two

Chemistry – *Jessica Sitomer*

handfuls of lemons. Matt looks back at the other side as Chemistry snatches it from his grasp.

With the utmost seriousness, Chemistry asks, "Question 17: How many of the numbers in your phone are for people who have seen you naked?" Rusty and Eli burst into laughter.

Matt alleges, "That's not really a question."

"It absolutely is," Chemistry responds earnestly, "An important one." She says with even more gravity.

"Well, it's not one I'm going to answer."

"I'll skip it," Chemistry shakes her head, "But your unwillingness to answer is an answer."

"Next!" Matt yells to the sky.

"If you held a world record, what would it likely be for?"

Rusty and Eli simultaneously call out, "Working late." Matt laughs as Chemistry writes their answer on her paper.

"If you could be on any reality game show, which would you pick?" Chemistry's face contorts, confused by the question.

"Does Beat Bobby Flay count as a game show?" Eli asks.

Rusty teases, "How about The Bachelor?"

"Stop," Matt chides him, "Hands down, Survivor."

"You'd definitely win the bug-eating round," Rusty says.

Chemistry interrupts, "I don't know what any of that means, so that question doesn't help my cause."

"And just what is your cause?" Matt suddenly wonders if this is more than Chemistry playing with him.

"I'm the one asking the questions," she insists.

Matt digs, "But these are not exactly HR-approved. Why do you need to know them to work here?"

"It's important to me to know the type of person I work for. These reveal

who you are and if I share the same mission as this restaurant." The guys look at her with zero comprehension, so she continues, "How long could you survive without your phone?"

"Let's hope I never have to find out," Matt says.

"Is this a compellation of Cosmo quizzes?" Rusty asks. Chemistry looks at him, puzzled, then gets back to Matt.

"If you could go back to school for one year, which grade would you choose?"

Chemistry – *Jessica Sitomer*

Matt thinks about this and thoughtfully answers, "My last year of school."

Chemistry writes that down and asks, "Why?" Without looking up, she says again, "Why?" When he doesn't answer, she looks up. He is looking off, far away from this moment. "Matt?" she asks gently.

Matt taps the bar, "That's enough fun for now. We've got a restaurant to open." He walks to the kitchen as Chemistry writes a big question mark next to 'school.' Maybe he was hurt in school and can't get past it. Perhaps I should whip up some instant matches to get him back in action, then... oh, what does Lust say? Get his juices flowing. Yes! Then he'll see he's still got it, and I can get that model to cross his path again...poof! This is an excellent plan.

Chemistry spends the next seven hours making fantastical concoctions for women of all types. After giving Matt his nightly Sazerac with her special touch of "saz." Chemistry watches Matt nurse the drink all night as women flock to him while he continues doing business as usual, utterly oblivious to the adoring women around him. There's something about him, she thinks, as one of the girls attempts to flirt with Matt. She's hit with a sudden wave of jealousy. What is that? No! Chemistry shakes off the feeling. Frustration! She insists to herself. That's it, I'm feeling very frustrated... very frustrated. She shakes a cocktail with extra force.

At the end of the night, Chemistry barges into Matt's office, where he is tallying the night's totals. She startles him both with her lack of manners and her sudden outburst.

"I watched a woman almost hiccup herself to death, and you didn't make any effort to get her a glass of water."

Matt, confused, says, "You seem unreasonably upset. Do you want to take a seat?"

"No, I don't want a seat," she says, pushing the rolling chair out of her way as she leans over his desk.

Matt stands, hoping to calm her, "Okay, I recall no such event of hiccups, and as a bartender, shouldn't you have given her some water?"

Chemistry paces like a caged animal, "Matt, a woman feinted at your feet!"

"Two guys helped her to a chair, and she was fine. Eli gave her some fruit juice."

"You should have given her the fruit juice! You should have felt compelled to give her fruit juice. And the girl who kept asking you to dance?"

Chemistry – *Jessica Sitomer*

"Was drunk! There is no dance floor, no dance music. I intentionally designed the aesthetic that way. Please stop trying to turn my place into something it's not! Stop trying to make me want something I don't!"

"But you do!"

Matt, now irritated, sits back down. "I hired you because I thought you were what the people wanted... you and your colored drinks... Misty likes you, and she is a good judge of character... except for Josh. But Chemmie, you don't know me at all, and you came in with your questions and your prying, which I must admit feels very personal."

"It is personal, Matt. I know there is so much more for you—"

Matt, losing his patience, exclaims, "Enough, Chemmie! You are my bartender, not my meddling mother, so if you want to keep your job, please stop trying to set me up or change me! This is who I am, your boss. No more overstepping." He walks from behind the desk, around her, and out the door into the kitchen. She takes a deep, calming breath, which she learned in yoga, and heads after him to the kitchen.

Chemistry – *Jessica Sitomer*

With determination, she pushes the kitchen door open with all her strength, hitting Eli, causing him to knock into Joshua and fall on the floor. Joshua snaps at her, "Do you mind? I'm cooking staff dinner!"

Eli gets up and says to no one in particular, "I'm fine."

Joshua's nasty attitude takes the namaste right out of her, and Chemistry points at Matt, "I will not! I will not give up on you! I will not stop meddling! You have a lesson to learn that is holding you back from love. A lesson I'm now convinced somehow ties to your last year of school. I know it."

Joshua winces, "Shut up, Chemmie, you are way out of line."

"No, you shut up, Joshua! I've only had one file, and I know all about you. You are a man whore who is happy to sabotage any happiness Matt craves because you're a narcissist."

Matt seethes through gritted teeth, "Chemmie, stop talking."

Joshua gets in Chemmie's face, "Who the hell are you?" Chemistry holds her ground. "That was not a rhetorical question, so let me answer it. You're a lowly bartender who sleeps on someone's couch, clearly has no life, and you're obsessed with him."

Chemistry – *Jessica Sitomer*

Joshua points at Matt. "He doesn't want you!" Chemmie doesn't flinch. "But if it gets you to shut up, so we can get back to normalcy here," he leans into Chemistry's ear and whispers, "I'll give you a night you'll never forget."

Chemistry is so shaken that she slaps Joshua's face, leaving a red handprint. He touches his stinging cheek and smirks at her, "I may not forget it either."

Matt's eyes blaze with anger as he pushes Joshua up against a wall, "What did you say to her!"

"Matt, stop!" Chemistry says, "Don't be like him."

The entire staff squirm in discomfort as the boiling water in the pot starts to spill over and sizzle. Joshua shakes Matt off with a smug laugh as he walks back to Chemistry. "I don't know who you think you are talking to," Joshua spits his words, "But listen closely. You are fired."

Chemistry turns to Matt, "Is this what you want? Is this your successful dynamic? You do all the work, and he gets all the credit, all the women, while you get bags under your eyes and a kiss goodnight from a dog?"

Matt's eyes change as rage floods through him. Without moving a muscle in his body except for his jaw, he coolly replies, "I made myself crystal clear in there. " He points toward his office, "You are, indeed, fired."

The staff try to calm him as he storms out of the kitchen. With a shit-eating grin, Joshua walks over to Chemistry and gets too close for comfort. In a very measured tone, he says, "You heard the man, you're fired, go."

"I'll apologize," she says.

Joshua grabs her by the arms and pushes her against the stove, "Go!" Chemistry cries out as the back of her arm is burned by the pot of boiling water. Joshua lets go of her and steps back as she clutches her arm in pain. "And don't even think of suing me. You'd only hurt Matt, and clearly, you don't want to do that." He, too, leaves the kitchen as Eli rushes to her aid.

"Let me see." Eli gently pulls a stunned Chemistry away from the stove and sits her on a chair. A server hands him the first aid kit, and he removes the burn cream. Eli takes hold of her hand, gripping her arm, and gently places it on her lap. In her trancelike state of disillusionment, she lets him. He checks the flesh on the back of her arm, but there's no burn mark. "That's strange," Eli says, "I could smell the burn. I thought it was going to be a third degree, but your skin is--"

Chemistry snaps out of her haze, "I've been fired. I should go!" She rushes out the back door and finds herself in tears. Fearful that the worried staff will follow her, she runs and runs and runs.

Chemistry – *Jessica Sitomer*

Chapter 10

Chemistry runs into the opulent lobby of The Plaza, buzzing with activity. Determined and brisk, she makes her way through the crowd, her destination fixed on the elevators. Mother Nature steps into her path, "Where are you off to in such a hurry?"

Chemistry wipes her eyes with the flesh of her palms, "I'm going back up."

Mother Nature arches an eyebrow, her tone gentle, "The case is closed?"

"As far as I'm concerned," Chemistry says in her most professional tone. "He can't learn his lesson because he doesn't want to."

Mother Nature offers a wise perspective. "Chemistry, no one wants to learn their lessons. That requires growth, and growth comes from trying new things. People are attached to comfort, as are all living things in nature."

"He's comfortable all right, partnered with a self-important, arrogant... and the women, he really couldn't care less, which is a shame because he's handsome and talented, and he loves his dog."

"Oh." Mother Nature can't help but tease, "So you like him. That complicates things."

"What did I just say to indicate that?!"

Mother Nature, ever the master of intrigue, "This could be interesting."

After only realizing she hasn't caught her breath yet, Chemistry sits on a plush lobby seat, closes her eyes, and takes three deep yoga breaths. Mother Nature sits across from her, happy that Chemistry has herself learned something new. Chemistry opens her eyes, still counting her breath as she recalls the past hour. "Matt was so angry. I don't even know what I said. He didn't raise his voice, but his eyes... made me shiver."

"Oh... so he likes you. That makes things easier."

"What did I just say to indicate that?"

"Where there is rage, there is passion. You can fix this."

"How?"

"Who's the matchmaker here? You like him. He likes you. Go fix it."

Chemistry speaks in a hushed, defeated tone. "I've done everything I can. He doesn't want love. I've given him every opportunity."

Mother Nature suggests, "You haven't done everything."

"I can show you the list. He's a workaholic. The only woman he talks to without his 'work persona' is his neighbor."

Mother Nature drags out the word in a leading way, "And?"

"And?" Chemistry responds. Mother Nature gives her a knowing look. "Well, of course, he talks to me. I haven't given him any choice," Chemistry sniffs.

"I suppose it takes one to know one."

"What does that mean?"

"You came down here to teach him his lesson. So, teach him," Mother Nature winks.

A hint of skepticism colors Chemistry's response. "Are you suggesting that I manipulate him into falling for me so I can teach him his lesson?"

Mother Nature offers a more nuanced plan. "No. I was thinking you would go on a nice date with him. Show him a fun time--"

Chemistry admonishes the plan. "Then devastate him when I'm done."

Mother Nature counters with a kinder option. "Or just tell him you had fun, but your heart belongs to someone else."

Chemistry – *Jessica Sitomer*

Chemistry puffs up a bit defensive as she acknowledges the statement's truth. "Which is true."

"You don't have to remind me," Mother Nature rolls her eyes. Off Chemistry's scowl, "Oh, He's a big boy. He'll be fine."

"If I give him my all, personally teach him his lesson… I could really hurt him."

"Isn't it in the pain that they learn?" Mother Nature points out.

Chemistry grumbles, "And to think, all these mortals give you credit for being nurturing," Chemistry closes her eyes, takes a deep breath, and pulls herself together. Without acknowledging Mother Nature, she leaves The Plaza to confront her complicated mission.

As Mother Nature continues through the lobby, she passes a wilting flower centerpiece, her gaze lingering on a handsome bellhop. As she checks him out, the flowers miraculously perk up, blooming with newfound vitality. Mother Nature revels in the moment. "I can be very nurturing." The bellhop, smitten by her presence, smiles in response.

Chemistry – *Jessica Sitomer*

Chemistry sits on a central park bench, running calculations as day turns to night. Behind her, Lust, Style, Confidence, Humor, and Knowledge stand watch. Tourists and locals have different reactions as they pass the mismatched group. Despite standing for five nights and five days, none leave Chemistry, even if she refuses to acknowledge their presence. As the sun sets in the park, the group grows restless. Humor breaks the days of silence.

"Perhaps this is the time for pulling out the rubber band?" Humor offers.

Lust, stupefied, responds, "I thought comics were supposed to have good timing."

Knowledge adds, "I just wish she would let us help. I brought Men Are from Mars, Women Are from Venus, and Freud's Three Essays on the Theory of Sexuality." Knowledge proudly displays the books.

"I don't even think Dior could help our girl right now," Style says, "and there's not a woman on Earth who wouldn't swoon for Dior."

"That's it," claps Confidence, "She's not a woman on Earth. She's a badass!"

Chemistry – *Jessica Sitomer*

Knowledge reaches into his coat. "I brought that too. You Are a Badass! It's been a best seller for over five years."

Confidence grabs the book from him and rounds the bench, dropping the book on Chemistry's lap. "You are a Bad Ass! You Got This! Make Shift Happen!"

"Confidence, please stop yelling book titles at me," Chemistry pleads.

Knowledge interjects, "They've all been bestsellers on Amazon."

"I don't know what Amazon is. I don't know who Matt is!" Chemistry sobs.

Humor jokes, "Well, he's not Amazon."

A collective "SHUSH" makes Humor sulk away as the rest of the staff awkwardly watch their boss break down. They shove one another, trying to get someone to say something to her. They push Lust out in front.

"Umm, I'm not great with chicks who cry." Lust starts. Style reaches over his shoulder and hands him a LV pocket square to hand to her. Chemistry takes it, wipes her eyes, and blows her nose. Style gasps at the violation of fashion and turns away. Lust treads uncharacteristically lightly, "We've watched you work equations for days. It's not like you to struggle like this. Maybe you have a blind spot?"

"A blind spot?" she asks.

"A blind spot," Knowledge explains as if in a spelling bee, "is an area in your range of vision that you cannot see properly but which you really should be able to see."

"Thank you, Knowledge. I know what a blind spot is. I don't see how it applies to this case." Chemistry says.

"You're both workaholics," Confidence points out.

Chemistry lashes out, "I'm not a workaholic! I have a job, that's all I have. What else is there? It's Eternity. We do our jobs."

"Some of us do more than our jobs," Lust points out, "Style shops, Knowledge reads, Humor... I'm still unclear how he got hired, and Confidence, well, she," Confidence does an awkward cartwheel, "She does that stuff. And me, well, let's say I..."

"You just made my point. You are all doing your jobs. That... stuff... is your research."

"I did luck out in the research department," Lust winks at her, "But what about your research? We do ours down here to keep up with what's current. You do yours by hiding in a lab."

Chemistry – *Jessica Sitomer*

"It's never failed me before."

"Until now," Lust says.

She sighs, "Until now." Chemistry takes a moment to pull herself together, then looks at Lust, "When did you get so smart?"

Lust replies in his typical lascivious tone. "I have sex with a lot of Ivey Leaguers." Chemistry shakes her head and finally looks up at her crew, wiping her eyes on the pocket square, leaning in to blow her nose again as Style grabs it.

Chemistry sounding young and small, "How do I get him to forgive me when I don't know why he's so mad?"

Knowledge pulls out The Wisdom of Forgiveness by the Dalai Lama. "You probably don't have time to read this," Chemistry shakes her head. Confidence kneels in front of her and takes her hands. Chemistry fidgets, causing Confidence to hold tighter and look Chemistry in the eyes. "You follow your heart," Confidence says.

"My heart?" Chemistry asks, "But my heart is broken."

Humor yells, "Even a broken clock is right twice a day."

Lust turns to see Humor peeking out from behind a bush. "Are you still here?" He signals the

Chemistry – *Jessica Sitomer*

rest, "Alright, gang, let's head back up. We're not helping. Let her go back to her equations." They leave.

Chemistry sits in silence. She puts her hand to her chest and then drops it in her lap. Nothing, she thinks as she pulls out her phone. "Hey Siri, how do I open my heart, Shakra?"

"Here's what I found on the web," Siri says.

"What is the web?" Chemistry asks, but no response. She rolls her eyes, "Hey Siri, what is the web?"

"It doesn't look like you have an app named 'web.' You can search for it in the App Store." Chemistry drops the phone back in her bag, wishing Misty was around. She stands up, desperate for some inspiration, and heads out of the park.

Chemistry molds herself into a corner as she watches through Bacchus' window. It's a packed Saturday night. Rusty is behind the bar, pouring classic drinks and decanting wine. The special must be lobster with a pairing of saffron & caviar because almost everyone has ordered it. Expensive pairing,

Chemistry – *Jessica Sitomer*

Chemistry thinks, as her hand touches her heart and the memory of the life she once lived brings back sweet and salty memories.

She watches Matt, calm as ever, deliver grilled cheese sandwiches to Mr. and Mrs. Topel, only instead of curly fries, Mrs. Topel receives the saffron & caviar. Chemistry watches her turn her nose up to it as Matt points to the combo, explaining something about the dish that upsets the Topels. Matt seems to be asking her to try it, but Mrs. Topel pushes the plate away. Matt smiles and takes the plate. His expression reads curly fries are on the way. But as he leaves the table, Mr. Topel grabs his chest, then his left arm, and his face twists in pain. Mrs. Topel shrieks. Chemistry watches as Matt drops the plate. It crashes to the floor, breaking and splattering its contents. As Mr. Topel curls over, Matt rushes to his side and yells out orders.

Chemistry pushes her way through the door, running to the table. She hears patrons calling 911, Mrs. Topel screaming, and Matt counting out compressions. She moves through the crowd around them and drops to her knees, "How can I help?"

"Can you get an aspirin?" Matt pleads.

Chemistry – *Jessica Sitomer*

Chemistry stands and calls to the crowd, "Does anyone have an aspirin?" she listens to the murmurs, "Anyone?!" She looks down at Mr. Topel, "Please! Not sure what it is, but I need aspirin!" She feels a nudge under her arm. She looks down at her bag and finds a bottle of aspirin has popped to the top. She examines the label for a moment. Hmmm, that's aspirin. Makes sense. Opening it, she takes out two aspirins as quickly as she can.

"Crush them up!" Matt insists. She does so on a napkin. Matt momentarily stops compressions and shakes the aspirin under Mr. Topel's tongue just as the medics arrive on the scene to take over.

The Upper West Side ER waiting room, stark under the harsh fluorescent lights, thrums with a quiet urgency. Rows of plastic chairs are sparsely occupied by a young mother cradling a feverish child, an elderly man clutching his chest, and a college student with a bandaged hand, all unified by their shared apprehension. The muted hum of medical equipment and the distant murmur of doctors' voices filter through the sterile air. A man in a tuxedo makes demands on a nurse who attempts to reassure him that everything that can be done is being done. As she walks away, the man paces, his fingers gripping his hair in frustration. Chemistry sits between Mrs. Topel and Matt. Matt, hunched over, his elbows on his thighs face down, also grips his fingers in his hair. It must be a man thing, she thinks. Mrs. Topel is stoic. Chemistry feels Mrs. Topel put her hand on hers.

"It's my fault," Mrs. Topel says quietly.

"Unless you poisoned him, it's not your fault," Chemistry assures her. Matt looks up at her with a 'what the fuck' kind of response was that?' Chemistry shrugs her shoulders awkwardly with wide eyes, raised eyebrows, and her mouth drawn back in an uneasy grimace. They both turn to Mrs. Topel, whose expression and posture have not changed.

Matt leans forward and says to Mrs. Topel, "I'm sorry. I shouldn't have said anything about the healing properties of Saffron."

Chemistry remembers the scene she witnessed in the restaurant, "That would hardly cause a heart attack, Matt." Again, he looks at her as if she's never had human interaction. They sit in silence.

Chemistry – *Jessica Sitomer*

"The doctors told me I have Cancer," Mrs. Topel tells Chemistry. "It's so slow growing, and something else would kill me first. But he doesn't want to live without me. He died of a broken heart." Matt stands up, rolling his neck in discomfort.

"He hasn't died yet," Chemistry assures her. Once again, Matt snaps his head toward Chemistry and mouths, "Yet?!?" She mouths back, "Well, he hasn't!"

Still unmoved and in the same quiet tone, Mrs. Topel says, "You two are such a nice couple. I hope you have a long life together."

Matt quickly corrects, "Oh, we're not a couple."

Ignoring Matt, Mrs. Topel says, "There is a comfort in knowing that if his heart stops tonight, mine will stop tomorrow."

Uncomfortable with the conversation, Matt insists, "I'm going to get an update."

Chemistry looks down at Mrs. Topel's hands on hers and piles her right hand on top. Mrs. Topel moves for the first time to look at Chemistry. "You understand?" Mrs. Topel asks.

"I do, too well. It makes me wonder why people long so desperately to fall in love, knowing it will end so painfully." Chemistry thinks, and why I'm a part of it.

Chemistry – *Jessica Sitomer*

Mrs. Topel smiles, "Pain is the price we pay for the gift of loving so deeply. It is a price that, with time, you realize was worth the cost."

"I know you're right about most relationships, but you and Mr. Topel are soulmates, and that pain is unbearable."

"I don't believe in soulmates. Love is love."

"Not true. An entire department is committed to matching soulmates, and I'm questioning why. Suddenly, my entire life's work seems brutal."

Confused, Mrs. Topel is about to question Chemistry, when Matt approaches with a doctor. "He will only speak to you," Matt says with an underlying tone of desperation.

The two women stand as the doctor addresses Mr. Topel, "Mrs. Topel, your husband experienced a cardiac arrest, which is a severe condition. However, thanks to the immediate medical intervention, he is now stable and doing well. He will need some time to recover, and we will monitor him closely to ensure there are no complications. We'll also run tests to determine the cause and prevent future episodes. For now, you can see him and be with him as he recovers."

"Thank you, Doctor," she says as she follows him.

Chemistry – *Jessica Sitomer*

Matt looks at Chemistry, "That's a relief." He sits. "I'm going to wait here and see that she gets home."

Chemistry sits. "I'll wait with you... in case she needs someone to stay with her." They sit in a long silence.

"Your aspirin may have saved him," Matt says.

"Your grilled cheese may have killed him," Chemistry says.

"Wow." Matt moves a seat away from Chemistry. Afraid she made him angry again, she searches her bag for a peace offering.

"I'm not great with people," she acknowledges. He rolls his eyes, recognizing the obvious. "Well," she digs deeper into her bag, "I bought you an apology gift. I'm not sure what I said to make you mad the other night, but I'm so sorry." She hands him a box, which he recognizes immediately.

"You bought me a knife?"

"It's a Moritaka."

"I know what it is. But, how do you?"

"They've been around for over 700 years, even longer than me." Noticing his confused expression, she searches for a save, "Misty says you're always chopping things, so you can never have too many knives, right?"

"This is too much."

Chemistry – *Jessica Sitomer*

"I don't think so... if your eyes could have turned red and shot flames at me, I think they would have."

Matt breathes a heavy sigh. "I'm sorry I scared you. I wasn't really angry at you." He pauses, "Josh and I have a complicated partnership, and you saying it out loud triggered years of pent-up... well, let's just say that Josh and I don't acknowledge our 'dynamic,' and it works for us."

Chemistry wants to scream Does It?! but her new mission has nothing to do with Josh. She has reformulated her plan, and this truce has her back on track. She remains silent.

"Thank you for the gift." He smiles at her. She smiles back. "I'll be right back." He says as he walks to the nurses' station. Chemistry stands and watches as he speaks to a woman at the desk. He hands her his credit card. When he returns, he says, "I've upgraded them to a private suite so she can stay with him as long as they're here."

"That was really kind of you," Chemistry says.

Matt looks away sheepishly. They stand like a couple of teenagers at their first dance. Matt breaks the silence, "Misty's been worried sick about you. Can I take you back to the brownstone, or have you found other arrangements?"

"You can take me back," Chemistry says.

"It's been a long night," Matt states, "I'll get us a cab."

"I think I'm going to walk." Chemistry steps toward the exit. The doors automatically slide open.

"It's over 20 blocks!" Matt calls after her, but she's already walking in the wrong direction down the street. Matt runs after her and physically turns her around, pointing her in the right direction.

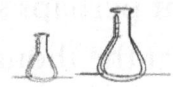

The muted remnants of the nightlife blend with the serene residential quiet on the Upper West Side. Chemistry and Matt pass the occasional dog walker but otherwise have the street to themselves.

Chemistry breaks the silence. "You care about the Topels."

Matt narrowly avoids chewing gum stuck to the sidewalk, "They remind me of my parents."

"You've never mentioned your parents... oh wait, yes, you did when you compared me to your meddling mom."

"Well, she meddles because she cares."

"I get that."

Chemistry – *Jessica Sitomer*

Matt stops short, but Chemistry doesn't notice until she hears him say, "I don't. Why do you care? You don't even know me."

She backs up and pulls him by the arm to get him moving again, "This is me trying to get to know you." She lets go of his arm once they are back in their walking rhythm, "Back to your parents. Where are they?"

Matt is tempted to argue but starts to wonder if Josh is correct, and if perhaps she does have a crush on him. He softens at the thought, "Florida. They've been married 35 years."

"Siblings?"

"None."

"College?"

"I like these questions much better than the Cosmo ones."

Chemistry sings, "Avoiding."

Matt laughs but doesn't answer the question. Chemistry stops at the corner, seeing the don't walk sign. Matt continues across the street since there are no cars in sight. When he reaches the other side, he realizes he's alone and calls to Chemistry, "What are you doing?"

"The sign says don't walk."

Chemistry – *Jessica Sitomer*

"In Manhattan, the signs are suggestions," he tells her. She hesitates and stalls, "Come on! Be a rule breaker," he dares her. Without overthinking, she runs across the street, looking in every direction. When she reaches the other side, she breathes like she just got away with a bank robbery. Matt can't help but be charmed by her peculiarity.

"Your turn," Matt says, "Parents?"

"Died."

"Sorry."

"It was a long time ago."

"Just because it was a long time ago, doesn't make it--"

"I'm starving!" Chemistry says as they pass a tipsy couple eating pizza slices.

Matt looks at his watch. It's 2 am. "The Wolfe closes in an hour, and it's 15 blocks away. I'll get a cab..."

"Or we can run?"

"Run?" Before he can get an answer, Chemistry is running at full speed.

The Wolfe's once lively dining room now exudes a hushed intimacy that only late hours can conjure. The soft, golden glow from vintage chandeliers casts long shadows, dancing lazily on the exposed

Chemistry – *Jessica Sitomer*

brick walls. The tables, covered in crisp white linens, bear the remnants of an evening well-spent—half-empty wine glasses, crumpled napkins, and the lingering aroma of rich, decadent dishes.

The murmur of conversations has faded, replaced by the soothing strains of a jazz playlist that mingles seamlessly with the occasional clink of silverware being collected by the tireless waitstaff. The bartenders, moving with the practiced ease of seasoned artisans, polish the last of the glassware, their reflections distorted in the bottles of top-shelf spirits that line the backlit shelves.

A few patrons linger at the bar, their faces illuminated by the warm, amber light. They are the night's die-hards—laughing softly, sharing secrets and stolen glances over the final sips of their cocktails.

The restaurant's large windows offer a view of the quiet street outside. The occasional taxi glides past, its headlights slicing through the darkness, briefly illuminating Chemistry's face as she stares at the menu.

"What's with the furrowed brow?" Matt asks, still out of breath from running and unsure why Chemistry is neither winded nor sweaty. He removes his suit jacket, unbuttons his cuffs, and pushes up his sleeves.

Chemistry reads from the menu, "Tomato braised meatballs, Vegan. Point Judith Calamari Frito, Gluten-Free... I know what a tomato and a meatball are. What is a Vegan?"

Surprised she can keep a straight face, Matt plays along, "A person who doesn't eat food derived from animals."

"Then why are they ordering a meatball? And Calamari, Frito? I know that's fried, but what is Gluten-Free?"

"Why do I have the chilling feeling that you are not messing with me?"

"Because I'm not?"

"Where have you been living for the past decade?"

Realizing she's out of touch, she submits, "Fine, I'll try the Gluten Free."

"Not on my watch. People don't eat that unless they have to." The waitress comes over, and Matt orders, "We'll have the Truffle Deviled Eggs, Cashew Brussel Sprouts, Seared Octopus... the octopus was delivered..." he looks at his watch, "an hour ago, right?" The surprised waitress nods yes. "Baby

Chemistry – *Jessica Sitomer*

Smash Burgers...Artichoke and Goat Cheese Croquettes..."

"Are we expecting more people to join us?" Chemistry asks.

"Quality control, want to report back to Brendan," Matt half-jokes.

"So, you're turning a late-night snack into work?"

"Restauranteurs are a tight-knit and competitive group." Matt removes his wallet and hands the waitress a twenty, "Will you bring me a peeled carrot?" She looks back and forth at the two as if they're up to something kinky. Matt immediately recognizes the oddity of his request, "A gift I have to try out." She takes the twenty with raised brows and heads to the kitchen

The waitress brings the peeled carrot on a plate. Like a kid with a new model airplane kit, Matt slowly opens the box, puts the history booklet aside, pulls the knife from the sheath and paper, and admires it from multiple angles. His eyes twinkle as he removes the carrot from the plate, wields his new blade, and cuts the carrot into 2-inch pieces. He whistles at the thrill of it, slices the base of a piece, and sets it on the table.

Chemistry – *Jessica Sitomer*

"Ready?" Matt asks.

"I don't know what's happening here," Chemistry answers, looking at the waitress for help. Her eyes tell Chemistry that she's just as stumped.

With speed and precision, Matt slices the carrot pieces, stacks them into matchstick proportions, and kisses the knife's blade. "I'm in love."

Chemistry murmurs, "That would be great if your soulmate was a knife."

"What's that?" Matt asks as a busboy brings the Deviled Eggs and places them on the table.

Chemistry covers, "I said, 'Great, you should make it your wife.'"

"If only," Matt says dreamily.

Not sure if she's confused or disturbed, Chemistry says, "You and I have very different interpretations of love." This breaks Matt's spell as he laughs. Chemistry feels a slight lurch in her stomach at the joyous sound of his laugh. He takes a bite of a deviled egg, nods approvingly, and then juliennes the rest of the carrot in record time. He slides a plate to the table's edge, pushes the carrot pieces onto it, and then swaps the plate for the Octopus, which another busboy is dropping.

"You're not going to eat the carrot?" the waitress asks. Matt shakes his head no, as if she were asking something preposterous. The waitress walks away, saying, "Hella expensive carrot."

As they enter the hall of the brownstone, Chemistry and Matt slow their pace, knowing the evening is ending.

Chemistry stops walking, "Can I ask you something serious?"

Matt smiles, hoping this is her weak attempt to stall, "That would be great because everything else you ask me is ridiculous."

She swats him impishly, feeling proud that she can now recognize his sarcasm as playful, maybe even a little flirtatious. Her heart does a little flip. Is he flirting with me? The notion startles her. She swallows hard and chokes on her saliva, sending her into a coughing fit.

"Are you okay?" Concerned, Matt pulls her from behind into his chest and lifts her arms above her head.

For a moment, she lets herself melt into him. His body feels safe and warm, very warm, hot even, then she stiffens, frightened of what she's feeling...lust?

"What are you doing?" she untangles herself from his hold, her cough gone as she slows her breath.

Matt blushes, "You were coughing, but I... my mom used to tell me to put my hands over my head to stop the coughing," he overthinks the words spilling out of his mouth but can't seem to stop, "Which I found confusing because she would also tell me to cover my mouth," he watches as Chemistry composes herself a good foot away from him, "Obviously you can't cover your mouth and put your hands over your head at the same time... obviously," Matt feels confused by his stammering as he forces himself to stop talking. There is a long pause of awkward silence, to which Matt responds with a change of subject, "You had a serious question."

"I did?" she asks. Unbeknownst to Matt, Chemistry hadn't heard a word of his rambling because she had been staring at his mouth, watching his lips, thinking thoughts, and suddenly she was thinking them again. Pull yourself together, Chemistry, she scolds herself, then Confidence's voice fills her head. You've Got This! Chemistry remembers his question, "I did." She confirms, "Why do you cut food up only to throw it away?"

"To stay sharp," Matt explains.

Chemistry smiles at his answer and then does a little tap dance that she's seen Humor do a thousand times as she delivers his infamous comedic line when a joke is told but doesn't land, "Ba dump bump."

Matt looks at her curiously, trying to solve the puzzle of this complex yet childlike woman he suddenly wanted so badly.

"I knew there was something different about you. I couldn't put my finger on it," he says, solving the puzzle. "Now I know what it is."

"You do?" Chemistry worries.

"You're funny!" he declares.

"I am?"

"You just have terrible comedic timing," he laughs and steps closer to her.

"I learned from the best," she admits.

"See? I have no idea what that means." The pace of his words slows, sounding entranced and seductive. "Yet it's completely and utterly charming." Chemistry takes a step back for each word he says as he approaches her. "Adorable," his voice deepens, "and very, very..." Chemistry finds herself backed against his door. "Beautiful," he says with a husky voice as he cups her face in his hands. He moves in for a kiss. Chemistry's eyes widen.

"When was the last time you were kissed?" she blurts.

Matt shakes his head and says under his breath, "Truly terrible timing." He looks into her eyes and sees her panic. He wants to put her at ease. "Like... four hundred years ago," he jokes.

"Me too!" Chemistry says with excitement, then catches herself, "Wait, that can't be right." She begins counting on her fingers.

"Are you going to do math, or are you gonna kiss me?" He leans in and traces her cheekbone with his finger. Again, Chemistry's eyes widen in alarm. Matt is confused. "Did I misread the situation here?" he asks, trying to undo what she clearly wants to be undone, "I'm sorry, that's probably the late hour and the ginger and cinnamon talking... two very bewitching spices." He steps back, giving her space, "Tonight was... refreshing. Go get some sleep."

Worried she's messed up her plan, Chemistry says, "Matt, wait..." But he smiles and nods at her as he slips into his apartment and closes the door as far as it will go. Chemistry shakes her head, discouraged, as she walks through Misty's open door.

Chapter 11

The following day, Chemistry sits on her cot behind her curtain, looking out the window. She hears a rustle in the kitchen and gets up to surprise Misty. To her shock, she finds Eli unpacking groceries and putting them in Misty's fridge.

"Oh, hi, Chemmie," he says as if this is normal.

"Eli, what are you doing here?" she asks.

"Every week, I restock Misty's food."

"She never told me that."

"She doesn't know," he says, "It's one of the ways I take care of her until her affections catch up with mine."

"Where does she think it comes from?" Chemistry asks as she watches him put fruit in refrigerator bins, vegetables on the bottom shelf, and Kombucha on the side door. He shrugs, not knowing the answer, and moves to the counter, removing a loaf of molding bread from a basket, tosses it in the garbage, and replaces it with a freshly baked loaf. He also hangs a bunch of bananas. He stacks cans of beans, almond butter, and bags of lentils in a cupboard.

"Eli, how long have you been working for Matt?"

From Misty's room, a groggy voice calls, "Hello?"

"Misty's up, gotta go, don't tell her I was here."

Misty calls again louder, "Hello?" as Eli hurries out the door.

"It's me, Misty," Chemistry calls back. A thud and a scuffle are heard from the bedroom as the dogs precede Misty in running out to greet her. Misty is still knotting the tie on her purple flowered robe when she throws her arms around Chemistry in a giant hug. The dogs jump up on both women, scratching their legs with sharp nails.

"Off!" Misty commands, "you all need pedicures today!" Then steps back from Chemistry and plops on the couch, "Where have you been?"

Chemistry sits beside her on the couch, "I was fired, so I thought I should stay away."

"Not from me! I was worried. But I saged the whole apartment anticipating your return, so there are no negative vibes here. We'll get you a job in no time." She jumps up and grabs the Sunday Times from the counter, which Chemistry now assumes

Chemistry – *Jessica Sitomer*

Eli delivered as well, and asks, "Where did that come from?"

"The paper?"

Chemistry points, "The paper, the bananas, the fresh bread?"

"I guess it's the Brownies."

"The what?"

"Brownies, the little fairies that come at night and clean your house, fill your fridge, and leave fresh flowers." Misty looks around for fresh flowers and spots them still in a paper bag on the floor. "Hmmm, they must've been in a rush. Can you put them in some water for me?"

Chemistry, wanting to be a gracious guest, obliges her but questions, "I don't think Brownie fairies are real."

Playfully mocking Chemistry, Misty answers, "Then where do you suppose the flowers you're holding appeared from?"

Realizing she won't win this battle, Chemistry changes the subject. "Why do you think Matt doesn't have a girlfriend?"

"He's too busy. Can you cut me a slice of the fresh bread and add some almond butter? Should be in the cupboard behind you." Chemistry knows precisely where the almond butter is, takes it out, and then looks through the drawers for a knife. When she finds one, she slices into the bread.

"Okay, he's busy," Chemistry agrees as she spreads the almond butter, "but he's a grown man. Does he have a lot of? How do I say it... intercourse friends?"

"No!" Misty insists, defending his honor, as Chemistry brings her the plate. Misty takes the bread and leaves Chemistry standing with the plate. After watching Misty devour her breakfast, she brings the plate to the sink, rinses it, and places it on a drying rack.

"Misty, you're going to tell me that a handsome, successful, kind man like Matt has no...?" Again, Chemistry searches for a word.

"Game?" Misty offers.

"Huh?"

"Girlfriends," Misty offers.

"Yes, let's go with that," Chemistry says.

"None! I don't get it either, but I stopped bugging him about it long ago, and if you don't want to make him mad again, you won't either."

Chemistry sits back on the couch, "He told you how mad he got with me?" Misty nods, grimacing. "I wish I could figure him out."

Chemistry – *Jessica Sitomer*

Misty swallows the last bite of bread and opens the paper, looking for the jobs section. "I don't even know if they list jobs here anymore. Everything's online," Misty says as she gets distracted by one of the dogs chewing on its paw. "Snappy, no!" A ringing comes from Chemistry's sleeping area, but she doesn't acknowledge it. The ringing persists. "Chemmie, your phone is ringing," Misty says.

"My what?"

"Your phone? The thing you answer when it rings so you can talk to the person on the other end... you're acting weird this morning."

Chemistry rises and follows the noise.

When she finds the ringing from the iPhoneXXX, she sees Knowledge's face on the screen and without knowing any better, presses a green button.

"Hello," he says.

"What is this?" she questions.

"Facetime."

"That means nothing to me."

"Chemistry, you are screwing it all up down there. I can help you over Facetime."

"Stop saying Facetime!"

A nosey Misty pokes her head behind the sheet and sees the little boy's face on the phone.

"Who's that adorable little guy?" she cries with glee.

Chemistry introduces, "Knowle—"

"Nephew," Knowledge interrupts, "I'm her nephew."

"Well, aren't you mature in your Sunday bowtie," Misty says.

"He always dresses like that," Chemistry chides.

"He does?" Misty asks, surprised.

Knowledge changes the subject, "You're a pretty lady." He gives her a big, toothless grin, "I should go. I'm sending help."

"What?!" Chemistry shouts as the screen goes blank.

"Cool phone!" Misty says, looking it over. There's a knock on the door.

"Oh no!" Chemistry cries out from behind the sheet, yelling, "I don't need any help. I've got everything under..." She steps on a dog toy, which wheezes out a drawn-out squeak. All the dogs come running, including Lola, who was in Misty's room. Regaining her balance, she looks up, expecting to see one of her staff, but freezes when she sees Matt standing in the doorway. Chemistry picks up the toy and pretends to be engrossed in playing with the dogs. She throws it toward a corner, and the

Chemistry – *Jessica Sitomer*

dogs go on the chase. She avoids eye contact while Matt who is fumbling with his tie. Last night's easy banter is replaced with stilted conversation. Excited by the tension, Misty, spying from behind the curtain, slips away to give them privacy.

Matt's voice, a little too bright, says, "Morning,"

Chemistry replies, her tone overly casual, "Morning." They both know the moment they almost kissed is lingering in the air, unspoken yet palpable. Chemistry's mind races, replaying the scene. "Sleep well?" Chemistry asks, breaking the silence but immediately regretting the cliché question.

"Yeah, you?" Matt responds, glancing at her and then quickly looking away.

"Fine," Chemistry says, her eyes finally meeting his for a split second before looking away. The comfortable rhythm of the night before is missing, replaced by a new, awkward dance. They both try to act as if nothing happened, but the charged silence speaks volumes. The moment stretches on, filled with unspoken questions and hesitant glances, making it clear that their relationship has changed, even if neither of them is ready to acknowledge it.

"I wanted to see if you and Misty wanted to grab some breakfast," he says, then instantly regrets it when he notices Chemistry's eyes widen in absolute horror! "Or not," he corrects.

"Definitely not," a man's voice interrupts from behind Matt. Entering the apartment in a stained t-shirt that reads One tequila, Two tequila, Three tequila floor with a googly-eyed worm, Lust continues, "She hates food." With a panicked expression, she shakes her head, 'not true' to Matt. "I've come to take the old lady home," Lust declares. "Come 'ere, Woman." Chemistry winces.

"And you are?" Matt asks.

"Bud," Lust says, outstretching his hand for a firm shake, "Weisner. He points at Chemistry, "Her boy--" Misty springs from behind the curtain, eager for the drama. "Brother, her boy brother," Lust insists, then makes his way through the apartment to Misty, "And who is this scrumptious creature?" Misty blushes and giggles.

"Bud," Chemistry demands through gritted teeth, "What are you doing here?"

"I came to take you home to St. Louis. You have no job and are not making any progress. We need you back up North," Lust points to the sky. "Things are getting messy without you."

"Missouri is South," Matt corrects as he looks at Lust like a suspect.

"North, South, East, West," Lust looks Misty over, "It's all titties to me. Let's go Sis."

"Hold on, she's not going anywhere. She has a job," Matt says.

"I do?" Chemistry asks.

"She does?" Lust and Misty both ask.

"She works for me," Matt assures.

"Oh," Lust struts around, "Mother Nnnnn... said you'd been fired."

"She was, but that was an overreaction," Matt looks at Chemistry, "She is welcome back if that's what she wants." A huge smile grows on Chemistry's face as she nods yes, YES! Matt turns to Lust, who has torn himself away from Misty to sit on the couch ogling over magazines, "It looks like she's staying." Lust continues to turn pages, panting as if they were Playboy, "Which means you can go back to St. Louis, right Chemmie?"

That gets Lust's attention. He imitates Matt, "Is that right, Chemmie?"

"Yes," Chemistry says with disdain, "you can go."

Lust claps his hands together and pops up. With a second thought, he decides to commandeer the magazine. As he leaves, from behind Matt and Misty, Lust mouths, "You're welcome" to Chemistry, who is relieved to see him go. The three remain silent. Matt wipes off Misty's counter. Misty straightens Chemistry's curtain. Chemistry watches at a complete loss for words. Matt breaks the silence.

"So, your brother seemed... extroverted," he says.

Misty jumps in, "And your nephew is so--"

Chemistry cuts her off, turning to Matt, "We should go on a date."

"What?" Matt and Misty both say.

"Yes," Chemistry paces, thinking through equations in her head. "The job offer is excellent, but it's too soon. Joshua does not like me." She stops and looks at Matt. "But I think you do." The five words hang in the air as Matt stands, mouth agape and with no response. "Unless I'm wrong," she continues.

"No!" Misty yells, "You're right, this is right! Right, Matt?"

Matt remembers the sting of rejection the night before and his conversation with himself about staying focused on business. He nods his head 'right,' but his face reads 'overwhelmed.'

"It can be friendly, no pressure," Chemistry suggests, "How about tonight?"

Matt considered the logistics, his brow furrowing. "Nights are too busy. How about a morning? Fridays are slow, and we could get out of the city and-- Oh wait, I can't Friday. I have a work thing. Monday afternoon? No. That's not good either. Hey Siri, what's on my calendar next week?"

Siri's robotic voice begins, "Grand Master Chef, you have 35 events until..."

Matt quickly silences the phone.

Amused, Chemistry inquires, "Grand Master, what?"

Embarrassed, Matt shakes his head, "I don't know why she calls me that. Someone must have reprogrammed her." Chemistry stares at him, waiting for him to return to the topic, "What does yours call you?"

Chemistry shoots back, "Don't change the subject, Matt! Your calendar's full. Always full. It takes a near-death experience to get you out of that restaurant!" She plops onto the sofa, in a fetal position, and puts a pillow over her face. Misty makes a prodding motion to him to get back in there. Matt ponders for a moment when a solution strikes him.

"Friday!" Matt exclaims.

Chemistry peeks out from under the pillow.

"I have to be back for a meeting, but we've got the morning and early afternoon," Matt elaborates.

Chemistry – *Jessica Sitomer*

With a grin, Chemistry agrees, "Friday it is then. Something fun!"

"Fun," Matt repeats, making his way out of the apartment. Chemistry leaps off the couch, and she and Misty dance around the room, their infectious enthusiasm spreading to the dogs, who join in the merriment. She sings joyfully, "We're going out Friday. He's gonna learn his less… We're gonna have a good time." Amidst the jubilance, one of the little dogs playfully humps her leg. Chemistry shakes him off with a laugh. "Not that good," she quips.

Misty picks up the little dog, "But here's to hoping." He licks her face.

A dog walker goes by with a pack of puppies as Chemistry waits patiently on the stoop, anticipation bubbling within her. Friday morning is quaint and bright, though loud horns blare on the NYC streets, and pedestrians yell at the cab drivers. The door creaks open, revealing a dashing yet academic-looking Matt dressed in a sports coat and slacks.

Chemistry smiles at him, "You look handsome. Where are we going?"

"Someplace fun," Matt says, his chest puffing up with pride.

Chemistry can't quite put her finger on it, and then a realization dawns, making her chuckle. Matt looks at her with a quizzical expression.

"Fun? Well then, the 'MIT look' will not work," she teases.

"Says the girl in glasses, whose hair is never out of that tight bun," he retorts.

"Touché," she says, "it seems neither of us get out much. Let's make a stop before we go."

The Saks Fifth Avenue shoe department is lively. Style is surrounded by boxes, attempting to force her foot into a shoe that is too small. Frustration etched across her face, she looks around, then discreetly waves her hand over her foot and slides it right in.

A voice behind her, accompanied by a hint of playful accusation, interrupts her efforts. "Cheater."

Startled, Style whips around, and her tense demeanor gives way to relief when she realizes it's Chemistry.

"Right on time," Style remarks with a hint of cynicism.

Chemistry – *Jessica Sitomer*

Chemistry is unperturbed by Style's tone, "He's over there." She points discreetly toward Matt, who stands amidst racks of casual menswear, contemplating his next outfit.

Matt stands before a three-way mirror, sporting a fresh ensemble of Tommy Bahama wear. A couple of young women with bunches of Saks bags pass by, whispering and giggling as a blush comes over their faces when Matt looks their way. Style's discerning eye quickly appraises his new look.

"Not only does that say, 'I'm taking a few hours off,'" Style begins with a twinkle in her eye, "but the color brings out your eyes, and the pants bring out your—"

Matt, slightly self-conscious, interjects, "Yeah, you don't think they're too snug in the back there?"

Style reassures him, "It's called contouring. When you've got it, flaunt it."

Impressed with Style's styling expertise, Matt admires himself in the mirror. His eyes catch hers as she watches him. "You do great work," he says.

Style, desperately appreciating the acknowledgment, teases Matt with a hint of mischief. "I'm the best. Are you ready for another surprise?"

Chemistry – *Jessica Sitomer*

Matt, intrigued by the prospect, responds with genuine curiosity, "I don't think there's room for me to put anything else on—"

Before he could finish his thought, Chemistry makes her entrance, looking like she did straight out of Matt's vivid dream. Gone are the glasses, replaced by long, flowing hair, carefully applied makeup, and an enticing sundress complemented by a matching scarf.

Always observant and attuned to Matt's preferences, Style leans closer and whispers, "You strike me as a legs man."

Utterly captivated by Chemistry's transformation, Matt nods in agreement, his eyes fixed on her like a moth drawn to a flame.

As Chemistry approaches, her presence casting a beguiling spell, she stops in front of Matt with a quirky yet alluring demeanor. "Ready to go?"

Matt, his enchantment clear, replies with unwavering enthusiasm, "Absolutely. I'll go pay for all of this."

With Matt off to settle the bill for his newfound attire, Chemistry's sharp eye catches a couple engaged in a heated argument nearby. She glances at Style, who is about to remove the tag from Chemistry's dress.

Chemistry – *Jessica Sitomer*

"Is everyone keeping up with their workload?" Chemistry inquires, her voice tinged with a hint of warning.

Style, sensing the weight of the implication, hesitates for a moment. "Of course we are."

"Because you know the ramifications," Chemistry warns.

Style rolls her eyes, then casually leaves the tag hanging in defiance.

Half an hour later, the sun casts long shadows across the Henry Hudson Parkway. Matt holds the steering wheel of his car as they approach the iconic George Washington Bridge. Classic 70s rock plays on the radio. Chemistry's head is entirely out of the window, her scarf dancing in the wind, and an exhilarated grin stretches across her face like a happy Labrador.

As the massive steel structure approaches, Matt can't help but chuckle, "Never been on a bridge before?"

Chemistry calls him through the wind, her eyes still glued to the bridge. "I'm just enjoying it before it becomes obsolete."

Chemistry – *Jessica Sitomer*

Matt shoots her an odd look, raising an eyebrow. "Well, let's hope that's not within the next five hours. I've got to get—"

Chemistry interrupts, "Back for your meeting. Got it! The world won't end if you leave your job for a while."

Suddenly, a thunderclap cracks through the sky, and the city behind them darkens ominously. In the opposite lane, Chemistry spots Lust cruising by in a convertible filled with stunning women, her brow wrinkles. The sunny day begins to shift into shades of gray.

They arrive at Six Flags Great Adventure, where the theme park bustles with families donning tourist t-shirts, groups of teenagers, and kids letting out ear-piercing shrieks. Chemistry munches on cotton candy, her gaze fixed on the towering roller coaster in front of her and the chorus of terrified screams from its passengers.

"Look at that thing! No wonder so many people have nightmares about them," she remarks between mouthfuls of sugary fluff.

Chemistry – *Jessica Sitomer*

"You've never been on a roller coaster?" Matt asks.

Chemistry shakes her head no as she stuffs another wad of cotton candy in her mouth.

Matt grins mischievously and stops at the entrance to the ride. "Come on..."

She tries to pull away, but Matt firmly holds onto her wrist. "You don't think I drove to Jersey for a ride on the merry-go-round, do you?" Chemistry continues to resist, but Matt's determination prevails.

Matt and Chemistry sit in the front row of the roller coaster, their hearts pounding with anticipation. As the coaster careens down a steep hill, Chemistry unleashes a torrent of ecstatic screams while Matt throws his hands in the air, embracing the wild thrill.

Exiting the Scream Machine, Chemistry licks her lips, her cheeks aching from smiling. Matt can't help but laugh. "So?"

"Again!" Chemistry exclaims.

Noticing the tag on her dress, he tucks it in and takes the opportunity to put his arm around her. The mood around them seems to be deteriorating as two young punks start a fistfight nearby. Matt glances at them as they walk past.

Chemistry – *Jessica Sitomer*

"What's with people? Isn't this supposed to be the happiest place on earth?"

One of the punks, mid-fight, responds to Matt, "That's Disneyland, ya pretty boy ninny!"

The other punk smacks his opponent upside his head, "Ninny? Who are you, my grandma?"

Ignoring the brawl, Chemistry pulls Matt away.

Throughout the day, they share moments of amusement and wonder. Standing in line, Chemistry savors a chocolate-covered banana on a stick, watching as twins in front of them celebrate passing the height requirement, only to be turned away by the grouchy ride operator.

Chemistry introduces Matt to Bugs Bunny and, nearby, observes as Wile E. Coyote trips an older man with a cane. When their eyes meet, Wile E. points to a young kid, and the older man smacks the kid's butt with his cane.

Chemistry and Matt revel in the chaos of bumper cars, their laughter standing out amidst the surrounding road rage. The day unfolds like a vivid montage of joy and absurdity, a brief escape from the encroaching gloom in the world around them.

Chemistry – *Jessica Sitomer*

Underneath the golden rays of the late afternoon sun, Matt approaches the corndog stand with an appetite for a classic fairground treat. Chemistry, beside him, exchanges a discreet signal with Humor, approaching them with a camera in hand.

"Picture for the happy couple?" Humor inquires, grinning.

"Oh, we're not a—"

Matt cuts Chemistry off with a good-natured nod. "Sure."

With that, Matt wraps his arm around Chemistry, and both flash genuine smiles as Humor snaps a Polaroid. He slides the instant capture under his armpit, a wry glint in his eye.

"What do you call a deer with no eye?" Humor asks.

Matt, being polite, responds, "Don't know."

"No-eye-deer," Humor delivers the punchline, causing a chuckle. "What do you call a fish with no eye?"

Matt guesses, "No-eye-fish?"

Humor replies with a flourish, "Fshhhh. Bah dump bump!"

Matt grins at Humor, "Funny guy," but he leans in and whispers to Chemistry, "Not so much."

Chemistry – *Jessica Sitomer*

Humor hands the developed photograph to Matt, who shows it to Chemistry before tucking it in his pocket.

"Thank you... very much," Chemistry acknowledges, attempting to be polite.

"That's ten bucks," Humor declares.

"For a Polaroid? You must be joking," says Matt.

"Not this time," Humor replies.

Matt protests but reaches into his pocket and hands over a ten-dollar bill. Humor's smile persists as he overstays his welcome.

"Outstanding job," Chemistry concedes. Her patience is wearing thin. "You can go now."

Humor theatrically takes a bow before finally sauntering away. Meanwhile, a young man hands Chemistry a corndog.

"I don't know if I can eat. I'm still a little nauseous from that plunge—" Chemistry starts, but can't resist the smell of the fried dough on the hotdog. She takes a big bite, letting grease dribble down her arm. Matt watches her with amusement.

"Mmmmmm. Lots of stuff on sticks at this place," she comments, taking another indulgent bite.

Matt decides to share a tidbit of trivia. "There's a lot of controversy about who invented the original hotdog on a stick. Did you know that in Australia, they're called Pluto Pups?"

"I did not," Chemistry replies with a hint of intrigue. "You're quite passionate about food, aren't you, Grand Master Chef?"

Matt chuckles at the title. "That's an understatement. And how about you? Passionate about food coloring?"

A thoughtful look crosses Chemistry's face. "No." She pauses, reflecting, then continues, "I guess I lost my passion a long time ago."

Matt leans in closer, genuinely interested. "What were you passionate about?"

She hesitates, worried her answer might sound clichéd, but Matt encourages her with a subtle nod. "I was a poet—but like I said, that was a long time ago."

A genuine smile spreads across Matt's face as he gazes deeply into her eyes. Chemistry, feeling self-conscious, turns her gaze away. Matt gently reaches out and turns her face back toward him. Slowly, she closes her eyes as he leans in for a kiss. Just as their lips are about to meet, Matt's phone rings, and he glances at his watch in frustration.

Chemistry – *Jessica Sitomer*

"Damn it!" Matt answers the phone, his tone agitated. "I'm on my way! I know! I know! Stall them!"

He hangs up abruptly, giving Chemistry a frustrated look, "Let's go." He dashes off toward the parking lot. Chemistry must sprint to catch up with him.

After a silent drive back to the city, the lively ambiance of Bacchus's kitchen is momentarily disrupted as Matt barges in through the back door, with Chemistry following closely behind. The rich aroma of roasting meats and freshly baked bread fills the air, mingling with the sizzle of pans and the chatter of busy staff. Matt hurriedly opens a closet and retrieves his 'emergency suit.'

"You know, Matt, you need to..." Chemistry begins, but her sentence drifts off as Matt undresses right in front of her.

Matt removes his shirt with the ease of someone accustomed to quick wardrobe changes. Watching him, Chemistry momentarily loses her train of thought.

"To what?" he challenges. He pulls on his dress shirt, buttoning it up methodically. The crisp fabric rustles with each movement.

Chemistry regains her composure. "To loosen up," she suggests, her concern for his rigid demeanor evident.

Matt's face tightens with irritation. "I have investors out there who will decide if I do or do not get money for a second restaurant. Look, I'm not blaming you, but this is what happens when I try to date. I can't do both!"

Chemistry offers a different perspective. "You're late. I'm sorry, but Matt, we were having a great time, and if these guys say no, others will say yes." Impressed by her newfound insight, she takes a shawl from her bag and wraps it around her shoulders. The soft fabric brushes against her skin, a comforting gesture. A thought crosses her mind. "Besides," she continues, "I have an idea."

Matt, willing to listen, gathers the staff around to hear Chemistry's plan. Willing to try, he nods with apprehension. Without further delay, as Matt follows, she leads the way into the dining room.

Five investors sit around a round table in the dining room, each with multiple glasses to avoid mixing different wines. The specific glassware designed to enhance the aroma and flavor of the wine is different from what has their attention fully captured. It's also not the air, thick with the rich scent of samples of aromatic elements like fruits, herbs, and spices to help identify specific scents and flavors in the wines or the small bites to demonstrate how different foods can complement the wines. No, they are entranced by something that has Joshua looking ready to explode with impatience.

Chemistry occupies a chair, wearing the short, alluring sundress that strategically exposes her mid-thigh. Her shawl drapes over her shoulders, and the light whimsy fabric contrasts with the modern decor. She smiles at the captivated men. She holds a wine glass in her hand, which Matt is about to fill.

"Gentlemen, thank you for your patience," Matt begins, his tone confident. "This presentation will be worth the wait and give you a sampling of suggestions from the discerning sommelier I'd hire for our next restaurant. Our first offering is a truly supple bottle of wine."

While Rusty pours wine for the investors, he glances occasionally over his shoulder to ensure he doesn't miss anything. The men raise their glasses,

Chemistry – *Jessica Sitomer*

eager to hear and see more. The sound of clinking glasses echoes softly through the room.

"You see, it begins 'closed up' in aroma when you first open the bottle," Matt explains. "It must sit in the open air. Then, as you swirl it in the glass..." Chemistry demonstrates this by swirling her glass, the liquid sloshing gently against the sides, as Matt gracefully removes her shawl. The delicate fragrance of the wine starts to fill the room.

"You allow the aroma to 'open up like a flower,'" Matt continues, circling her bare shoulders. Chemistry releases an appreciative gasp as she lifts the glass to her lips and takes a sip. The investors follow suit, clearly intrigued. "When you taste it," Matt continues, his eyes locked with Chemistry's, "it should 'caress the inside of one's mouth.'" He emphasizes his point by letting his fingers glide over her skin, the touch soft and deliberate. Chemistry holds his gaze momentarily before savoring another sip of wine, and the investors mirror her actions.

"If you 'quickly swallow,'" Matt teases, "you miss the complexity of the wine."

Chemistry giggles, her laughter a light, melodic sound that fills the room. Joshua, on the other hand, rolls his eyes in exasperation. Matt opens another bottle of wine and begins pouring for the investors. "Look for the 'legs' on the glass."

The investors are mesmerized as Chemistry runs her finger down her leg, her smooth skin catching the light. Matt continues, "See how smooth the wine is?" All but Joshua nod in agreement. Matt and Chemistry finally break their intense gaze, returning their focus to the task.

The kitchen at Bacchus buzzes with intensity, a symphony of clattering pans, sizzling oil, and Joshua's sharp orders at the pass. The tension in the room seems to thicken as Matt steps in, his face set in a mask of calm, but underneath, the cracks are forming.

Joshua doesn't waste a second. "What the hell, Matt? You walk in late and expect everything to run smoothly?"

Matt keeps his voice steady, knowing all eyes are on them. "Relax, Josh. It worked out." His words are calm, but there's a flicker in his eyes, a conflict brewing that he's struggling to contain.

Joshua's voice rises. "Worked out? You show up late with the fired bartender, throwing us under the bus in front of investors? This is serious!"

Chemistry – *Jessica Sitomer*

Matt meets his partner's gaze, his jaw tight. "I handled it." He can feel the weight of the kitchen staff's stares, but his mind isn't on Joshua's words—it's on Chemistry, standing just a few feet away, her presence pulling at him like a magnet.

Chemistry steps forward, still wearing that bright, easy smile. "They finished another bottle of wine. Can I bring out some food?" Her tone is light, unaware of the storm brewing between the two men.

Joshua cuts in before Matt can speak. "I'll handle it." He turns to Chemistry, "You're done here. Go home."

Matt's stomach twists. He wants to shout at Joshua, to tell him to back off, but he knows he can't—his team is watching. "Josh, stop." His voice wavers slightly, and he feels the room closing in. "This isn't your decision."

Joshua's eyes narrow, but he steps back, throwing his hands up in mock surrender. "Fine. It's your call, Matt. But you know what I think."

Matt looks at Chemistry, his heart racing, but his face remains neutral. His thoughts are a jumble—I don't want you to go. Stay. Please, stay. But his mouth says, "Chemmie, I had a great

Chemistry – *Jessica Sitomer*

day. Thanks for everything." He's trying hard to be professional, but every word feels like a lie.

Chemistry's smile falters. "What's going on?" she asks, her eyes flicking between the two men.

Matt's throat tightens. He forces the words out, each one a betrayal. "It's nothing. Just... it's not the right time." His voice is too steady and cold for what he feels.

She shakes her head, hurt flashing in her eyes. "When will you learn there's more to life than this?"

Matt feels a surge of panic, his heart thudding in his chest. He wants to reach out and tell her he knows there's more—she is the more. But instead, he says, "I don't want more than this." The words are wrong, and he knows it. But he can't let her see the truth—not here, not now.

Chemistry's expression hardens. "Fine. But when this all falls apart, and it will, because he's not your partner, he's here for himself. Your happiness means nothing to him. Remember what you gave up." Her voice is cold and final, and she nods to Joshua, which cuts Matt deeper than he thought possible. When Joshua laughs, it breaks Matt.

"Please leave," Matt snaps, his voice louder than intended. The kitchen staff pauses, their eyes on him, but all he sees is her walking away.

Joshua calls out, "Back to work!" The kitchen noise resumes, but for Matt, everything feels distant, like he's stuck in a slow-motion spiral. He watches Chemistry leave through the alley door, his chest tight with regret.

Eli, sensing the shift, steps up quietly. "Vince Lombardi said, 'The price of success is hard work and dedication.'"

Matt barely hears him. His mind is racing, replaying the moment, the words he didn't say. He can't go after her, not now. "Good advice, Eli," he mutters, his voice hollow.

Eli pauses. "But he also said, 'Behind every great man, there's a woman.'" He says it softly, knowing what Matt needs to hear.

Matt looks at the door where she just left, his heart in his throat. "I can't go after her, Eli. Not with everything on the line." Eli nods, pretending to understand.

The kitchen hums on, the chaos continuing around him, but Matt is still—his hands on the edge of the counter, gripping it like it's the only thing keeping him from falling apart. Then he straightens up and heads back into the restaurant. Eli tells one of the servers he'll be back and follows Chemistry.

Chemistry – *Jessica Sitomer*

The alleyway behind Bacchus stretches narrow and long, bordered by tall brick walls adorned with faded graffiti and old posters peeling at the edges. Stacks of crates and boxes line on one side, remnants of the day's deliveries waiting to be discarded, while near the back door of the restaurant, a cluster of metal trash bins stands, their lids slightly askew, offering a feast to the occasional rat or stray cat that stalk the shadows. The alley serves as a getaway for hurried cigarette breaks, whispered conversations, and stolen moments of solitude for the restaurant staff. Chemistry is almost to the city street.

"Chemmie, wait," Eli calls. Hearing him, she stops and looks back. Eli pulls some paper from his apron and jogs to her. Offering them to her, "You're good for him."

Chemistry sifts through the once crumpled and discarded papers, which Eli has smoothed to the best he could get them. "What are these?" she asks.

"Matt has a journal. He writes random notes." As Chemistry looks through them, he says, "I believe the ones he crumples and throws away are the most meaningful. They are too hard for him to look at, so he tears them out. I find them when I throw out his trash and save them."

Chemistry – *Jessica Sitomer*

She shuffles them and asks, "What's a ghost restaurant? It's on a lot of these." Eli shrugs, not knowing. "Thanks, Eli," she smiles at him. He salutes her, then turns and jogs back to the restaurant. Chemistry looks at the crumpled paper that says, 'ghost restaurant,' an idea forming as she pulls out her phone, "Hey Siri, what is a ghost restaurant?"

Inside Matt's apartment, the clock reads 4:03 AM. Lola is luxuriously sprawled in the middle of his unkempt bed. The room bears the unmistakable signs of restless slumber, with pillows askew and blankets bunched up.

Matt walks into his bedroom and discovers Lola. He can't help but smile. He leans in to pet her affectionately.

"Lola, look at this bed. Off!"

Lola promptly jumps off the bed, her tail wagging in response. Matt straightens a few pillows and adjusts the disheveled blanket. As he lifts the blanket, his casual routine is abruptly interrupted by a jarring discovery—a body hidden beneath.

Chemistry – *Jessica Sitomer*

Startled, he yells, and the person beneath the blanket screams, leaping out of bed. In the dim light, Matt can hardly make out the figure. He quickly flicks on the bedroom light. To his astonishment, it's Chemistry. "What are you doing in my bed?" Matt exclaims in disbelief.

Chemistry, disoriented and still half-asleep, stammers, "I was waiting for you, and it got late."

Matt's aggravation boils over. "Let me rephrase that. What are you doing in my apartment?!"

Her mind foggy from sleep, Chemistry replies, "The door was open."

Matt's tone is stern as he clarifies, "It's always open."

Unperturbed, Chemistry attempts to convey her intent. "I wanted to apologize for earlier."

Matt, however, remains uninterested in her apologies. He is all business, declaring, "I'm not interested in your apologies. You humiliated me in front of my staff!"

Chemistry pleads with him to understand. "If you could just forget about the restaurant for one minute—"

Matt, fueled by anger, grabs her by the arm and forcefully leads her toward the bedroom door.

"Unhand me!" Chemistry demands, her patience wearing thin.

Mocking her choice of words, Matt retorts, "'Unhand me?' What is this, Medieval times?"

They reach the living room, where Matt continues to usher her toward the front door. "That 'restaurant' has been my dream since I was eight years old. You may not understand that--"

"Believe me, I know a thing or two about dreams," Chemistry interjects, her voice laced with empathy.

Matt, however, is unwavering. He appeals to her in earnest. "Then do me a favor—stay out of mine!"

With finality, he pushes her out of the apartment and closes the door behind her, leaving Chemistry standing in the hallway.

"Goodnight," Matt calls out firmly from the other side of the door.

A tense silence hangs in the air as they lock eyes through the warped doorframe. Then, Chemistry pushes her way back into the apartment, clutches Matt's face, and passionately kisses his lips. The moment their lips part, Chemistry feels a warm sensation through her whole body. A wave of uncertainty crashes over her, and an awkward smile appears as she searches Matt's eyes, wondering if he

Chemistry – *Jessica Sitomer*

felt the same whirlwind of emotions that now tangle inside her. Unable to read him, her vulnerability feels unbearable. With an air of defiance, she straightens her shirt and walks out, leaving Matt utterly stunned in the middle of his living room.

Chemistry – *Jessica Sitomer*

Chapter 12

The soft morning light gently filters into Misty's cozy apartment, where Chemistry lies asleep on her cot. Stretching languidly, she blinks her eyes open, gradually rousing from slumber. Lola pants nearby, her warm breath a soothing presence.

Chemistry, still in a state of half-sleep, closes her eyes again. A smile forms from the corners of her mouth as a growing appreciation for sleep returns to her consciousness. A small dog's whine interrupts her fleeting moment of tranquility. She opens her eyes again, only to be met with an unexpected sight—a lineup of dogs, hanging tongues, and pants of various lengths, all neatly arranged in her line of sight.

Her gaze travels upward, tracing the line of pants, until she locks eyes with the source of her bewilderment—Matt. He stands before her, holding a cup of coffee and a croissant.

Chemistry – *Jessica Sitomer*

"You kissed me last night," Matt states matter-of-factly.

Chemistry, unperturbed, replies with a hint of playfulness, "You noticed."

Matt can't help but acknowledge the truth. "Hard to miss."

Chemistry teases him with a grin. "Not the romantic reaction I was looking for—"

Before she can finish her thought, Matt jumps in, fingers gripping his hair, words tumbling out rapidly, "Look, I'm not good at this. I like you-- I really liked that kiss, but how does this work? I will constantly be disappointing you-- I don't have time. I have to stay focused. You don't understand the stress of the perfection needed."

Chemistry sits up, pats the cot, coaxing him to sit beside her, and says, "I happen to be very familiar with the stresses of perfectionism, so why don't we take the pressure off? Maybe no kissing for now?" Matt's face falls, "We can focus on something you're passionate about while we get to know each other."

"The only things I'm passionate about are restaurants."

"Okay, so something in your industry, like," she pauses as if thinking up an idea, "a ghost restaurant."

Chemistry – *Jessica Sitomer*

In alarm, Matt jumps to his feet, "How do you know about Ghost Restaurants?"

"I didn't," she explains, "I heard someone say it yesterday in your restaurant and asked Siri what it was."

"Who said it!?"

"I'm not sure--"

Matt drops to the floor and takes Chemistry's hands. "I need you to think hard. Was it Joshua? One of the investors?"

Noticing his anxiety, "Um...no, it was a patron."

He lets out a long sigh as he leans up against the cot, looking out the window. "I've been thinking of what would have been possible if I hadn't worked with Josh. How I could make it without him."

Chemistry slides off the cot so she is sitting side by side with him. "Can't you tell the investors that the menu is yours?" Matt shakes his head no. His neck drops between his knees. Chemistry awkwardly reaches for his back and rubs it. He looks up at her. She pulls her hand back. "As a friend... with no kissing at all... explain to me what a ghost restaurant would look like with you in charge."

His eyes turn back to the window, and now there is a glint of a spark in them. The corners of his mouth begin to turn up. "You really want to know?"

"Absolutely," she says. Matt jumps up and offers her his hand. She accepts as he helps her to her feet, and they head out of Misty's apartment.

Matt pushes his door open and walks with purpose to his kitchen cabinets. He pulls open two, revealing stacks of notebooks and journals years in the making. Grabbing the one on top, he brings it to the couch and plops down, patting the seat next to him. Chemistry gives him a 'one-minute' sign and pulls a random journal from his cabinet. The cover, worn and stained from countless hours in the kitchen, hints at the rich contents within. Inside, vibrant sketches of dishes bursting with color and detail, each one evidence of Matt's artistry. Saffron-yellow risottos, ruby-red beet carpaccio, and emerald-green pesto swirls are rendered with a painter's precision, making the pages come alive.

Scattered among the drawings are handwritten notes in Matt's elegant script. Ideas for new flavor combinations, techniques to perfect, and ingredients to experiment with are jotted down with excitement and curiosity. 'Lemon verbena foam for the seabass,' one note reads next to a quick sketch of the dish. Another page features an intricate drawing of a dessert, a delicate chocolate sphere, and a suggestion to pair it with raspberry coulis and edible gold leaf. Chemistry closes the journal and places it back where she found it.

She joins him on the couch, where he is flipping through the journal until he finds a detailed sketch of a kitchen layout. Stations are carefully mapped out, from the sauté section to the pastry corner, each with annotations on workflow improvements and equipment placements. 'Move the prep table closer to the walk-in,' says one note alongside a detailed diagram.

Chemistry gently takes it from him and turns the pages with reverence. The journal is a blend of artistic inspiration and practical planning. Matt turns ahead and says, "I'm trying to decide between these four menus. He hands the journal to her.

Chemistry reads them, "Whimsical." She looks over the offerings, like Fairy Garden Flatbread paired with Rosé and Pixie Dust Poppers paired with a Pinot Noir, and then turns the page to "Molecular Gastronomy." What in the world is that, and what is a Liquid Olive Sphere? She continues reading over dishes she can't make heads or tails of, like Tomato Water Ravioli and Spherified Pea Risotto. On the next page, she finds a Farm to Table. Great! Farms, I know. She recognizes many, like the

Chemistry – *Jessica Sitomer*

Creamy Cauliflower Soup paired with a Viognier and the Garlic Mashed Potatoes paired with a Chardonnay, but what is Kale and Quinoa, and why would he grill a peach? The desserts were equally as vexing. Chocolate Avocado Mousse paired with a Port Wine? Ooo! A Galette! That one, I know. Peach and Basil Sorbet? How do those ingredients mix? She realizes her face is contorted, and Matt is watching, so she gives him a big smile and a happy nod as she turns the page to read the final menu. Instagramable? Not knowing what the word means or any of the beautifully described dishes with words like 'rainbow,' 'glaze,' and 'zest,' she says, "Matt, these look incredible! I know nothing about wine or what most of these dishes are, but they're so poetic, making me want to try everything." Matt tilts his head at her thinking.

"What if you did? What if I bring ingredients home every night to experiment and refine?" Matt jumps up with excitement. "We can spend time together without me feeling guilty."

"You sure know how to charm a girl," jokes Chemistry, "But I'm in. I really want to try the chocolate avocado mousse because, logically, those two do not go together."

Chemistry – *Jessica Sitomer*

"Food isn't about logic. It's imagination and chemistry," Matt grins.

Hmmm, Chemistry nods her head in approval. This may be easier than I thought, she thinks, as she turns the pages and Matt opens cabinets, drawers, his fridge, and freezer, taking a quick inventory.

In the pristine kitchen of his apartment, Matt moves with practiced precision. Chemistry watches as he places ingredients in exact formation on the marble countertop. Matt's hands move deftly, slicing into the ripe avocados with a sharp knife, the blade gliding through the creamy green flesh. He scoops the avocado into a sleek, stainless steel mixing bowl, its rich color vibrant against the polished surface. The room is filled with a delicate, nutty aroma as he adds a generous pour of pure maple syrup, the amber liquid pooling over the avocados.

Matt reaches for the Valrhona Dutch Processed cocoa powder with a soft hum, measuring out spoonfuls of the dark, velvety powder. The cocoa dusts the avocados, creating a stark contrast of color

Chemistry – *Jessica Sitomer*

and hinting at the decadent treat to come. He sprinkles a pinch of sea salt, the delicate crystals catching the light. Chemistry can't help but notice his concentration, the measuring, and the concocting, which feel familiar to her. As he works, the sounds of the city outside, louder than usual, fade into the background.

Switching on the food processor, the kitchen fills with a low, steady whir as the blades blend the ingredients into a smooth, creamy mousse. Matt watches intently, the corners of his mouth curling into a satisfied smile. He has a certain Zen in his act of creation.

"All you need is a lab coat," Chemistry jokes.

"This apron is my lab coat," he says with a serious tone.

She turns away, mimicking him softly. "This apron is my lab--" She catches herself, realizing she is acting like Style. Instead of hovering, she decides to look through his notebooks.

Matt completely entranced, pauses the machine and dips a spoon into the mixture, bringing it to his lips. The taste is heavenly – the deep, rich chocolate perfectly balanced by the subtle, creamy avocado and the hint of sweetness from the maple syrup. He nods to himself, pleased with the result.

Chemistry – *Jessica Sitomer*

Matt carefully spoons the mousse into a delicate glass ramekin, the dark chocolate mixture settling with a slight jiggle. He tops it with a sprinkle of shaved dark chocolate and a single raspberry, the bright red fruit adding a pop of color. "It's not chilled, but taste," he offers her a spoonful. Chemistry sniffs it, then closes her eyes as she tastes the mousse, her lips curling into a smile. The rich chocolate and creamy avocado meld perfectly, a luxurious blend of flavors dancing on her tongue. She savors the velvety texture, letting out a soft, contented sigh as Matt dumps the rest of the mousse in the garbage.

"What are you doing?" Alarmed, Chemistry investigates the trash bin, discovering days of chopped vegetables decaying as the layers get deeper.

"That was just my first trial. It's not even close."

"But there are famines, people starving," Chemistry's voice is almost childlike.

"Wow, that's dramatic. This is my process. It's just an avocado."

"That is perfectly good food!"

"Not perfect enough!" he yells with way more emotion than is appropriate for this moment, which he quickly realizes. The momentary joy he'd been feeling has been replaced by reality. "What are we doing? I can't do this. This industry is so competitive. It's so stressful."

"You know what solves that?" Chemistry swipes some chocolate from the side of the mixer and dots his nose. "Balance. Letting someone in. Letting someone love you. Someone you can laugh with, blow off steam, and relax with."

Matt wipes the chocolate from his nose, unmoved by her playfulness, too caught up in the reality of his life. "Relax? There's no time for that. Josh wants a star. A star!"

"You are a star."

"A Michelin Star."

"Alexa, what's a Michelin Star?" Chemistry laughs.

Alexa answers, "Michelin stars are used in a three-star rating system in fine dining to determine the overall food quality. One Michelin star determines--"

"Alexa, off!" Matt laughs.

"I don't understand. How does Joshua get the star when you created the food?" she asks.

"To the world, he's the chef, and a star is what he wants."

"What do you want?" Chemistry whispers.

Chemistry – *Jessica Sitomer*

Matt doesn't have to think about it, "I want people to love my food."

Chemistry opens the garbage, sticks her finger in the mousse, and sucks it off her finger, "I'm just getting to know your food, but this..." She takes a bigger fingerful of the mousse and eats it, "this could be love."

"You just ate garbage food. I don't know whether to be disgusted or flattered." She smiles at him, her toothy grin smudged in chocolate. "Leaning toward disgusted," he jokes. She swats him and asks what's next. He points toward the sink, and the dishwashing begins.

At Bacchus, the prep crew is in bright and early, checking deliveries, breaking down boxes, and prepping vegetables and proteins. The kitchen hums with the soft thud of knives on cutting boards and the hiss of gas burners flaring to life. Matt walks in, taking in the scene with a satisfied nod. He spots one of his Stagiaires. The culinary intern is working unpaid for the chance to learn from the best, so Matt walks over to give him a lesson.

Chemistry – *Jessica Sitomer*

The kid is hunched over a pile of carrots, cutting furiously but unevenly. Matt steps up with a smile. "Here, let me show you something," he says, gently guiding the Stage's hand. "You want every piece the same size, like this." He demonstrates a few clean, precise cuts, and the Stage watches in awe. "It helps them cook evenly," Matt explains.

He greets the saucier next, patting him on the back before dipping a spoon into a pot of rich, bubbling sauce. One taste, and he moans in appreciation, his eyes closing in approval. "Perfection," he mutters as the saucier beams with pride. I've got a good thing here. He thinks to himself. Chemmie's rushing me and the process. Look at these guys. I should enjoy my success and grow responsibly.

With a strong feeling of satisfaction that he hadn't felt in a long time, he tells the team to have a great day and walks to the serenity of his office. After allowing himself to enjoy the feeling of accomplishment, he opens his desk, pulls out his journal, removes the elastic, and pulls the ribbon to open his last entry, which reads Ghost Restaurant. He tears it out, crumples it, and throws it in the trash.

Without warning, Josh, bounding with energy, barges into Matt's office, startling Matt. "You're up early," Matt states the obvious.

"Haven't been to bed yet," Josh corrects, pacing like a caffeinated toddler, "I want to do a menu of all my dishes from the show- we can create a huge marketing campaign around it- people will come from everywhere—"

"Whoa! What are you talking about? We have a menu."

"Yeah, yeah, we have a menu, but it's nothing special," Joshua tosses out as Matt winces. "I'm talking about a menu of all my dishes from the show. We can give them names that tie into my persona, "Joshua's Juicy Jambalaya. Joshua's Manic Mole Poblano."

"That Mole got you kicked you off the show," Matt reminds him.

Josh mimics, "For too much chocolate flavor. Who puts 'too much' and 'chocolate' in the same sentence? You can never have enough chocolate!" Joshua stops pacing, "I should have a desk in here."

Matt stands, "Josh, you need to get some sleep."

"I need you to design my menu," Josh insists.

"Josh," Matt tries to be delicate, "No one wants to eat those dishes," then accidentally blurts out, "The judges didn't want to eat those dishes."

Joshua paces like a storm cloud on the verge of bursting, each step charged with electric tension. "You are so jealous. You always have been. And you're so wrong!"

"I'm not wrong, Josh."

"It's Joshua! And the investors think it's a fantastic idea and will blow this place up, probably making it a franchise. We'll have to change the name to stand out—we were throwing around Joshua's Joint, but we want something more sophisticated." Joshua starts mumbling words to substitute for Joint.

Matt is momentarily stunned. "Did you meet with my contacts? My investors?" Matt questions with a tone of years of resentment.

"They're our investors, and after your amateur hour, I felt it was important to wine and dine them, get them back, give them something provocative to consider--'The Joshua Experience,'" Joshua dramatically stretches his jazz hands as if revealing the signage.

Chemistry – *Jessica Sitomer*

Using all his restraint, Matt puts his journal back in his drawer, locks it, puts his key in his pocket, and storms out of the office.

Amsterdam Avenue is busy with people walking toward subway entrances. Matt walks fast, his steps heavy. A man with his nose in his phone knocks into Matt and curses at him. Matt forges forward, encountering one rude person after another.

As he passes his corner bodega, he grabs a green pepper, two carrots, and an onion, "I'll get you later, Mr. Sanchez," Matt calls, and Mr. Sanchez waves to him.

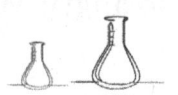

Matt chops and chops in his kitchen. He nearly cuts himself but continues to chop. When he's done, he looks at the three piles as if they were maggots. Chemistry walks in just as he's about to slide all the pieces into the trash. "Noooooooo," she pleads playfully, "Make an omelet."

"I don't want to make a fucking omelet!" Matt shouts. His tone paralyzes Chemistry.

Chemistry – *Jessica Sitomer*

Misty comes running in, her pack of barking dogs in tow, "What's wrong?" she cries.

Matt roars, though more to himself than the women. "He steals everything from me!"

"We should go," Misty whispers, taking a dazed Chemistry by the arm and pulling her out the door. The dogs quietly follow.

Once the women are in Misty's apartment and Misty has settled Chemistry on the couch, she says, "I'll make us chamomile tea." A labrador jumps up next to Chemistry and licks her face until she snaps out of shock.

As Misty brings the tea, Chemistry says, "I've never seen anyone so angry. Who was he talking about?"

"Joshua, I'm sure. They go through this every other month or so," Misty explains, "though he does seem uncharacteristically upset."

"The way he lashed out at me," Chemistry says, trying to work out a puzzle in her mind, "I'm still missing something... Something deep... and dark. Maybe even I can't--"

Misty takes Chemistry's shoulders and shakes her, "Buck up, Girlie! This has nothing to do with you. He was not lashing out at you. He's mad at

Chemistry – *Jessica Sitomer*

Joshua, and you happened to be there. The dogs and I talked, and we think you've been perfect for him." She slides the teacup toward Chemistry, "Drink up. Tea makes everything better."

The half-empty teacup on Chemistry's bedside warms in the sunshine the following day as Chemistry tosses and turns on her cot. Evidence of a night of work surrounds her. She picks up an equation, taps the pen tip on it searching for something, and then tosses it to the floor where it lands next to the iPhoneXXX. Chemistry grabs the phone and scrolls through. Nothing? she thinks, then types WHERE IS EVERYBODY?! SOMEONE RESPOND TO ME I NEED HELP! Three dots flash in response when an aroma of buttery richness and savory notes fills the air. She leans off her cot and around the curtain to see what it is, startled to find Matt standing a foot from her, holding a plate with a steaming omelet. She shoves the phone into her bag.

As she retreats behind her curtain, Chemistry complains, "The lack of privacy around here is insufferable." Matt reaches his hand straight ahead, holding the plate so the food is visible to her, but he is not. She stares at it, then takes it with a huff.

"Fork?" Matt's other hand produces a fork wrapped in a napkin. She takes it, smells the omelet, then takes a forkful. She sighs with pleasure as the creamy eggs, butter, and herbs melt in her mouth.

"I keep finding myself apologizing at your mercy," Matt says, the curtain still between them, "I've never behaved like this, and I don't know why you keep forgiving me."

With a stuffed mouth, she mumbles, "Clearly, it's your cooking." She swallows, "And I haven't forgiven you." She pushes the curtain aside to find him sitting on the floor, his back to her. She watches as his head drops in shame. She slides off the cot and sits back-to-back with him. "Talk to me," she whispers, "Help me understand."

"It's just work stuff," he blows off.

"After the way you snapped last night, 'just work stuff' doesn't cut it anymore." Matt remains still, silent. Chemistry shakes her head in frustration, then swings around and lifts his face to meet hers, "You scared me."

He looks away. "I know," his voice so quiet it's barely audible. The weight of his words hangs in the air, heavy with remorse. They sit silently, neither looking at the other, when Lola lumbers in and drops to the floor between them, panting heavily.

Matt strokes Lola's back, "My emotional support dog."

Chemistry tries to muster a smile, "Do you share your emotional problems with her?"

"Don't need to," Matt pats Lola on the head, "She gets it."

"Must be nice for her."

"Can't beat unconditional love," Matt says.

Chemistry looks at him, "Just because she's a dog doesn't mean it's unconditional. She loves you because you love her, and she feels it. When you're sad, she feels it. When you're angry, she feels it."

"And she loves me anyway," Matt says.

"Yes, that's what love is. Loving someone through whatever they're going through... their success, their pain, their illness," Chemistry turns away, fighting back tears. She swallows hard and composes herself, "but that means sharing it all. I can forgive your anger but can't forgive you shutting me out."

Matt stays quiet for a moment, then stands up. "I'm sorry you feel that way. Come on, Lola." He walks out of the apartment with Lola by his side and disappears into his apartment.

Discouraged, Chemistry gets up and reaches into her bag for the phone. Nothing. She types

Chemistry – *Jessica Sitomer*

HELLO?!?! I KNOW YOU'RE THERE. I SAW THE DOTS! She waits, but no one responds. What am I going to do? After a moment, she picks up a pen and writes on her unused napkin:

> In the quiet dawn, whispers of the heart,
> Unconditional love, a timeless art,
> Boundless, steadfast, an eternal arc,
> It's worth the effort for the spark.

She gets dressed and tiptoes around the dogs to avoid disturbing Misty. Looking through drawers, she finds a roll of clear tape, rips off an inch, and secures half of it to the napkin. She grabs her bag, heads out of the apartment, tapes the poem to Matt's door, and leaves.

Chapter 13

The poems continue as the days go by. She walks the NY streets. She writes them while sitting on benches and subway cars. She explores the city she's only seen in dreams, inspiring her words. Every day, she returns and tapes a poem to Matt's door. Though they haven't spoken in weeks, the poem is always gone when she returns with her newest one. One day, on a walk with Misty and her pack of dogs, Chemistry notices how dirty everything seems. She sees couples fighting and strangers yelling at each other.

"Is it me, or is everyone grouchy?" Chemistry asks.

Misty ponders, "The season is changing. New Yorkers get angry when it's cold. They also get angry when it's too hot... and when spring only seems to last two weeks. They get angry when the leaves fall from the trees because who doesn't like to watch the changing leaves? They just don't last long enough."

"So, you're saying this is Mother Nature's fault," Chemistry confirms.

"Oh, for sure. New Yorkers are the best people, but climate change is irritating. Do I put my thermostat down to 72 when I know it will drop to 40 tonight? These are real-time problems."

"Okay, just making sure this is typical behavior."

"Absolutely," Misty reassures.

A grizzled man walks by, "Hey, your dog just took a dump. Clean it up."

Misty snaps, "I have eyes, Sir, I HAVE EYES!" She reaches into her pocket, pulls out a bag, and looks around. In her doggie voice, she asks, "Which one of you made big business?"

"Maybe we should go back to the apartment," Chemistry suggests. Misty agrees and rallies the dogs.

The pack pulls Misty to her apartment as Chemistry lags. She whispers to her bag, "I need tape." A roll of tape pops up, and she tears off a piece. She pulls a napkin from her pocket and approaches Matt's door. She tapes it, but as she reaches to stick the

Chemistry – *Jessica Sitomer*

poem on the door, Matt opens it, and they are face to face. They stand in awkward silence.

Chemistry self-consciously sticks the poem to Matt's suit jacket. "Busted. These have been from me."

"I figured," Matt says with no emotion. He pulls the napkin off his chest and reads it aloud, "Can we be okay again, like we were before? In the quiet of the night, can we heal and soar? Through the scars and tears, can we find the light? In the dawn of new hope, can we set things right?"

Chemistry apologizes, "On the nose, I know. Wasn't feeling very inspired today."

"It's good," he smiles. "They're all good. It's been like getting a fortune cookie every day."

"Really? Like the restaurant you took me to with the cookie and the paper inside?"

"Yes... the fortune cookie," Matt reinforces.

"Huh. That would be cool for your Ghost Restaurant. I could write a different food poem each day... and people would come to collect them."

"Like McDonald's Happy Meals?" Matt asks. Chemistry can't make out if he said it with disdain or consideration. She mentally notes that she should ask Siri what a McDonald's is and what makes their meals happy.

"What about a vegan heart-shaped pastry with a poem sticking out?" she brainstorms.

Matt's expression changes as he considers this, "Like a Hershey's kiss?"

"Like a Vegan kiss," Chemistry adds, not knowing if she is hiding her lack of understanding of his references.

"A Vegan kiss..." He thinks for a moment, "gluten-free flour, sugar, salt, water, coconut oil, and I can infuse with different flavors daily," growing more excited. And I wouldn't charge for them, for surprise and delight... Eventually, it would become an expectation, but occasionally, I can change the cookie. It would be great for Instagram..." Chemistry forms a big smile. "What?" he asks her.

"I've never seen you this animated. You're happy."

Matt reigns himself in and centers himself, "Well, one day. Not now. The restaurant's doing well."

"You could try it out there," she suggests.

"No!" Matt snaps, though not at her. He shuts down again.

"No," she realizes, "because anything you do there will be associated with..." She doesn't need to say his name. He shakes his head yes. "Well, if you ever want to play around with the cookies or the menu ideas... that was really fun."

"Okay," he answers noncommittedly and begins to walk away. You can keep writing me poems if you want." She nods in agreement. "Food ones if you want to practice," he suggests.

"Practice?" she feigns insult, then recites a poem off the top of her head, "In each bite, a balm for the soul's deep ache," with each word, she steps closer to him, "Food heals with love that only," with her last words they are close enough to kiss, "warmth can make." They stand that way for too long, each turning breathlessly away without the other noticing. As they turn back to each other, Chemistry thinks, gosh, he has nice lips. Very. Nice. Lips.

"If I remember, I'll bring home some ingredients tonight," he says, warming to her again.

"I hope you remember," Chemistry says, then gives an awkward wave, mentally scolding her dorkiness, and continues back to Misty's apartment.

On the stoop of the brownstone, Chemistry writes. Her pen flows with ideas. She looks up at the sky,

Chemistry – *Jessica Sitomer*

remembering in her youth how there had been so many stars. With the lights of Manhattan blocking any celestial possibilities, she wonders if the stars are gone or not visible from New York.

"You're out late," Matt says, startling her.

"You've got me writing again."

"Let's hear," he prods, placing a brown bag on a step. Then, he takes a seat on the stairs below her.

She shifts uncomfortably, "These aren't about food. They're personal."

"Aren't you always insisting I open up?" Matt reminds her.

"Yes, 'you' need to open up."

"How about you read me the last poem you wrote, and I'll tell you about the first girl who broke my heart."

Chemistry's interest is peaked. She takes a breath, "In the city lights, the stars are lost to sight. I yearn for their glow. Their absence fills my heart with quiet sighs and memories. Do you see them?"

Matt looks up at the Manhattan sky, a deep navy canvas punctuated by the faintest stars struggling against the city's bright haze. The moon hangs low, casting a silver glow on the silent streets. Streetlights flicker softly. "I think I do," he whispers. A taxi driver flies by, holding his hand on the horn, ruining the tranquility.

"Okay, you owe me a story," Chemistry insists.

"Fine," Matt drones. "Her name was Lizzie McGuire," he says thoughtfully, then looks to Chemistry for a reaction. Chemistry only encourages him to continue. "You probably know her as Hilary Duff, and when I found out she was dating the guy from Good Charlotte... well, my eleven-year-old heart just broke."

Chemistry put her hand on his knee. "You had your first heartbreak when you were only eleven?"

"Chemmie, are you being serious right now?"

"Are you? That is a trauma."

"Chemmie! I'm talking about my childhood crush on Hilary Duff, the actress from the Disney Channel?"

Chemistry turns her pad over, shielding it from his eyes, "I read you my poem, and you didn't tell me about your first heartbreak?"

He senses her irritation, "I mean, I was bummed." Chemistry turns away, "Can we go inside? I brought home some ingredients, and I don't want them to spoil." He picks up the paper bag and heads for the front door. As he puts his key in the lock, he realizes Chemistry is still seated. As the door opens, he says, "Come on, don't be mad. I thought you'd laugh. Come inside." Frustrated, Chemistry realizes she must use every opportunity she has with him if she's going to finish the case.

Inside Matt's apartment, Chemistry and Matt are welcomed by the sight of Lola, a remote control clutched between her teeth. Matt doesn't hesitate. He takes the remote, tosses it onto the couch, and leads Chemistry into the kitchen.

He pulls a glass container from the bag and dips his finger into it, then offers his finger to Chemistry. "Taste this," he urges.

She looked at his finger, puzzled momentarily, before realizing his intention. She gently touches her tongue to his finger, savoring the tiny taste. Matt nonchalantly sucks the remaining bit off his finger. "Good, huh?" he asks. "But wait!"

With deft movements, he adds spices, mixes ingredients, and prepares an irresistible dish. Chemistry watches him with a growing appreciation for his culinary skills.

He offers her another taste. This time, she dips her finger into the mixture. A relished "Mmmm" escapes her lips, and her eyes open wide with delight.

Chemistry – *Jessica Sitomer*

Matt is in his element as he delves into the fridge, opening more glass containers, and skillfully dices, slices, adds, and mixes ingredients. The scent of the meal to come fills the air.

Matt takes Chemistry's hand and leads her to the colorful blanket on the floor, adorned with an array of intriguing foods. Chemistry and Matt sit side by side, their shoes kicked off and sleeves casually pushed up. They both wear expressions of ease and contentment.

"Your restaurant seems to be doing well. You could probably afford a dining room table," Chemistry suggests.

He laughs, "I never eat here."

"Then why is there so much food in your fridge?"

"When I get mad or have a problem to solve, cooking is where I find my zone," he says.

"Your zone?" she questions.

"Yeah, like, my flow. I'm in the zone." He dives deeper, "Have you ever had a problem to solve that was beyond frustrating, and you feel like if you don't fix it or make the right decision, you'll blow everything you worked for?"

"Yes!" Chemistry shouts, then laughs.

Chemistry – *Jessica Sitomer*

"How do you work through it?" he asks, "What takes your mind off of everything so the answer comes to you?"

"Math."

"Math?" he asks.

"Well, science... chemistry specifically, equations... the right math, the right formula, is always the answer," she says, then takes a bite of a flaky savory puff. It's so delicious that she stuffs the rest in her mouth. She grabs a piece of watermelon covered in a white yogurt sauce and topped with some type of crumble. She finishes it with a moan and digs into a spinach and cheese crepe.

Matt's eyes twinkle with amusement as he observes Chemistry savoring her food as if every bite were her last. She suddenly notices she's the only one eating. "You're not having any?"

A wry grin plays on his lips. "I don't enjoy my food nearly as much as I enjoy watching you enjoy it," he confesses, his voice tinged with affection. "When's the last time you had a home-cooked meal?"

Her mouth still half-full, "Not including your omelet?"

"That wasn't a meal, that was eggs."

"Ooof... Hundreds of years ago," she replies between bites, the food disappearing with astonishing speed.

"So, I take it you don't cook?" Matt inquires, intrigued by her voracious appetite.

She shakes her head 'no' vigorously, causing her mouthful of food to sway in rhythm. Her next gulp of bottled water is equally enthusiastic.

"You are a very mysterious woman," Matt remarks, his tone thoughtful. "Let me show you something that every civilized person should know." He reaches for the cheese board and a knife, pushes it in front of her, and sits behind her. He puts the knife in her right hand and grabs a celery stick with his left, placing it on the board. "This is the most basic knife skill. The chop." He places his hand over hers and helps her chop the celery. He grabs a carrot stick and helps her chop that.

Her breathing quickens, and she pays no attention to the knife. He doesn't see, but her eyes are closed, and her mouth is moving as he guides her hand, "No kissing, no kissing, no kissing--"

Matt interrupts, "You know you're talking out loud, right?"

She thinks, What? No! "I wasn't saying anything." She drops the knife and puts some carrot pieces in her mouth. "I was just wondering how you learned to cook like this."

Matt allows her to shift the conversation. "I went to culinary school."

"What?! Then why aren't you the chef?" Chemistry inquires.

"I dropped out," Matt admits with a shrug. "But I met Josh there, so it was worth it. I've got a better mind for business. But I was there long enough to learn a thing or two. Like those smoked oysters you ate? Aphrodisiacs. Everyone knows that, right?"

Matt's hand finds its way to Chemistry's foot, and he begins tracing it with his finger, his touch gentle and knowing. "But adding that bit of mint zest causes a tingling in the most sensitive part of a woman's foot," he continues, his voice laced with playful sensuality.

Chemistry watches, intrigued and amused, as his finger continues its journey. She is unsure whether the food or his touch is causing the unique sensations he's describing.

"I certainly knew nothing about it," she admits with a smile, her eyes fixed on his hand.

She pulls her leg away when he reaches her calf, momentarily breaking their connection.

Chemistry – *Jessica Sitomer*

"Relax," Matt encourages, trying to put her at ease.

"I can't," she confesses, her vulnerability evident.

Matt is genuinely concerned. "Why not?"

Chemistry hesitates for a moment, searching for words. "I don't feel like I should."

With a gentle smile, he tries to reassure her. "Oh, that's just the chickpeas. The lucky thing about chickpeas, though, is that shrimp counter the tension they cause."

He picks up a shrimp by the tail and holds it in front of her mouth, a mischievous glint in his eye. When she doesn't take it, he brushes it teasingly over her lips.

In a moment of panic, Chemistry accidentally knocks over her water bottle. It spins around and lands squarely on Matt.

"You know what that means," he says, a suggestive grin on his lips.

"I should get some paper towels?" Chemistry guesses, slightly flustered.

Matt, however, has something else in mind. "I wasn't referring to the spill. I was referring to the bottle you spun, now pointed directly at me." Chemistry appears puzzled, prompting Matt to elaborate. "You never played spin the bottle when you were a kid?"

With a whimsical smile, Chemistry replies, "There were no bottles when I was a kid. We just harvested rain in big containers." Matt looks at her, curious about her comment. "Sorry. Weird joke," she babbles.

"Not as bad as my Hilary Duff joke. I'm sorry about that," he offers a supportive smile, and Chemistry's gaze softens. She begins clearing the plates, but Matt places a hand on hers, stopping her.

"Oh no, you don't. Watch," he says with a playful glint in his eye. "It's an easy game. You spin the bottle..."

He spins the bottle, and it lands on Lola. Matt leans in and gets a big, wet kiss.

Chemistry picks up the bottle, her fingers trembling slightly, and nervously peels the label off its neck.

"Let me take that," Matt suggests. He places the bottle on the floor and wraps the label around her finger like a makeshift ring." There. Now I've made an honest woman out of you. Spin," he urges, eager to continue their playful game.

Chemistry – *Jessica Sitomer*

Chemistry hesitates, not making a move. Matt leans forward and spins the bottle again. It lands on Chemistry.

"Rules are rules," he declares with a charming grin.

As he moves in closer, Chemistry begins to speak, her words tinged with uncertainty, "You know, maybe it's the chickpeas, but I'm having these overwhelmingly strong feelings for you right now, which I know are inappropriate because—"

Before she can finish her sentence, Matt leans in and kisses her. The kiss is passionate and unyielding. She feels hummingbirds, waterfalls, and rose petals until the moment is abruptly interrupted when Lola decides to join the affectionate exchange, slathering both their faces with her enthusiastic canine affection.

The moment their lips part, a wave of uncertainty crashes over Chemistry. Her smile falters as she searches Matt's eyes, wondering if he feels the same whirlwind of emotions that now tangle inside her.

Matt quips, brushing away the dog's wet kiss, "Lola, how unromantic was that?" Chemistry takes advantage of the moment.

Chemistry – *Jessica Sitomer*

"Why don't we take her for a walk?" Chemistry suggests, hoping to prolong their time together but avoid what was most definitely against her rules.

Matt nods, not wanting to push her too quickly. "Lola, you want to go for a walk?"

Lola responds with an enthusiastic tail wag and a spirited head tilt.

"I'd say that's a yes," Matt chuckles. "Where's your leash?"

Lola dashes to a nearby chair, fetches her leash, and brings it to Matt, her tail wagging in anticipation.

"Good girl," Matt praises as he attaches the leash. "Now, if I could just train you to bus tables."

With the leash secured, they leave the apartment, ready to enjoy a leisurely walk.

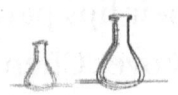

The trio of Matt, Chemistry, and Lola wander along the tranquil streets of New York. The city that never sleeps has taken a break, and the quietness envelopes them like a comforting shroud.

Deep in thought, Chemistry hears Matt say, "You haven't heard a word I said, have you?"

Chemistry – *Jessica Sitomer*

She breaks her silence, her voice soft and thoughtful. "You left school because of the 'stiletto,' didn't you?"

Matt's eyes dart to her. A faint surprise colors his features. "Why do you say that?"

She observes him, a knowing look in her eyes. "You really love cooking, and people don't usually give up on something they love unless they've been hurt by something else they love."

Matt halts in his tracks as Lola curiously sniffs a fire hydrant. He chuckles, "How cliché."

Chemistry's response carries a trace of hurt. "There is nothing cliché about a broken heart."

Matt quirks an eyebrow, a mischievous glint in his eye as he points to Lola. "I was talking to Lola." He grins as she relieves herself on the hydrant. "Why are you so sensitive? Someone break your heart?"

Her tone shifts, taking on a melancholy note. "Not intentionally... He died."

Matt's demeanor shifts to one of empathy. "Oh... This is one of those awkward moments where--"

She interrupts with a small smile. "It doesn't need to be. It was a really long time ago."

"How long were you together?" he asks.

"A few years, we were young. He was troubled."

Chemistry – *Jessica Sitomer*

Matt takes this in. "Did he…" She nods yes. "That's kind of fucked up," Matt says sympathetically.

"He was my soulmate. And then he died… and everything I believed about my future was gone… permanently… and my heart just broke." Then, in a whisper, "It killed me."

They walk in silence for a few minutes, Lola between them. Finally, Chemistry breaks the silence, "And your stiletto?"

"Emily," he shares.

"Emily. What happened there?"

"Josh."

"Josh?" she asks, bewildered.

"He's got this charisma but not a lot of integrity. Emily, Josh, and I were in a lab group together, and while I was busy putting in 70 hours of kitchen time, he was busy moving in on her. I felt so betrayed by them that when I found out, I left."

Lola stops to sniff a tree bark. Chemistry stares at Matt, waiting for him to say more.

His head lowers with shame as he admits, "Not only had he taken my girl, but he'd also taken credit for our final dish, which won an award and landed him on a reality show."

Chemistry – *Jessica Sitomer*

Chemistry steps back in disgust, "Why on Earth are you working with him then?"

"Well, his cooking sucks, but his charm kept him on the show until there were only four, and it would've been criminal to eliminate anyone else. Lola begins walking again, and they join her. Matt shakes his head, then, "I have big dreams, Chemmie. I have contacts, and Josh is a name. He also knew he couldn't succeed independently, so he apologized to me, which hasn't turned out so badly."

"Not so badly? You're miserable!"

"Some days." A smile creeps over his face, "Mr. and Mrs. Topel were back for their grilled cheeses tonight. I made it with tofu. He didn't know the difference. That's what matters."

His sentiment touches Chemistry. She asks, "How much would it cost to open the Ghost Restaurant?"

"Pffff... Chemmie, who knows, it could be twenty grand, it could be fifty-"

"Don't give me that 'who knows' I know, you know, to the penny."

A sheepish grin gives him away, "If I want to do it my way? Five hundred thousand."

"That's more than twenty or fifty," she nods.

Chemistry – *Jessica Sitomer*

"Yep," he concurs as they find themselves back at the brownstone. "We should get some sleep." They walk up the stairs and into the brownstone.

Sitting on her cot, she pulls over her bag, slides it away with her foot, pulls it back toward her, then away, then toward, then away, grabs it, and hisses into it, "I need five hundred thousand dollars."

Fifty stacks of $100 Federal Reserve notes in $10,000 straps shoot out like popcorn. Chemistry, collecting them nervously, looks around her, then to the bag, and asks, "I need a duffle." A Louis Vuitton duffle pops out. Chemistry sighs, "Style, something less conspicuous." A run-of-the-mill blue duffle sticks out of her bag. She pulls it out and stuffs the Louis back in. "Thank you." Quickly, she fills the duffle with the money and hides it under her cot, covering it with a crocheted blanket.

Chapter 14

Eli breaks down boxes in the back alley behind Bacchus and flings them into the recycle dumpster.

"Pssst," a sound comes from behind one of the trash dumpsters. Eli looks up and around. Seeing no one, he returns to the boxes. "Pssssssssst!" he hears again. This time, when he looks around, he sees a woman's hand beckoning him toward the last dumpster.

"Me?" Eli asks.

Chemistry sticks her head out cautiously, "Yes, you," she mouths. Eli speed walks to her in the most obvious way. She pulls him behind the dumpster with her. "I need your help. What else have you found in Matt's trash regarding the Ghost Restaurant?"

"I gave you what I have, but he keeps his journal in a locked drawer in his office." Eli informs her, "We can wait until he leaves, sneak in, and pick the lock--"

Chemistry – *Jessica Sitomer*

"I have a better idea. You leave before Matt, right?" Eli nods, obviously, "Great. Meet me at his apartment."

"Normally, I'd think you were up to no good, this business is cutthroat, and I'm loyal to Matt," Eli points and wags his finger at her, "but I've got a really great feeling about you. I'll see you at midnight." He jumps up and yells into the air, "I'll bring my lock pick."

Chemistry waits by the brownstone door to let Eli in. He is right on time. As she pulls the door closed behind him, he shows off three different lock picking kits, "This one I got in a Sherlock Homes gift store, this one--"

Chemistry presses her finger to her lips, "Shhh, we don't need those." Eli follows her to Matt's door, which, like the others, he notices are not closed due to warping.

"Huh, I always thought Misty left her door open out of friendliness," Eli says.

"She does," Chemistry smiles at him, "Come on." She checks to be sure no one is watching, then ushers him in, closing the door as far as she can. They stand in the dark the only light is coming through the tiny slit in the front door.

"What's the plan?" Eli asks.

"I know where he keeps his journal about the Ghost Restaurant, but I have no idea what to do with it," she replies.

"What do you want to do with it?" Eli asks.

"I want to see his plan, build on it, and show him that he can do it independently without Josh."

"I love that plan. I love that plan so much. Please tell me I'm part of the plan," Eli begs. "'Take me with you!' Spiderman 2."

"There will be no spiders involved, but you will be," Chemistry assures him. "You're the key to this entire plan."

"I'm so excited. I don't even have a quote, "I am the key!"

"Right, but I'm going to need you to calm down, and... do you have a flashlight?"

"Of course, on my phone," Eli presses the flashlight on, and Chemistry takes it, leading him to the kitchen cabinet. She takes down the journal, and they look at it under the light.

"We have to retain as much of this as we can, so we can reference his ideas, making him feel like moving forward with his plan is his idea," Chemistry explains.

Chemistry – *Jessica Sitomer*

"Or again, I've got a camera on my phone. I can take pictures, and we can go somewhere we won't be caught," Eli suggests.

"I knew you were the right man for this job," Chemistry says as she turns pages, and he takes photos with his phone.

"Stop!" Eli says in a hushed warning, "We've got to hide."

"Hide? Matt won't be home for hours."

"Not Matt," he licks his finger, puts it in the air, and then smells it. With reverence, he sighs, "It's Misty."

"Eli--" Chemistry begins to talk as he covers her mouth and pulls her behind the kitchen island just as Misty turns the light on.

"We can look, Lola, but I don't think it's in here," Misty says as Lola trots around sniffing, and Misty pulls up the couch cushions. Not finding what they're looking for, Misty heads toward the kitchen island. Eli pulls a crouching Chemistry around in sync with Misty's steps so they are never in her sight. Then SQUWEEEEEEEEEEEEEE fills the air as Eli's eyes bulge, and Chemistry looks at him in alarm. Lola beats Misty to the squeaky toy as Eli puts it in her mouth, and Misty walks back around to meet Lola just in time For Eli and Chemistry to get to the opposite side of the island.

"Good Girl!" Misty says, "Now, next time you borrow Mr. Wilbur Whisky Von Doodle's toy, you have to bring it back." Lola groans, looking back at Eli and Chemistry, who are hand-signaling her to follow Misty. She does, and Misty turns off the light and shuts the door.

Chemistry prods, "That was too close. We need to finish up." But Eli puts one finger up, gesturing her to wait as he takes deep breaths of air. "What are you doing?" she whispers.

"Taking all of her air into my lungs."

"Oh, Eli, I don't have time for this. I already have one impossible case," she apologizes. "Please take the rest of the pictures."

When he's done, Chemistry returns the journal precisely as they found it, and they sneak out. Chemistry heads for Misty's apartment, but Eli doesn't move.

"Ummm, I can't go in there, 'She's' in there. It's not time yet," Eli insists.

"And I don't have time to bargain, so you lead the way." Chemistry follows him out of the brownstone to the street.

Chemistry – *Jessica Sitomer*

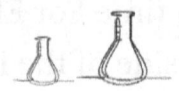

Eli leads Chemistry to a wrought iron gate on West 89th Street between Amsterdam and Columbus Avenues and introduces her to the West Side Community Garden. She looks through the reddish iron at the lush gardens inside when she hears Eli murmur, "Yes!" Turning toward him, she discovers he has picked the lock to the gate.

"Matt's apartment was one thing, but breaking into a community garden? I can't," Chemistry argues.

"Come on, Chemmie. Inside is the inspiration of magical proportions. You just have to believe," Eli coaxes her as he enters. Chemistry looks around. "Are there security cameras? I've seen nightmares about those."

"It was getting vandalized in 2023, but I don't think they ever installed cameras. Anyway, we're protected." Eli moves his hands as if creating an invisible cloak over them

"Eli, are you... how do I put this? From here?" she asks, "because you have this 'otherworldly realm' thing about you."

"Thank you," he answers as he sits on a wooden bench. "I am from this realm, though I think I'm more in tune with it than the average person. Like how I know Misty will love me. I absolutely know."

Chemistry laughs affectionately, "I hope you're right because I can't pull any strings for you. I am a by-the-book girl."

"Speaking of books," Eli says as he opens his photo album in his phone, "let's start here."

Chemistry looks at the picture with confusion: " It's his idea for the kitchen floor plan, pretty brilliant. Since it's vegan, the only cross-contamination he has to worry about is severe allergies like tree nuts, but people with allergies tend to be very aware and carry EpiPens."

"So, the kitchen floor plan is ready," she confirms. He nods yes, "What else would he need to get it started other than the funding and a location?"

Eli laughs, "Oh, other than that?" He scrolls through the photos, "He's thought of menus, wine pairings, distributors... Oh, look," he shows her a note that he magnifies on the screen, "He even mentions the community garden to buy produce." Eli continues to scroll, "He hasn't landed on a name yet, but has a list of them... oh look, cute little cookies in hearts and stars with paper coming out like a fortune cookie meets a Hershey's kiss. He'll probably have his logo on the paper."

"I bet he has something more creative planned."

"You're probably right." Eli's expression looks pained, "He's going to need powerful word of mouth and gorilla marketing, tons of social media, since he can't use Joshua's name. I researched it, and most Chefs who've done these had great success during the pandemic, but they're not really trending anymore. He'd have to have a twist on it, turn it into a hybrid of sorts," Eli contemplates, "It's almost a waste since Matt's strength is that he's such a people person."

"That's true," Chemistry thinks, "What if the plan is to start as a ghost restaurant, and then at a certain milestone, the money that he makes goes into building out the restaurant behind the scenes, all the while having a contest, because when they reveal who the Chef is, whoever guessed, eats free for life."

"But no one knows Matt's food."

"Not true, they do. They think it's Joshua's, so not only does Matt get to open a restaurant, but anyone who guesses the chef is Joshua will realize it was Matt's menu. Word will get around. Matt will get the credit he deserves, and Joshua will be revealed as the fraud he is."

"Wow, that's... that's..."

"Math," she beams, "The perfect equation."

"I was going to say a little devious, but if two plus two equals four, then who am I to argue such an acute angle?"

"This can work," Chemistry says.

"Yeah. How do we get Matt to believe he came up with the idea?" Eli asks.

"Show me those menus again," Chemistry requests, watching Eli scroll back in his phone.

Matt walks into the brownstone, rolling his neck after his long day, when he sees Chemistry standing by his door.

"What are you doing up so late?" he questions.

"Remember that menu you showed me?" Before he can answer, she continues, "I mean, what is Carrot Ginger Caviar? Or Deconstructed Gazpacho? What is Spherified Pea risotto, and am I even pronouncing that right?"

He laughs, "You're not." He pushes his door open, but Chemistry doesn't enter. She lingers in the doorway.

Chemistry – *Jessica Sitomer*

"What are liquid smoke jackfruit tacos... What's carrot air?"

"Are you coming in? Because I have to shower," he says, unbuttoning his shirt. "And how do you remember those dishes?"

"How could I forget those dishes?" She looks at her forearm to see what else is written on it, not noticing that Matt has removed his button-down and is now pulling his undershirt over his head. She looks up and sees his naked torso as she clutches her non-existent pearls and gasps, "Nitro Coconut Ice Cream with Mango Pearls!" She squeaks and runs to Misty's apartment, straight to her cot, pulls the curtain, and hides under her sheet.

The next morning, Chemistry is sitting on Misty's couch as Misty performs acupuncture on a Jack Russel Terrier. Matt walks in and puts a plate in front of Chemistry. The dish's centerpiece is a small glass bowl filled with orange pearls, resembling caviar.

He says, "These pearls are made from a carrot and ginger mixture using a spherification technique, giving them a delicate, bead-like appearance." The pearls are garnished with a small sprig of fresh dill, adding a touch of color and freshness. A puddle of vibrant orange sauce surrounds the caviar. Green leaves and herb sprigs are placed artistically on the plate, adding a visual balance and fresh elements to the dish. Matt points to small, light-colored crumbles scattered around the plate, "Crunchy ginger popcorn," he announces proudly. Silver dragees and small, metallic-colored candy decorations add a touch of elegance and sparkle to the dish, enhancing its visual appeal without significantly altering the flavor.

 Chemistry stares at the plate as Matt hands her a spoon. She takes it entranced and then says, "I can't eat this... it's too beautiful." Matt smiles with his entire face.

 "I couldn't stop thinking about your questions last night. There are so many people who have no idea what is possible for them to taste. Go on... taste it for them," Matt encourages, "learn what Carrot Ginger Caviar is and how it feels on your tongue and in your nasal passages."

 Misty turns away from the dog and scolds, "Matt, you just went from sexy tongue food to nasal passages. Do not put that in the menu description."

Chemistry – *Jessica Sitomer*

"Misty, food touches all your senses. Come here," Matt insists.

Misty considers the dog, "Bogart, stay! If you move, you will stab yourself," Misty says as the dog whimpers on his back, his legs in the air with needles sticking out of him like a porcupine. Misty joins Chemistry on the couch.

"Okay ladies, pinch your nose so you can't smell and stare at the dish... and don't stop until I tell you," Matt instructs. A line of dogs surround them, staring at the plate with desire, their olfactory systems screaming, CARROT!

Chemistry and Misty pinch their noses and stare. As seconds turn into a minute, Chemistry licks her lips. Misty's breathing quickens, and the dogs each have a string of drool forming from their mouths. "Now, without a word... Misty," he adds in warning, "close your eyes and let go of your nose." They both do as they're told. Matt picks up a piece of popcorn in each hand and tells them to take a big inhale and hold it at the top. They do, but Misty breaks the silence.

"Whoa! That cleared my sinuses."

"Shhhhh!" Matt insists, "Keep your eyes closed." Matt grabs another spoon from Misty's counter. He scoops two spoonfuls of the pearls and holds them under their noses, "Take another deep breath," they do, "And another, but this time let the scent go all the way to your brain and allow your brain to send the signals to your stomach. Chemistry takes a deep breath in and smiles with delight.

"Wooooo!" Misty interrupts again, "That scent just went right through my stomach down to my, woooo, I think I'm having a foodgasm." Chemistry can't help but open her eyes and turn to Misty with a look she usually reserves for Lust.

"Focus, Misty, or you are out of the experiment," Matt warns, but he can't help but beam at her reaction. "Keeping your eyes closed, I will hand you each a spoon. Taste it first with the front of your tongue, then let it move to the back and see how the flavor changes." He watches them do what he's asked, then instructs them to swallow when ready. When they do, he asks them how they feel with it in their stomach.

Chemistry's face lights up, "So happy."

"I feel enchanted," Misty adds.

"That, ladies, is how you eat food with your five senses... your eyes, nose, tastebuds, feelings, and ears."

"Our ears?" Chemistry questions.

Chemistry – *Jessica Sitomer*

"Talking about the meal is part of the fun, hearing what others think and feel," Matt explains.

Misty raises her hand to interrupt again. "My sixth sense is telling me that you have more in your apartment, and you better bring it in here for me." She tosses a piece of popcorn in her mouth. "Wooooo! I love that nasal passage clearing." She looks at the drooling dogs. "I'd better feed them."

As Matt leaves to get Misty a plate, Chemistry indulges her senses as she takes her time eating Matt's creation.

Chemistry catches Matt in the hallway as he's leaving for work. "Matt?" he turns to her. "Where did you get the carrots to make those?"

"From work."

"But who grew them?"

He laughs, "I don't remember if we sourced them from a vendor or a farmer's market this week. Why?"

"I was walking last night, and I saw this huge gate. When I looked through it, it looked like a garden."

Chemistry – *Jessica Sitomer*

"That was the West Side Community Garden. What they've preserved there is pretty spectacular. And the gardeners are passionate. You can taste it in their bounty."

Chemistry's tone is more suggestive than intended, "Ooooo, I want to taste their bounty,"

"Okay, umm. I'll make arrangements at the restaurant tomorrow, and I can take you at 10:30 before I head to work."

"It's a date!" Chemistry proclaims, then heads back to Misty's.

It's a date, Matt thinks to himself. He smiles while walking out with a spring in his step.

As Matt and Chemistry walk through the West Side Community Garden gates, she is dazzled by the difference between night and day. The vibrance of the colorful plants and flowers shows brightly in the sun. The fragrance of the Night Jasmine is gone, replaced by roses. Matt takes her hand and leads her toward 90th Street, where vegetable plots, communal herb beds, six children's school plots, a tool shed, and compost bins are in a closed garden area. One of the garden members waves to Matt and calls him over, tempting him with beans off the

Chemistry – *Jessica Sitomer*

vine. Matt squeezes Chemistry's hand and walks her over.

Matt makes introductions as the gardener gives them each samples of his ripened vegetables. Chemistry remarks that she can taste something different in the flavors but can't put her finger on it.

A woman approaches and says, "What you taste is nature at its best."

Recognizing the voice, Chemistry turns to see Mother Nature dressed in overalls, her hair in a messy bun with tendrils spilling out of the bandana that holds it all together. She points a three-claw rake at a tomato and tells them to pull one off and try. Matt reaches for one and savors the freshness. Chemistry stands rigidly, staring at Mother Nature as she looks Matt over. "Such a handsome young man you are," she tells Matt, "Do you mind if I borrow her? I have some purple basil she will flip over." Matt smiles at the woman and encourages Chemistry to go with her.

Mother Nature takes Chemistry out of sight and demands, "What are you doing here?"

"Me?" Chemistry accuses. "I'm doing what you told me. What are you doing here?"

"Creating a new heirloom zucchini." Mother Nature warns, "Chemistry if you haven't taught him his lesson yet, he won't learn it. You need to come back up." Chemistry shakes her head no, "Immediately!" Mother Nature insists.

"I just need more time... a few weeks. I know it's weird that I'm here--"

Mother Nature's sarcasm is in full force, "Because there's food? And he might ask you to eat something?"

"Because I've determined that the key to his connecting with his match is getting him away from his Chef, so he'll be happy and able to meet his match. Being here is helping build his confidence that he can make it on his own."

"That's a pretty big endeavor, Chemistry, even for you, with your staff nowhere to be seen."

"I have help!"

More sarcasm from Mother Nature, "You asked for help?"

"I did. And it's working. A few more weeks, please?"

Mother Nature raises a brow, "This city is a mess. It looks like a dump, and the rudeness is at an all-time high..."

Chemistry murmurs under her breath, "That's your fault."

Chemistry – *Jessica Sitomer*

"But…" Mother Nature says, then nods as the word hangs in the air, and she disappears into the garden.

Chemistry returns and finds Matt sitting on a bench, writing on a small notepad. "Whatcha writing?" she asks.

He looks up, a smile on his face, "Ideas."

She sits next to him, "I know, I feel them too, like, what if you opened that ghost restaurant as a tease for the actual restaurant to come? Have one of those social apps everyone uses to guess who the Chef is inside the kitchen." She sees Matt's wheels turn as he notes on his pad, "Use the money foodies spend to figure out the mystery chef to continue building out your actual restaurant, letting people know that whoever guesses correctly will eat free forever."

He looks up, "That's not ethical since they don't know my food."

"Don't they?" she asks.

"Well, they know it as Joshua's." She nods, signaling the truth, then watches him make the same connection she made the night before. "If they guess Joshua, then see it's me, that will reveal…" He says no more but writes furiously.

Chemistry – *Jessica Sitomer*

Before they leave, Matt buys ingredients from the gardeners. He and Chemistry say their goodbyes, and as they make their way through the gate back to 89th St, Matt calls Eli and tells him he's taking the day off and to please advise the front of the house. Matt no longer holds Chemistry's hand because he stops every few feet to write on his pad.

When they return to the brownstone, he asks Chemistry if she could spend the day with him so he can bounce ideas off her. Without hesitation she agrees with a huge smile.

Sketches, papers, and drawings cover the floor of Matt's living room. Lola sits on her bed, watching the pair point at papers and rearrange. She only moves hours later when Matt cuts carrots and parsnips. He tosses a carrot chunk, which she catches in her mouth, then sits to stand by for more.

Chemistry does her equations, knowing Matt is engrossed and not to be disturbed while in his zone. Finally, he calls her over. He has plated a generous spoonful of parsnip puree. She watches as he uses an immersion blender to blend a carrot juice and lecithin mixture at the surface to incorporate air and create foam. It takes a few minutes as Chemistry watches a light, airy foam forming on top. Matt adds a pinch of salt to the foam and gently mixes it. He looks up at her, "Carrot air, Mademoiselle." Using a spoon, he gently scoops the carrot air on the parsnip puree and garnishes it with microgreens. He pushes the plate toward her and hands her a clean spoon.

Chemistry tastes it, her eyes roll back in her head, and she moans. Matt interrupts her ecstasy with an insecure "It's just my first pass. I could make the air lighter."

"Matt," she says, "Artists are always perfecting, but to me, this is perfect… almost." She drizzles olive oil on the plate, swirls the parsnip and carrot in it, and tastes, nodding her head, "Yes!"

"You're pretty good at this for someone who didn't know what a corndog was," he considers.

"It's just chemistry," she shrugs. He laughs, and the sound fills her with joy. "I know you are just starting, but you said you cook because you want people to love your food. I love this!" An uncomfortable grin shows on his face. She continues, "I didn't know how to taste food this morning. Now I'm salivating at what you'll make next. What if... and it's an 'if' so let it ruminate... what if, when the restaurant opens, you gave lessons on food tasting? You could charge full price five days a week, so on the sixth day, you can have a community day, an inexpensive tasting so the average person can try elevated food." Matt wants to argue, but she says, "What if local growers contributed to the dishes that day, or 'save the planet people' sponsored the sixth day?"

"Save the planet, people?" he laughs.

"You're right. The people who are destroying the planet should sponsor." They both laugh.

"And on the seventh day?" he enquires.

She moves in close to him, looking right in his eyes. "And on the seventh day, you rest." He stares at her, mesmerized and inspired, then pulls her face to his and gives her a delicate kiss. Her eyes close as his kiss grows more passionate. Then he sweeps her up and takes her to his bedroom.

In the intimate space of Matt's bedroom, Chemistry and Matt lay side by side on his bed, fully clothed. Every light is on. Their gazes wander the ceiling, and Matt casually inches closer until their arms touch. Chemistry wiggles away, but Matt persists, gently placing his arm next to hers. His touch sends a wave of warmth through her, yet the familiarity of closeness feels foreign. She turns her face toward the lamp, swallowing the uncertainty rising in her throat.

"Are you avoiding me?" Matt teases.

She hesitates before replying, her voice filled with vulnerability. "No... yes... it's been a really long time."

Matt reassures her with a gentle smile. "That's okay."

Chemistry confesses with a hint of self-deprecation, "No, you don't understand. A really long time."

The weight of her confession settles between them, and the air grows still for a moment. Matt reaches out, his fingers brushing hers. "Hey... it doesn't matter how long it's been. We'll figure this out together."

"You're sweet," she says, "But I feel like a..."

Matt's playful side emerges. "They do say after a year you regain virgin status... very sexy."

An innocent private smile tugs at her lips, and then she murmurs, "Do they say anything about it closing up permanently?"

Chemistry – *Jessica Sitomer*

He responds with a reassuring smile, leaning in to nuzzle her neck as Lust's face appears on the 80" TV screen with an 'are you kidding me' look. Chemistry stifles a scream, and it comes out in a yelp. Matt attempts to lift his head, but she shoves it into her chest. Matt moans with anticipation as Chemistry's eyes widen, and Lust gives her two thumbs up. She squirms for the remote, holding Matt's head tightly to her body. With a press of the button, Lust is gone. She releases her grip on Matt.

"Dominant. Surprising," he says. Lust pops back on the screen with Knowledge, and they high-five. Chemistry's eyes bulge. She grabs the remote, turns it off, and accidentally pushes Matt off the bed.

"Sorry. Sorry. Can you please get me a glass of water?" she asks. His bewildered expression softens as he untangles himself from the bedding, puts the blanket back on the bed, and nods. As he leaves the room, Lust and Knowledge pop on screen again. "With ice cubes, please," she calls to Matt, then back to the TV screen. "What are you doing?"

Lust rants, "What are we? What are you doing other than floundering around, and I mean flounder like the fish? 'Does it close up permanently?" Have you learned nothing from watching me?"

She hears Matt coming toward the bedroom. "Actually, can you make me a cup of tea? A hot one, but not from your machine. Can you boil it in a kettle? Please!"

Knowledge laughs, "I brought the original Kama Sutra, completely illustrated."

"Would you get him out of here? He's seven!" Chemistry demands.

"What was that, Chem?" Matt calls from the other room.

"Uhhh, do you have any seven-layer cake?" she calls back.

Lust and Knowledge argue on the screen. Lust puts his hand over Knowledge's face as the little boy tries throwing punches but can't reach.

"No," Matt replies, "I have some chocolate chip cookies."

Lust gives Knowledge a final shove out of the picture and yells after him to leave the book. He turns back to Chemistry and gestures with his finger to stall Matt.

"Could you bake me one?" she calls. Lust throws his hands up and rolls his eyes. "I'm kidding!" she retracts, then puts her hands up, desperate for ideas. Lust mirrors her body language because he's never been in this situation.

"I have ice cream, "Matt offers.

"Yes! Ice cream sounds great." Lust shakes his head and pulls his hands apart like, 'stretch it out, "a... a... sundae," she adds. Lust nods, impressed. Empowered, she calls out, "With twelve toppings!"

"Twelve?" Matt asks.

"At least! Surprise me, make me the world's greatest sundae, and take as long as you need." She falls back into the pillow.

"Okay, listen," Lust says, "a lot has changed since you've had sex." Chemistry puts her face in her hands, "Don't be a prude," he says, then looks at her concerned, "You have had sex. I mean, you were married--"

"Yes, I've had sex!" she spits out.

"Have you..." Lust gestures toward his mouth, sticking his tongue into his cheek.

"You're disgusting," Chemistry says.

Matt calls from the other room, "What was that?"

"Nothing," Chemistry calls. I was just—" The TV goes black as Matt walks in carrying a tray holding two bowls of ice cream and twelve shot glasses filled with toppings ranging from sweet to savory, fruit to nuts to chocolate chips.

He places it on his end table. "I was going to whip up some cream, but I thought that was cliché."

Without hesitation, Chemistry pulls his face to hers and kisses him. He kisses her back and lays her on the bed. As he rolls his body to cover hers, she pulls back, her voice trembling. "Wait." After briefly pausing, she continues, "I'm probably not going to be very good at this."

Matt's gaze is warm and tender. "That's okay. I'll be good enough for both of us." They share a laugh that eases the tension in the room.

"I don't remember what to do," she confesses, her uncertainty bare.

Matt teases, "It's just biology."

"That's not my department," she panics.

Matt, still smiling, leans in closer. "Well, it's mine."

"Listen, I tried yoga, I'm not flexible, I can't do all those positions..."

"What positions?" he teases.

"The ones in the Kama Sutra."

"Oh, Chemmie, no one reads that."

"I know a seven-year-old who's read it twice!"

"Well, he should be taken away from his parents."

Chemistry – *Jessica Sitomer*

"Matt, I'm serious. I don't remember how to do this." Even as the words leave her lips, Chemistry dislikes how vulnerable she feels. For centuries, she was the one with all the answers, but in Matt's presence, she was adrift. Opening herself up terrified her.

He whispers, " Close your eyes, and tell me when you do." She closes her eyes, and his kisses graze her eyelids and the tip of her nose. Just as she lifts her lips to meet his, he moves to her fingertips, caressing each one gently before trailing up her arm. She shivers as his lips journey down to her toes, ankle, and calf.

He reaches for a remote, which turns off all the lights, plunging the room into darkness. In the quiet, his kisses continue their sensual exploration.

Chemistry's voice, tinged with longing, breaks the silence with a whisper, "I remember."

Chemistry – *Jessica Sitomer*

Chapter 15

Simultaneously, the vast laboratory appears eerily vacant in Eternity, its usual bustling energy replaced by an unsettling silence. Rows of empty workstations and abandoned experiments stretch before the solitary figure of Inspiration. Her determined gaze is fixed upon the hundreds of scattered files beneath a data chute.

With a whirlwind of ideas constantly spinning in her mind, Inspiration meticulously sorts through the files. She picks up a stack of documents, her fingers dancing across them as if deciphering some secret code. Her sharp mind races to connect the dots as she shuffles through the paperwork.

Suddenly, a single file slips out of the chute onto the top of the pile, slipping off to the floor. She bends down, her eyes scanning the document's title. It reads "MATT DURAND." Inspiration's heart races and her eyes widen with admiration.

Chemistry – *Jessica Sitomer*

"She did it," Inspiration says, her voice a hushed but reverent whisper. "She did it!" she yells, swiftly opening the file and revealing a photograph of Matt's next match. Inspiration's excitement grows as she studies the image, absorbing every detail with intense focus.

"Perfect," she murmurs to herself. With newfound purpose, she leaves the cart of files behind, her footsteps echoing through the deserted lab as she hurries toward the exit.

A man screaming profanities on the street wakes Chemistry. Matt is already awake, watching her sleep. Now, a shrill woman is heard cursing.

Chemistry yawns, "Is it me, or has everyone become ruder?"

"Nah, they were always rude, but now that you're in love, their negativity pulls you out of the bubble, so you notice it more," Matt says, kissing her cheek, neck, and shoulder.

"Am I?" she teases.

"In love?" he asks, "I guess. I don't know. Are you?" He continues to kiss down her back. She turns

Chemistry – *Jessica Sitomer*

on her side and looks out the window, allowing him more space to caress. Entranced by his kisses and the room's warmth, she watches a pigeon land gracefully on the windowsill. She observes the bird with tranquility, her eyes following its every movement. Another pigeon joins the first, and Chemistry can't help but smile as they share a moment.

The first pigeon coos at its new companion, a gentle exchange that warms Chemistry's heart. Suddenly, the second pigeon pecks the first on the head. The startled bird takes flight and disappears into the cloudy morning. Matt stretches, "I hate that I have to go to work today." He lifts the sheet, exposing his naked body as he walks to the shower. Chemistry's eyes follow him like a schoolgirl peeking through a hole in the wall to the boy's locker room. "Want to join me?" he turns and asks.

"No, that would only make you later," she says.

"Such a rule follower," he jests.

"Fine, I'll be right in," she promises.

When she hears the shower jets, she slips out of bed and goes to the window. She gazes at the gloomy day, where trash and leaves swirl in the gusty wind. As she turns her gaze, a figure materializes before her—Mother Nature. Chemistry blinks, but just as quickly, the enigmatic figure vanishes.

Quickly and quietly, Chemistry dresses herself. "On second thought, I'm going to get some fresh air," she calls and leaves the room before he can counteroffer.

Chemistry walks towards the park. The city has fallen into a palpable gloom, and the decline is impossible to ignore. Angry and miserable people drag their feet through the streets, their expressions reflecting the prevailing desolation.

Papers spin in the wind, and cars seem to target pedestrians. The city's cacophony reaches new levels, with car horns adding to the symphony of chaos. A barking dog startles Chemistry as she walks. Then, amidst the discord, a familiar voice.

Misty's voice rings out, "Chemmie, there you are."

Chemistry turns to see Misty, accompanied by her pack of energetic dogs. She continues on her path, taking in the troubling scene when Misty joins her. The dogs bark in an enthusiastic chorus.

"We were worried when you didn't come home last night," Misty confesses.

Chemistry – *Jessica Sitomer*

A pudgy bald man walks past them, his annoyance evident. "Get those mangy mutts out of our city! They're crappin' all over the place!" he grumbles.

Misty stops and turns, and the dogs follow suit. "I'll light a candle for you, Sir. It'll be black, but I'll light it!" she retorts, catching herself. "Ooo. People are bringing out the worst in me lately."

Chemistry comes to an abrupt stop in front of a newsstand. The tabloid headlines blast stories of celebrity breakups. Magazines like Newsweek and Time ask, "WHERE IS THE LOVE?" Chemistry's gaze shifts from the sensational headlines to the grim state of the city. Finally, she absorbs the profound decline.

Just then, Mother Nature appears across the street.

Misty's concern is evident, "Are you okay?"

Chemistry briefly glances at Misty, then back across the street. Mother Nature has once again vanished.

"I've got to go," Chemistry responds with urgency.

As she hurries away, she collides with Eli.

"I know how this looks, but I'm not stalking her, I promise. It's happening," Eli insists.

Chemistry – *Jessica Sitomer*

"What?" Chemistry asks.

Eli makes a tiny space with his fingers. "She's this close to falling in love with me. I can feel it!"

"Oh, Eli. I sure hope she does. But if not, we'll find you someone perfect," Chemistry reassures him. "But I'm kind of in a rush. Are you going to be okay?"

Eli's face lights up with determination, "I'm going to be better than okay!"

Central Park has succumbed to a state of disrepair. Litter is scattered about, and homeless individuals wander through the neglected landscape. It is a far cry from the vibrancy she'd experienced only months ago.

Chemistry enters the park. Her thoughts echo as she tries to ignore the somber atmosphere. She finds Mother Nature seated on a bench, a sense of melancholy surrounding her. Chemistry walks over and sits beside her, a comforting presence respite from the gloom hanging in the air. As she settles in, a piece of crumpled paper swirls in the wind and lands gently on Chemistry's lap.

Chemistry's concern is evident, "What are you doing to the weather? It's miserable."

Chemistry – *Jessica Sitomer*

Mother Nature sighs softly. "It's not the weather, Dear, it's the mood."

"So, fix the mood," Chemistry urges.

"That's what I'm here to do," Mother Nature replies with a knowing smile.

A mother and her toddler stroll by, their expressions as grim as the surroundings. Mother Nature opens her purse, and a butterfly with a rainbow pattern emerges. It circles the toddler before bursting into a radiant rainbow behind the trees, accompanied by a faint glow of the sun that had been absent for days.

The mother crouches beside the toddler and points out the rainbow. The child's face lights up in awe. She runs towards it, her arms outstretched as if trying to touch the colorful spectacle. The mother chases after her with delight.

"We touch all of their lives," Mother Nature says, her voice filled with pride. "You... you show them the path to love."

More people notice and appreciate the rainbow, their expressions shifting from despair to delight. Mother Nature waves her hand, and the sun emerges, casting its brilliant rays upon the park. Smiles spread across everyone's faces.

Chemistry – *Jessica Sitomer*

"Your department is falling apart," Mother Nature continues solemnly. "The world is missing love. There are eight billion people who need you."

She produces the new Durand file and holds it out for Chemistry. The scientist in Chemistry can't resist as she takes it, opening it to reveal the picture of Matt's next match. She turns away, her emotions in turmoil.

"You did it. Now, come back and fix things up down here. That'll keep you so busy, you'll forget all about him," Mother Nature implores.

Fix things? Is that all I'm good for? Chemistry hesitates, considering the possibility. "Style comes down to shop from time to time. Maybe I could—"

"Style has an addiction. That's why she was chosen," Mother Nature interjects gently.

"Why was I chosen?" Chemistry asks, her voice tinged with uncertainty.

"Because you understand their pain," Mother Nature replies with a knowing smile.

Chemistry lets those words sink in, realizing the profound truth in them. Then, with determination in her eyes, she speaks professionally.

"If I stay with him, he'll settle for me, and he'll never meet his soulmate," Chemistry recognizes. She stares down at the file Mother Nature handed her, her fingers tracing the edges. The park seems brighter now, the once-gloomy clouds parting to reveal a soft, golden light filtering through the trees. People around her laugh and smile as they watch the rainbow Mother Nature created. But Chemistry's mind is elsewhere, spinning with questions and doubt.

"Eight billion people," she mutters. She closes her eyes and inhales, grounding herself in the cool air around her. The sun's warmth on her skin feels like a consolation, but she knows what to do.

The staff at Bacchus attempt to work while tension fills the air as Joshua and Matt engage in a heated argument that seems to have no end. "My personal life has nothing to do with this restaurant," Matt insists, his frustration evident.

"It does when you miss a day of work and then arrive late—again," Joshua retorts, his voice laced with exasperation.

"I wasn't late. I came in at 9:30. We've got two hours 'til lunch," Matt defends himself.

"But normally, you're here at 8," Joshua points out.

"How would you know? You don't roll out of some food groupie's bed until 10:30!" Matt shoots back, his irritation flaring.

"You're jealous! It always comes down to this, man. Don't blow our dream because my charisma pulls the people in," Joshua retorts, his voice tinged with frustration.

"Please! I designed every detail of this place. Every light fixture, every Italian glass—"

"Now you're gonna go tit for tat?" Joshua interrupts, exasperated. "We've planned this since school—"

"I've planned this since school. You've come along for the ride," Matt declares, his tone dismissive.

Joshua's patience wears thin. "I am tired of you taking credit for everything we created! They come because of me. They don't care what type of flower is on the table or what light bulb lights the food on their plate. They want a hot young chef to serve it to them!"

"Amazing. You actually believe your own hype," Matt scoffs.

Chemistry – *Jessica Sitomer*

"Not only do I believe it, I'm willing to bet my career on it!" Joshua declares with resolve.

"Meaning?" Matt probes.

"Meaning I can get a job in any restaurant I want. See what happens to this place without me," Joshua threatens, his voice laced with arrogance.

The door opens, and Chemistry walks in, unknowingly becoming a spectator to the tumultuous scene.

Joshua gives Chemistry an appraising look as he heads for the door. "Beautiful. Here's the wrecking ball now."

Matt, however, warns Joshua, "Watch it!"

"You watch it!" Joshua yells. He pauses as a calm comes over, and a smile plasters his face. He nods his head to himself. A decision has been made. "I quit. And I'm going to hurt you where you work and where you live," Joshua promises, his anger simmering under his smug smirk.

The door slams behind Joshua, and the room falls into an uncomfortable silence. Chemistry glances at Matt, her pulse quickening as she tries to understand what happened. This is serious. The thought buzzes in her mind like static, but she doesn't know what to say or how to help. The tension still lingers in the air, thick and suffocating.

Chemistry – *Jessica Sitomer*

Matt sits down, his face pale, his hands clenched into fists. Chemistry watches him, unsure if she should say something or stay silent. She chooses silence. The weight of Joshua's departure settles over them like a heavy blanket, stifling any attempt at conversation.

This is going to change everything. The realization sinks in slowly, and Chemistry breathes to clear her thoughts.

The staff whispers in discomfort when Eli breaks the silence, quoting, "Some cause happiness wherever they go, others whenever they go."

Matt, realizing the need to regain control, asserts, "The show's over. Back to work." The back-of-the-house staff returns to the kitchen. The front-of-the-house staff continues to set up as far from Matt as possible.

Chemistry settles into a chair. Matt sits beside her, the aftermath of the argument lingering in the air.

"What was that about?" Chemistry finally asks.

Matt sighs. "He just quit."

"I heard. Why?"

"He thinks he can find something better," Matt explains.

"What will you do?" Chemistry is concerned.

Matt contemplates his options. "Let the lawyers fight it out. Hire someone to take his place while I develop our new concept." They sit silently for a moment, the weight of the situation sinking in. "Or I could take his place," Matt suddenly declares, determination in his voice.

Chemistry is shocked but then smiles approvingly. "You? Matt, that's a great idea!"

"I should try, right? I gave it up for the wrong reasons, and if it works, I don't have to start over as a ghost," Matt admits.

"It's good that you figured it out," Chemistry says.

"Me? It was your dose of inspiration," Matt credits. Chemistry's expression changes abruptly. She seems to lose her composure, her face turning pale. She stumbles back but steadies herself on a nearby chair. "Hey, are you okay?" Matt asks, concerned. Lost in thought, Chemistry doesn't immediately respond. "Chemmie," Matt urges, snapping his fingers gently, "Come back down to Earth."

"What am I doing here?" she mumbles, her confusion evident. "I have to go... I can't stay..." she mutters, as if to herself.

"Chemmie, what's wrong?"

Chemistry – *Jessica Sitomer*

She holds back her tears. The Hostess brings her some water, but she won't take it. "Please don't make this harder."

"Make what harder? I don't know what you're talking about," Matt says, trying to make sense of her cryptic statements.

"Matt, I never said I was staying," she acknowledges, her voice quivering. This revelation stops him in his tracks. She tries to walk past him, but he catches her arm.

"What?" he asks. She doesn't reply, "What!" he asks again, the only word he seems to be able to muster.

Trying to calm him, "Here, in New York, I never told you I was staying."

"But we planned and..."

"I helped you plan because I believe in you, but restaurants are your passion, not mine.

She recognizes the anger she's seen before in him as betrayal, "And you're telling me this now as everything's falling apart?"

"That's just it. Everything's coming together for you, you'll see."

Trying to calm himself, "Fine, fine.. you're right. You never said you were staying, but can't you?" Tears well up in Chemistry's eyes, and she struggles to contain her emotions. "Or I can go with you. Wherever you're going, I will go with you."

"You can't come with me. You have your restaurant," she says, her voice strained with sadness.

"I'll start over. I can do the ghost restaurant, wherever we-- " She shakes her head, no, but he won't give up. "You can write the poems," Matt insists, his determination unwavering. Then, suddenly realizing he doesn't know much about her, he asks, "Where are you going?"

"Matt, I don't want you to give up your dream for me. I want you to expand it so that there's room for a life," Chemistry implores.

"I get it. I want a life... with you," Matt confesses, his feelings laid bare.

"It's impossible," Chemistry replies, her voice tinged with regret. She pulls away from him.

"It is possible. I love you," Matt confesses, his voice cracking under the weight of the truth he's been holding. Chemistry's heart skips a beat as the words sink in, each syllable like a ripple spreading through her chest.

"I tried to fight it," Matt continues, his eyes searching hers as if afraid of what he'll find. "But from the moment I saw you... I knew."

Chemistry – *Jessica Sitomer*

Chemistry blinks, her mind racing to process the words and his voice's sincerity.

"There was a frog—" Matt starts, but the vulnerability in his expression juxtaposes the lighthearted tone of the comment as he steps toward her.

"A frog?" she repeats, her voice soft, as the moment's weight presses down on her.

"For Mr. Topel, it was electricity," Matt explains. The walls he's built are crumbling down. He takes a step closer, closing the distance between them, and in that quiet moment, the weight of everything left unsaid hangs in the air between them. Chemistry's breath hitches, and she allows herself to feel for the first time in a long time.

Chemistry's voice comes out in a whisper, "You're not making any sense."

"I know." He explains, "At first, I thought I was crazy. Seeing you in my dream, saving you. I wanted to talk, but I couldn't. There was a frog in my throat."

Chemistry is stunned back to reality as she trips, knocking a glass off a table. The glass shatters on the floor, and her hands tremble as she kneels to pick up the pieces.

He continues, "It's just an expression, but then you walked into my restaurant. You were real, and--"

Chemistry interrupts, her disbelief evident, "You remembered me... from your dream?"

"I felt it instantly. My throat closed. But all I could think of was my business and how you'd be a distraction from everything I'd worked so hard for," Matt confesses, his voice filled with regret. He watches her fumbling with the glass, "Leave it. Someone will clean it up."

She drops the shards of glass and walks away from him, pacing between the tables, trying to process the revelation.

This isn't making sense, she thinks. Chemistry pauses by the window, staring out at the city traffic. Her heart clenches like it hasn't in over four hundred years, and the sensation unsettles her. Why is this different? She keeps her distance, compartmentalizing her feelings, yet Matt slips past her defenses. She knows better—this wasn't in the plan. But then again, nothing has gone according to plan since meeting him.

Matt interrupts her thoughts, admitting, "Josh blames you for this. Heck, a few months ago, I would have blamed you. But you changed something in me, and now I want it all."

Chemistry – *Jessica Sitomer*

She turns away from the window and abruptly walks to him, taking his face in her hands. "Matt, you can have it all. Somewhere out there is your soulmate. I'm not her. I was just one of the 'files' that fall from the chute to teach you what you need to know so you'll be ready when you finally meet her," Chemistry explains. Matt is utterly confused by her words, struggling to grasp the significance. "And you will meet her. I'll make sure of it," she assures him, letting her hands fall to her sides. She opens the door to the restaurant, but Matt pushes it closed and pulls her close.

"I won't let go," he insists.

She kisses him gently, "I can't stay here, and trust me, you wouldn't want me to if you realized what you'd be giving up." The words tumble from her mouth, but her heart hesitates. How do I explain this? How do I make him understand without telling him how much this is breaking me?

"Now you're not making any sense," his weak smile pleading as his hand gently cups her face. Chemistry feels the familiar pull. She reminds herself that this was supposed to happen, repeating the words like a mantra in her head. But as his fingers linger against her skin, it feels less like work and more like desire. Don't forget why you're here, she urges herself, but her heart is already betraying her mind. I can't stay here! The thought flickers like a warning light in the back of her mind.

She pulls away from him, knowing she must do what's best for him, even if it's breaking her heart. "I can't let you settle. Please find her. You deserve to be with your soulmate." If I don't leave now, I'll never be able to.

She pulls the door open and runs out. He chases after her.

Chemistry runs through the congested streets of New York. People yell and curse at her as she knocks and struggles through the crowd.

Matt chases after her, equally determined to catch up. He, too, collides and pushes through the sea of people until he almost reaches her.

"Chemmie, wait!" he calls out, breathless from the chase.

Chemistry slows down but doesn't stop. She walks backward, looking back at him, her voice carrying over the street's cacophony.

"We are too busy to see what's in front of us, and then too soon it's gone, though not the ache that it leaves behind. Wait for her, Matt, trust me," she implores, her words filled with urgency.

"Because you're quoting Ana de Gournay I should trust you? You're starting to sound like Eli!" Matt retorts, his frustration evident.

Chemistry's heart skips a beat. "What did you say?"

"You sound as crazy as Eli!"

"No, before that."

"Ana de Gournay? You just quoted her," Matt replies, closing the distance between them.

Chemistry stands frozen in shock, her mind racing with the implications of Matt's words.

"How do you know that name?" she asks, her voice trembling.

"She's one of Eli's favorites. A famous poet married to a troubled artist who killed himself. Eli said after six months without him, she died of a broken heart," Matt explains, his voice tinged with sadness.

Chemistry is speechless as Matt continues towards her. However, his path abruptly collides with a woman carrying grocery bags. The bags fall, and groceries scatter amidst the busy street's walking feet. Without hesitation, Matt kneels to help her.

Chemistry watches, her heart sinking, as she quickly recognizes the woman as Matt's next

Chemistry – *Jessica Sitomer*

'Match' from Mother Nature's file. As he helps the woman collect her groceries, he looks right into her eyes, causing him to rub his own, just as Chemistry watches the Match touch the raised hair on the back of her neck. Matt smiles at the woman. Chemistry's chest tightens. The pang of jealousy is sharp and painful. The thought of letting him go suddenly feels unbearable. Crushed by the realization they had connected, Chemistry staggers back into the crowd, her world spinning with the weight of what she had just witnessed. It was inevitable. She tells herself this over and over again, but it does little to ease the ache in her chest. He's meant for her, not me. I should be relieved. This is how it's supposed to work. Her legs move automatically, her mind barely registering the busy street around her. So why does it feel like everything is falling apart? She brushes away a tear. I have to stop feeling. I have to let him go for his sake—and mine. Chemistry realizes she must go, must walks away from Matt, but each step feels like a weight pressing down on her. The streets of New York blur around her, the city's noise dimming into a distant hum. She pauses at a crosswalk, watching as cars rush by. "This is what he needs," she tells herself, though her lungs tighten with every breath. A pigeon flutters by, landing on a bench just ahead. She watches it coo and hop along the path, oblivious to the world's chaos.

The walk sign turns green, but Chemistry doesn't move. She stays still for a moment longer, letting the world swirl around her before taking the next step. She exhales slowly, allowing the tension to slip from her shoulders, but the weight remains in her chest. This is the right thing, she tells herself again, hoping it might feel true this time. After a long moment, she starts to run. As she dodges a man on his phone and stumbles, her breath coming in shallow gasps, she thinks, Keep running. Don't stop. But even as she pushes herself forward, her mind betrays her. Why are you running? You always run when things get complicated. You're supposed to be the one who helps people stay, not the one who bolts at the first sign of... a connection... they connected, Chemistry. Go back up! She steadies herself, straightens her clothes, and heads for the hotel.

Chemistry – *Jessica Sitomer*

Chemistry walks through the doors of The Plaza without acknowledging the doorman. Her eyes focused on her path to the elevator. Go! She disciplines herself and then dashes for the elevator, blocking anyone from joining her as the doors close. When the elevator door opens, Chemistry enters the world she's known for hundreds of years. She looks around at her dimly lit office. Her old habit instantly kicks in as her eyes dart to the large file bin under the chute, now filled to the brim. No more sleep. No more delicious food. The reality of her existence feels like a punch to the gut. No more Matt. Only files.

She walks to her desk and grabs the top file. A young woman in Ireland, she reads. Resigned to take her seat, she realizes she can't. Her eyes widen as she takes in the stacks of files on her chair, piled under her desk, hidden behind a file cabinet, and lined up against the wall. At first, it's a relief, a huge undertaking to keep her mind off... her heart clenches, and then anger kicks in. I never felt anything before I went down there! Anger, good! Resentment that I know how to do... she sucks in a breath fighting back the tears, when she hears her door open.

Chemistry – *Jessica Sitomer*

With glasses on and her hair pulled back in a tight bun, Inspiration emerges from behind, carrying an armful of files. She stops and almost drops the files when she sees Chemistry.

"You're back!" Inspiration says, unable to contain her excitement. "We weren't expecting you yet—" a sound from the chute interrupts her train of thought as another file drops. Inspiration rushes to grab it, but Chemistry puts her hand up, gesturing her to stop. She waves for Inspiration to hand over the pile in her arms. Inspiration steps forward and gives them to Chemistry. Their eyes meet, and Inspiration instinctively knows to turn around and leave.

Chemistry places the files on her desk, her hands trembling as she tries to steady her breath. Her legs feel weak beneath her, and she knows—there's no escaping the wave that's coming. Her eyes scan the room. The world feels too still, too empty without him. Five minutes. That's all I'm giving myself. She closes her eyes, leans against the desk, and slowly lowers herself to the floor. The cold tile presses against her palms, grounding her momentarily before the floodgates break.

Her shoulders tremble with the weight of the loss, the finality of it crashing down around her like

Chemistry – *Jessica Sitomer*

a tidal wave. I didn't think it would hurt this much. The thought slips through her mind like a whispered confession, one she's barely able to admit even to herself.

Tears fall unchecked, and for the first time in what feels like forever, Chemistry allows herself to be vulnerable, to let the pain wash over her without pushing it aside. There's no more running or denying how much she feels—how much she's lost. I used to be so strong, she berates herself between sobs. She realizes this isn't who I was before, burying her face in her hands. I'm weak now... She cries harder, feeling the vulnerability weigh down on her.

Chemistry's chest rises and falls with deep, uneven breaths as she leans against the desk, her face streaked with tears. The files scattered around her feet seem to mock her efforts. She wipes at her face hastily, trying to push the weight of her emotions back down where they belong. She feels the echo of the empty office around her, the thump of another file falling from the chute. She straightens up, her hands shaking as she clutches the corner of her desk. It's too much. She thinks but doesn't say it aloud. Her hands drop to her sides as she stands in the quiet, letting the ache in her chest

Chemistry – *Jessica Sitomer*

subside. She has time to gather herself. There's always time here. The moment stretches, and when she feels ready, she reaches for the nearest file and drops it. The work must continue, but she allows this pause before diving back into the endless flow of duties.

Chapter 16

"You're back!" Misty shrieks as Matt drags himself toward his apartment at 2 am. His feet feel like lead as Misty drags him, his eyes barely able to focus on anything but the thought of sleep.

"Not now, Misty. I need to sleep."

"No, you need to see something!" she pulls him. He has no strength to resist as she pulls him into her apartment to Chemistry's area, where the sheet no longer hangs, but there's a duffle bag with a note on the cot. On the note, it reads 'MATT.' His heart kicks faster when he sees the duffle bag with his name on it, but exhaustion fogs his reaction.

"What now?" he mutters, more to himself than to Misty.

"I'm not gonna lie, I looked in the bag."

"And?" Matt asks. She motions with her head for him to open the bag, her eyes bulging. Matt unzips the bag slowly, his heart thudding in his chest. He pulls back the zipper enough to glimpse the neat stacks of bills. His stomach drops. He looks at Misty, who insists.

"Nothing's going to jump out. Just open it!" she shrieks.

Matt unzips the bag and jumps back, "What the--?!"

"Right?"

"Misty, how much is in there?"

"I don't know. I didn't count it," She says, "Five hundred thousand dollars!"

"What? I thought you said you didn't count it?"

"I didn't," she swears, "But I read the note. She's gone, Matt. She's not coming back." She looks at him with sympathy and then tries to cheer him up, "but she wants you to finish your plan."

What was Chemmie thinking? His mind races. Five hundred thousand dollars? Had he misunderstood everything about her? He stares at the cash, the weight of her absence hitting him like a punch to the gut.

Misty interrupts his thoughts, "So, what's the plan?"

"The plan is to get that money back to her. Where is she?"

"I have no idea."

"Then, what's her number?"

"I don't know."

"You don't know her number?"

"You don't know her number."

"I never asked. She was always--"

"Here, I know." Misty finishes his sentence.

Matt stares at the bag, stacks of bills heavy in his hands. His mind can't keep up with what he is seeing. Chemmie is gone. But why leave this? And why leave him? He shakes his head, forcing a weak smile as Misty's conspiracy theories roll on, her voice barely cutting through the noise in his head.

"You think she's a gangster?" she asks.

Matt manages a chuckle, but the knot in his chest tightened. He drops the stack of cash like it burned him, muttering, "Doubt it. But, I'd take the gangster if it meant she'd come back... She was here for months, and we know nothing about her yet..."

"You're in love with her."

"Fuck." He whispers.

"Fudgsicle," Misty agrees.

"Can we agree we know her well enough to believe it's not stolen?"

"Yes, if..." Misty goes to the duffle and dumps it—the money piles on the floor. "There is no dye pack in here. We can rule out gangster, or is it the opposite, and the dye packs make her a government

Chemistry – *Jessica Sitomer*

informant?" Misty digs through them. "Nope, no dye pack. She's probably a princess or something."

Matt groans, already regretting this conversation, but he can't help the chuckle that escapes. "Yeah, right. Just a runaway princess with half a million in cash." The two stare at the money for a very, very long time. "Misty, I have to get some sleep. I've had the worst day of my life, and this," he motions to the money, "Has just made it worse. I don't care what you do with it, but I can't take it." He peels himself off the floor and forces his legs to take him home.

The lab is a flurry with months' worth of activity. With every Bunsen burner on, sounds of small explosions, shooting stars, butterflies, and birds of all types fill the air, and in the center of it all, Chemistry moves from station to station, gripped by urgency. She squeezes the droppers, her fingers working with practiced precision, but her mind is far from the formulas before her. No matter how fast she moves or how much she tries to focus, Matt's voice lingers in her thoughts, tugging at her with an insistent weight. The lab's sterile environment feels suffocating compared to the warmth she had felt with Matt. Her work had always been her anchor, the one constant. But now, for the first time, she feels untethered.

Behind her, she hears a file drop into the bin, but her reaction is anticipation rather than disappointment. She jumps up and grabs it. Her hope quickly fades as she examines its contents.

Mother Nature enters the lab. Her presence brings a momentary pause to the frenetic activity.

"I was in Paris today. Things are back to normal in the city of romance," Mother Nature remarks, trying to strike up a conversation.

"I tackled it first to set a good example," Chemistry replies, her tone weary and resigned.

"Brilliant planning as always," Mother Nature says, forcing a smile.

The chute opens again, and a stack of files pour into the bin. Chemistry looks at the growing pile with a sense of defeat.

"Am I being punished? For every two I complete, another six shoot out," she laments.

Mother Nature chuckles softly, understanding the toll this relentless workload has taken on Chemistry. "Things have been tough down there,

Chemistry – *Jessica Sitomer*

Sugar. You're in demand," Mother Nature comments, trying to offer some perspective. Chemistry rubs her temples. The stress is evident in her actions. "Why don't you ask your staff for help? You can't do all this by yourself," Mother Nature suggests.

Chemistry shakes her head adamantly. "No. I can't afford another mistake."

Mother Nature regards her with a knowing look. "I wouldn't call him a mistake."

"It never should have happened. That file never should have come back." More files drop. Chemistry grabs them.

"Chemistry, Matt, is a minuscule part of your existence."

Chemistry's grip tightens on the files she's holding. More files drop into the bin, and she swiftly grabs them, determined to complete her task unshaken.

"But he feels like the only part that matters," she confesses with a heavy heart, her emotions pressing down on her.

"For now," Mother Nature assures her, "but soon, he'll just be a tiny blip on your timeline." Chemistry nods, wanting to believe her.

Chapter 17

Bacchus is half full on a Saturday night. Most of the front-of-the-house staff have moved on except Eli, who pours complimentary wine for the guests. Mr. and Mrs. Topel arrive, and the hostess seats them at their table. Eli gives Mr. Topel a high five and fills their water glasses.

Like clockwork, Matt comes to their table, delivering grilled sandwiches and curly fries. Mrs. Topel winks at Matt, thrilled that her husband still hasn't figured out he's eating tofu.

Matt nods with a practiced smile, but his mind is elsewhere, on the empty tables and the fact that Bacchus isn't the bustling success it had once been. What the hell is he doing? Is this all he is now, serving tofu to unsuspecting diners?

Mrs. Topel launches into her usual playful banter, "I tried that vegan recipe you gave me." She points her fork at her husband, "He couldn't tell it wasn't meat." Matt forces a chuckle, grateful for the distraction.

"It was meat," Mr. Topel argues, "It stunk up the house, but it was meat."

"Maybe you should change the menu," Mrs. Topel suggests, "Bring in more customers. It's been slow the last couple of weeks."

Chef Alex, a talented Culinary Institute of America-trained chef, walks out of the kitchen and makes rounds greeting guests. "I've let Chef Alex try a few of his dishes. They're wonderful, and he's far better than Joshua, so it's not the food." Mr. Topel lets out a HUFF, and Mrs. Topel Shhhs him. "What?" Matt asks. Mrs. Topel shakes her head no. Mr. Topel throws his hands up. "What aren't you telling me?" Matt pushes.

"I hate to keep things from you, Matt, but Eli said it was to protect you." Mr. Topel shakes his head again. Matt looks at Eli, who has been observing the table. Matt points at Eli, then points at his office, mouthing NOW! Matt gives Mr. Topel a reassuring pat on the back and follows Eli to the office.

Immediately on the defense, Eli says, "I didn't tell him it was tofu. He was bound to figure it out."

Chemistry – *Jessica Sitomer*

"What is it you're protecting me from?" Matt demands.

"'Only a true best friend can protect you from your immortal enemies'- Richelle Mead,"

"Eli!"

"She wrote Vampire Academy," Eli says innocently, avoiding the subject. Looking around, "This office could use a coat of paint. The white isn't—"

"Eli!!!"

Eli vomits words, "Joshua has a reality show, and he's been trashing this place—trashing you—and is definitely lying. Lying a lot. So much lying." Matt tries to wrap his head around what he's hearing. Eli, uncomfortable with the silence, babbles on. "It's called the Joshua Experience. He gives these young chefs his recipes—your recipes and tells them how lame the dishes are, and they have to make the dishes 'star worthy,' and he votes the worst off, and each week the best version goes on the menu for his new restaurant."

Matt stares at Eli, trying to process what he's hearing. Joshua was using his recipes? A bitter laugh escapes him as the weight of it all crashes down. Of course, Joshua would take what isn't his and make a spectacle out of it. But the worst part isn't Joshua's betrayal. It's that tiny voice in Matt's head, whispering that maybe Joshua is right. Maybe his food isn't good enough to stand on its own. He feels a tightness in his chest, anger bubbling up, but Eli's following words hit him like a brick before he can voice it.

"And the winner gets to be his sous chef as they build a Michelin Star restaurant live... I mean, there are no guarantees."

Matt slowly claps his hands. "Brilliant. Absolutely brilliant. Think about it. He has a season's worth of dishes, opens his restaurant, then does another season, and another, each bringing new top chefs to the table to create the food that he can't. HA!" Matt laughs, "it's brilliant!" Eli sways, staring at the ceiling, thinking of things to say, but he closes his mouth before any words come. Matt walks over to him and pats him on the back, then with a tight side-hug, he says, "My friend looks like the writing is on the wall." Matt grabs a black marker and writes in giant letters on the wall 'We're Done!'

"Guess we won't be needing that paint job now." He throws down the marker and walks out of his office. Eli licks his palm to see if the ink will rub off, but it only causes a smudge and stains his hand.

Chemistry – *Jessica Sitomer*

Chemistry sits at her cluttered desk, with a pencil between her teeth, staring at a blank paper pad. The overflowing garbage pail next to her is a testament to her frustration, filled with crumpled papers that have failed to capture her brilliance.

Inspiration walks into the room, her eyes scanning the chaotic scene. "Hard case?" Inspiration enquires, studying the mess.

Chemistry sighs, pulling the pencil from her mouth. "It's not a case. It's a poem. Well, it's nothing at the moment."

She rips off the page she has been working on, crumples it, and tosses it carelessly onto the floor.

"I didn't take you for a poet," Inspiration remarks, curiosity in her voice.

"I'd forgotten how it felt to be inspired," Chemistry admits, her tone tinged with melancholy.

"And now you remember?" Inspiration probes further.

"I was writing poetry for Matt," Chemistry says, her eyes distant. Then, in awe, she continues, "He knew my name." Inspiration's brow furrows in confusion. Chemistry inquires with a small, mischievous smile. "What was your name down there?"

"Um, I thought I read on page 537 of the manual that I'm not supposed to say my name."

"Go ahead, break the rules. I won't tell anyone. Mine was Ana de Gournay. And he knew my name."

The revelation has Inspiration perplexed. "How is that possible? You've been gone over 400 years."

Chemistry shrugs, her expression pensive. "He didn't know it was me, but apparently, I'm famous. Knowledge showed me the poetry section in the library. Books of my work. They were hard to re-read, but I couldn't stop myself. They say misery loves company."

Inspiration offers a sympathetic look, recognizing the weight of the situation. "They also say getting back on the horse is good."

Chemistry smiles at the sentiment. "Do they? I never heard that one."

Inspiration chuckles. "After your time."

"And what horse are they saying I should get on?"

Glancing at the pad of paper on Chemistry's desk. "It appears you're already on it. I want to read it when it's done." Chemistry nods, her enthusiasm tempered by self-consciousness. Inspiration stealthily grabs a pile of files behind Chemistry, "I'll leave you to it then."

"Nope!" Chemistry says without turning around.

Inspiration warns in a sing-song style, "They're piling up again,"

"I'll get to them. I always do."

Inspiration shrugs and lets out a sigh of boredom as she stomps out of the office.

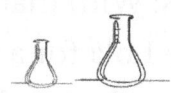

Matt sits on his couch, a heavy cloud of depression hanging over him. The living room is a mess, littered with restaurant magazines, most featuring Joshua's smug face on the cover. One magazine is turned to a headline that announced the unfortunate closing of Bacchus. Joshua's reality show is on television, although Matt has it muted.

"Who plates that way?" Matt asks the air in irritation.

Lola grabs the remote in her teeth and turns off the TV. She then turns her gaze toward Matt, her expressive eyes silently pleading for his attention. Matt glances at her, his own eyes clouded with misery.

"No," he mutters, his voice carrying the weight of his mood. Lola tilts her head to the side, her canine charms evident. Matt sighs, realizing he can't resist Lola's persistent request. "I don't feel like it."

Undeterred, Lola grabs her leash in her mouth and stares at him with an unwavering determination. After a moment of resistance, she lets out a sad woof, expressing her insistence. Matt can't help but chuckle at Lola's persistence.

"Fine," he relents. With that, he gets up from the couch, ready to take Lola for a much-needed walk. But Lola turns her head when he reaches for her leash. "What? I thought you wanted to go out. She walks into his bedroom. "What do you want from me?" he cries as he follows her into his room and sees her sitting in front of his full-length mirror. Lola whines and nudges him in front of it. Matt sees his reflection. Pajama bottoms, a stained white t-shirt, and hair that hasn't been brushed or washed, he realizes. Lola moves into the bathroom.

"Fine," Matt agrees, "but clearly, you don't have to go out that badly." Lola lowers her head but lifts her eyes. "I'll be quick."

Matt walks Lola along the Upper West Side streets and sees Eli in front of a store. He quickly turns to go in the other direction when he hears Eli call, "Matt!"

Matt attempts to keep walking but feels Lola's leash get taut as she is firmly seated on the sidewalk. He waves to Eli as Lola gets up and pulls Matt toward him. As he gets closer, his eyes are drawn to a real estate sign displayed in the storefront window.

"How cool is this space?" asks Eli, "And so close to the community garden."

"What does one have to do with the other?" Matt asks.

"I was just thinking if someone opened a take-out place here, people could take their food and eat in the garden." Eli looks at Matt, who has a god-smacked expression, "Sorry, I was just musing. How've you been? I've tried calling."

"Yeah, haven't been in the mood to talk," Matt says.

"We get together every week, front and back of the house. Meet at different restaurants. Many of us haven't landed anywhere yet, but we go places where those of us who have will feed us." Matt cups his eyes with his hands and presses his face against the glass to get a better look inside. "Have you thought about opening something?"

Chemistry – *Jessica Sitomer*

"I haven't been inspired since she left..." His words suspended between them.

"We all miss you, man, and believe in you. We'd follow you anywhere." Eli gives him a pat on the back and starts to walk away, then calls over his shoulder, "Right there would be perfect, walking distance for everyone."

Matt chuckles as Lola stands on her hind legs, almost as tall as her owner, and peers into the window. "It can't hurt to write down the number," he says to her as he peers into the window again, ideas starting to unfold. A wet tongue swipes the side of his face in agreement.

Chapter 18

Chemistry stands before a blackboard, chalk in hand, writing an extensive formula that seems to defy comprehension. Mother Nature storms in, followed by Chemistry's nervous staff.

Mother Nature demands, "Did you leave five hundred thousand dollars down there for him?"

Chemistry keeps writing. Without turning around she says, "I did." Her entire staff gasp.

"That is a complete abuse of your power!" Mother Nature accuses.

"Actually," Knowledge intercedes, "Most of what's minted today has no intrinsic value, so she left him a bunch of paper."

"Stay out of this!" Mother Nature warns. Knowledge hides behind Confidence.

"He's not wrong." Chemistry says, "That was my thought process behind it. He probably won't use it anyway, but if he does, it won't cause a stock market crash or anything."

Chemistry – *Jessica Sitomer*

"I don't even know what to say to you," Mother Nature admits.

"Nothing you can say now." She says petulantly, "Go cause a Tsunami or an Earthquake, as the things you do have actual consequences on hundreds of thousands of lives each year."

Mother Nature stands rigidly and then turns to go—the staff part like the Red Sea. Chemistry continues writing on the board as her staff leaves one at a time. Lust is the last to go but then turns back. "I want to let you know that I exercised restraint today," Lust announces proudly.

Chemistry, deep in thought, says nothing.

"How, you wonder?" Lust continues, undeterred. "I went down to pay a little 'booty call' to a shrink I met in Jersey... She was talking to that wacky dog masseuse you lived with who was blubbering like a baby over some chef."

Chemistry stops writing. Her interest is immediately piqued.

"I was going to put the moves on her. Depressed chicks are easy targets," Lust continues, "I can be irresistible, you know. But the poor girl had been pushed around a little, and this Joshua guy sounded like bad news. So, I backed off. Just thought you'd be proud."

Chemistry – *Jessica Sitomer*

He waits for a reaction from Chemistry, but she remains silent, lost in her thoughts. Disappointed, he walks for the door.

Just as he reaches for the handle, he hears, "Lust, you did good." She turns to face him, finally acknowledging him.

Excited, Lust spins around. "Yeah? I did good? You wanna 'do it'?"

Chemistry clarifies her statement with a wry smile. "I said good, not prodigious."

Lust scratches his head, somewhat bewildered. "I don't know what that means. But does it justify a kiss?"

Chemistry's smile only deepens, leaving Lust even more confused.

"Never mind," he mutters, hand back on the door handle. "You, with a smile, creeps me out."

Now in the central lab, Chemistry rises from behind a stack of books. She turns off the desk light, plunging the room into darkness. However, a sudden thwacking sound catches her attention, and she quickly flicks the light back on.

A single blue file has appeared in the file bin. She reaches for it and reads, her eyes reflecting a mix of gratitude and determination.

Chemistry – *Jessica Sitomer*

"Thank you," she whispers to the unseen forces at work. Without hesitation, she begins working on the intricate formula, her purpose unwavering in the face of the magical match ahead.

Armed with a plastic bag, Misty bends down to clean up the soiled papers left behind by the dogs. As she meticulously goes about her task, it becomes evident that the documents are old clippings featuring Joshua, now marred with dog pee stains. She collects the unsightly remnants and promptly stuffs them into the plastic bag before laying out more pictures of Joshua, a ritual she often engages in.

Amidst her task, a knock resounds at the door. Misty, plastic bag in hand, goes to answer it. She unlocks the newly fixed door and swings it open to reveal Eli standing there, clutching a substantial gift.

Misty blinks in surprise. "What's that?"

Eli struggles to find his words, his nerves getting the best of him. He finally manages to speak, though his words come out as a stuttered jumble.

Chemistry – *Jessica Sitomer*

He waits for a reaction from Chemistry, but she remains silent, lost in her thoughts. Disappointed, he walks for the door.

Just as he reaches for the handle, he hears, "Lust, you did good." She turns to face him, finally acknowledging him.

Excited, Lust spins around. "Yeah? I did good? You wanna 'do it'?"

Chemistry clarifies her statement with a wry smile. "I said good, not prodigious."

Lust scratches his head, somewhat bewildered. "I don't know what that means. But does it justify a kiss?"

Chemistry's smile only deepens, leaving Lust even more confused.

"Never mind," he mutters, hand back on the door handle. "You, with a smile, creeps me out."

Now in the central lab, Chemistry rises from behind a stack of books. She turns off the desk light, plunging the room into darkness. However, a sudden thwacking sound catches her attention, and she quickly flicks the light back on.

A single blue file has appeared in the file bin. She reaches for it and reads, her eyes reflecting a mix of gratitude and determination.

Chemistry – *Jessica Sitomer*

"Thank you," she whispers to the unseen forces at work. Without hesitation, she begins working on the intricate formula, her purpose unwavering in the face of the magical match ahead.

Armed with a plastic bag, Misty bends down to clean up the soiled papers left behind by the dogs. As she meticulously goes about her task, it becomes evident that the documents are old clippings featuring Joshua, now marred with dog pee stains. She collects the unsightly remnants and promptly stuffs them into the plastic bag before laying out more pictures of Joshua, a ritual she often engages in.

Amidst her task, a knock resounds at the door. Misty, plastic bag in hand, goes to answer it. She unlocks the newly fixed door and swings it open to reveal Eli standing there, clutching a substantial gift.

Misty blinks in surprise. "What's that?"

Eli struggles to find his words, his nerves getting the best of him. He finally manages to speak, though his words come out as a stuttered jumble.

Chemistry – *Jessica Sitomer*

"W-w-when one door closes another door opens, but we often look so long and so regretfully upon the closed door that we do not see the ones which open for us."

The dogs, excited by Eli's presence, begin to jump around and eagerly tear at the ribbons on the gift.

Misty looks closely at Eli, genuinely puzzled, then with sudden recognition, "You! You're always so nice to me. Why? I don't even care that you exist, and I care about everyone!"

Eli offers her the gift, and she takes it, walking to her couch. He follows her inside as she opens the present without looking at him. Inside the gift is an assortment of freshly baked dog biscuits in various shapes and sizes. Overwhelmed by the thoughtful gesture, Misty can't help but cry.

Eli, fidgeting nervously, tries to fill the silence. "You cannot prevent the birds of sorrow from flying over your head, but you can prevent them from building nests in your hair."

The gift deeply touches Misty, and her emotions surge as she reaches a breaking point. In a sudden and unexpected move, she leans in and kisses Eli.

Startled but not entirely displeased, Eli continues with another quote, "A kiss is a lovely trick designed by nature to stop speech when words become superfluous."

Tears still in her eyes, Misty hiccups. She giggles, but the hiccups don't stop, so between them, she speaks. "Once, just once, hiccup, I'd like to hear you say something in your own words."

Eli, his anxiety palpable, hesitates for a moment. Then, summoning all his courage, he blurts out, "Hi! I'm Eli—and I'm in love with you."

Their eyes lock, and a connection ignites between them. Misty's hiccups continue, but her tears are tears of joy. Misty hiccups once more, her voice soft and sincere. "That will do." With that, she kisses him again.

Chapter 19

The space where Matt had last seen Eli is now occupied. The windows are covered with signs that say, "Something Delicious is Haunting This Space," "Whispers of a Secret Menu... Coming Soon," "You Haven't Seen Anything Like This Before...#WhatsCookingBehindTheseDoors."

The signs invite people to take photos of them and share them on social media using the custom hashtag. The campaign drives intrigue and interaction as the crowds outside grow each day to await the daily clue.

Inside, a contractor gives orders to workers, walls are being painted, and a social media specialist interrupts Matt as he reviews plans with his architect.

"Today's clue is 'It's just Chemistry,'" she tells him.

Matt stiffens for a moment as a memory overtakes him. He shakes it off and gives her an approving nod. He is interrupted again before he can get back to the plans in front of him. A young man shares a handful of brochures.

"I'm going to need your choices on the biodegradable, compostable, and reusable packaging options sooner than later," he says.

"Misty?" Matt calls out.

Misty and Eli are camouflaged by stacks of boxes in a deep kiss when Matt's voice penetrates their love bubble. "Coming," she sings as she gives Eli one more kiss, then another.

"Misty!" Matt calls again. She scrambles through the maze of boxes and joins Matt, who hands off the brochures to her. "Sooner than later," he repeats the order from the young man to Misty.

Without hesitation, Misty inspects the pile. "Nope," she drops the brochure on the floor. "No," the young man grabs the paper before she can drop it, "Yes," she cheers, "Oooo, yes!" she says again, handing the two pages to Matt. "Hmmm," she examines a photo from multiple angles, "I still like this one if we use evaporating ink."

The young man rolls his eyes, "For the hundredth time, there is no such thing as evaporating ink."

Chemistry – *Jessica Sitomer*

"Then invent it," Misty insists, "Look at this place. Everything about it is magical."

Exasperated, he begs, "If I can't invent it in time for opening, do I have your approval for this one?"

Misty twitches her nose back and forth, then smiles, "Yes!"

"Finally!" the young man groans and hands the brochure to Matt for final approval.

"Now go invent it," Misty says, "I believe in you."

His voice laden with sarcasm as he replies, "I'll get right on it."

With a happy clap, Misty heads back to the box stacks.

A rarely seen smile edges Matt's face as he reviews the plans before him. He pats the architect on the back and says, "You did it. This could work."

The architect learned not to embellish once he got approval from Matt. This will work, he knows. After months of working with Matt, he wished the guy would enjoy the process more, but he rolls up the plans, shakes Matt's hand, and heads out the door, careful not to let the crowd get a peek.

Chemistry – *Jessica Sitomer*

The lab is on overload. Typical, beautifully composed formulas are blowing up or overflowing as Chemistry tries to stay ahead of her workload. Her eyes sting with exhaustion as she seals yet another jar. The sterile hum of the lab feels like a distant buzz, her hands moving automatically. But her mind... her mind is still on Matt.

She tries to bury herself in work and lose herself in formulas and files, but nothing erases how he looked at her the last time she saw him. She grips the table, her knuckles turning white. If she stays in this cycle long enough, maybe she'll forget. But the memory clings to her, and she feels misplaced for the first time in centuries. She barely hears the elevator door open as her team spills out laughing and hanging on each other as they walk. She welcomes the distraction.

"Where were you?" Chemistry asks, her voice carrying a tone of disapproval as she glances up from her workbench.

Humor replies with a carefree grin, "Jimmy Fallon's New Year's party. He's my hero."

Chemistry can't help but sigh and rub her temples in frustration. "That's productive," she mutters under her breath.

"Then invent it," Misty insists, "Look at this place. Everything about it is magical."

Exasperated, he begs, "If I can't invent it in time for opening, do I have your approval for this one?"

Misty twitches her nose back and forth, then smiles, "Yes!"

"Finally!" the young man groans and hands the brochure to Matt for final approval.

"Now go invent it," Misty says, "I believe in you."

His voice laden with sarcasm as he replies, "I'll get right on it."

With a happy clap, Misty heads back to the box stacks.

A rarely seen smile edges Matt's face as he reviews the plans before him. He pats the architect on the back and says, "You did it. This could work."

The architect learned not to embellish once he got approval from Matt. This will work, he knows. After months of working with Matt, he wished the guy would enjoy the process more, but he rolls up the plans, shakes Matt's hand, and heads out the door, careful not to let the crowd get a peek.

Chemistry – *Jessica Sitomer*

The lab is on overload. Typical, beautifully composed formulas are blowing up or overflowing as Chemistry tries to stay ahead of her workload. Her eyes sting with exhaustion as she seals yet another jar. The sterile hum of the lab feels like a distant buzz, her hands moving automatically. But her mind... her mind is still on Matt.

    She tries to bury herself in work and lose herself in formulas and files, but nothing erases how he looked at her the last time she saw him. She grips the table, her knuckles turning white. If she stays in this cycle long enough, maybe she'll forget. But the memory clings to her, and she feels misplaced for the first time in centuries. She barely hears the elevator door open as her team spills out laughing and hanging on each other as they walk. She welcomes the distraction.

    "Where were you?" Chemistry asks, her voice carrying a tone of disapproval as she glances up from her workbench.

    Humor replies with a carefree grin, "Jimmy Fallon's New Year's party. He's my hero."

    Chemistry can't help but sigh and rub her temples in frustration. "That's productive," she mutters under her breath.

Confidence, always quick to defend her impeccable actions, retorts, "That's not fair! You won't let us help. Indulging yourself in misery is self-defeating. You need to turn that frown around!"

Style chimes in with her perspective, "A sample sale always cheers me up."

Lust, eager to offer his solution, "Need a distraction from all that brooding? I'm great at providing one," a mischievous glint in his eye.

Chemistry winces. Ick! Make it stop. With a hint of resignation, Chemistry finally relents, "Fine! Work."

"Really?" the group says in unison, and before she can change her mind, they eagerly return to their respective lab stations. They all look through files, picking out the ones they want and tossing the rest on Inspiration's station. Inspiration doesn't seem to mind. Humor adds a file to the top and the pile is now taller than her. Reading the file, she can't help but raise a thought-provoking question.

"You know what doesn't make sense?" Inspiration muses aloud, drawing the attention of her companions. "If everyone is set up with perfect matches, then why isn't everyone happy?"

Knowledge provides an answer: "The initial attraction doesn't last forever. Our chemicals flood

Chemistry – *Jessica Sitomer*

their bodies, causing a rapid heartbeat and mood to soar. It can last up to four months."

"Down there, they call it 'the honeymoon period.'" Confidence elaborates.

Inspiration probes deeper, her gaze focused on Chemistry, "What happens when the honeymoon is over?"

Style, always attentive to human behavior, adds insight, "It's up to them. They can choose to try to make it work or start looking for someone else to try on."

Then, Inspiration poses a more personal question directed at Chemistry, "Or they can wind up miserable like Chemistry?"

Chemistry looks up as everybody else quickly looks back at their work.

Inspiration continues, "I read your poem."

Chemistry's face blushes, then turns to anger, "You had no right! That was—"

"You loved him so much, so why didn't you stay with him?" Inspiration demands.

Everyone stops what they're doing and looks at Chemistry. Chemistry looks around, her eyes meeting those of her colleagues. They all pause their work, waiting for her response.

"Because," Chemistry says, "I've had my soulmate, and Matt deserves the chance to find his."

The group contemplates her words. Satisfied, they resume their tasks. But Inspiration can't let go of her curiosity. She delves further into Chemistry's personal history. "How do you know?" Inspiration enquires, her voice filled with genuine interest, causing the others to pause again.

In unison, they chime in, "Because she knows everything!"

However, Inspiration isn't satisfied with their response. She seeks clarity, "No, how do you know you've had your soulmate?"

Once again, a hushed silence descends upon the room as everyone awaits Chemistry's answer.

For a moment, she is dumbfounded by the question. Then responds with heightened frustration. "I'm here, aren't I?" demands Chemistry.

Unsatisfied with this enigmatic reply, Inspiration presses, "So?"

"So!" Chemistry retorts with a hint of anger, "So? I died from a broken heart. I experienced the ultimate love to the point that it killed me. That's why I was picked, don't you think?"

Chemistry – *Jessica Sitomer*

The room remains silent as everyone exchanges thoughtful glances. Inspiration, undeterred, ventures an alternative perspective, "Not necessarily. You told me I was picked for my inspirational gifts and the pure goodness I personified. Regarding my inspirational gifts, I never even made it to my first symphony... but I'm here. Maybe the first guy wasn't your soulmate." The group looks back at Chemistry, who appears bewildered and distressed by the ongoing conversation.

Feeling overwhelmed, Chemistry abruptly storms out of the room, and Inspiration promptly follows.

Inspiration runs to catch up to Chemistry in the hallway, determined to confront her about her intentions.

"I quit!" Inspiration declares, her resolve unwavering.

Chemistry is taken aback. "You can't quit," she protests, a note of desperation creeping into her voice.

But Inspiration remains steadfast. "If this is what love does, I won't match them up! How can you, knowing how it feels?"

Chemistry – *Jessica Sitomer*

As Chemistry listens to Inspiration, she feels a pang of recognition. You used to be like her, so sure, so determined. But now you're not even sure what you believe anymore. The words of encouragement she wants to say die in her throat. How do I help her when I can't even help myself? Chemistry attempts to explain, "Look! We don't set them up knowing things will go wrong."

Undeterred, Inspiration persists, "Then why? What could they possibly learn that is worth it?"

As they stand off, Chemistry realizes she must convey their purpose's essence. She kneels closer to Inspiration's size and takes her hands in hers. "They learn about themselves so that when they meet the soulmate they were intended for, they recognize what makes them happy. Then they stick," she explains, hoping to make Inspiration understand.

The tension between them lingers as Inspiration contemplates her words. She can't help but question Chemistry's situation.

"And is this all you were intended for? Misery for eternity?" Inspiration asks. "Or did your now 'imperfect record' teach you that maybe there's more than striving for perfection?" Waiting for an answer that doesn't come, as Chemistry grapples with the profound question raised by the young girl, Inspiration continues, "I never had a soulmate, I never knew love, and I'm here! Explain that because nothing you've taught me so far substantiates my credibility!"

Chemistry contemplates what to say next. "Of course, you knew love. You died of a broken heart, just like me."

"Oh, please!" Inspiration rolls her eyes, "I died in a plane crash and wound up here." The look on Chemistry's face causes a strange unease in Inspiration. She waits for Chemistry to say something, but she doesn't. Unable to withstand the empathetic expression on Chemistry's face, Inspiration says again, "I did die in a plane crash. I remember it clearly." Then she adds with a touch of tween sarcasm, "You'd think they would spare you the cause of death up here."

"Inspiration--"

"Stop! What's your point? I remember! The plane was going down. I was terrified my mom was terrified. I was trying to keep her calm, and I was praying that we'd be okay. I was praying so hard!" She sighs, "But it didn't work," She closes her eyes and covers her ears, "The sound of the impact was unimaginable. It was crying, screeching metal, like even the plane was in pain. But people were alive. I could hear them wailing and screaming." Her voice gets caught in her throat, "But not my mom. She was silent. She was dead."

Chemistry puts her arms around Inspiration, who squirms out of her grasp and then accuses Chemistry, "Why isn't she here? Why me? Why me? She was the epitome of love. She sacrificed everything for me, including her grief over my dad. She was so strong..." her memory returns to the crash, "But I couldn't be that strong. I didn't want to live without her. I gave up. I'm weak." She whispers to Chemistry, "Why me?"

"You're not weak," Chemistry assures her, "Your heart is broken... so deeply that you, explicitly, can help others love just as deeply."

"But--" Inspiration says.

"In a situation where others would have been absorbed in their own fear, you turned your attention on your mom. You stayed calm, compassionate, and loving to comfort her until the end. That's not just bravery or love. That's pure goodness."

"Anyone would have done that."

"No one on that plane did it but you," Chemistry assures her. Inspiration remains unmoved. "Are you grateful for the love you had with your mom and dad?"

"Of course!" Inspiration demands.

"Then, despite the pain that love can cause, aren't you lucky to be able to create the formulas that gift love to others?"

Inspiration thinks long and hard. Chemistry doesn't leave her and doesn't interrupt her thoughts.

"Guess we are both destined for an eternity of misery," Inspiration states.

"No. You won't feel miserable when you see the impact you're having. You'll feel privileged."

"Privileged? That's the word to describe how you've been feeling since you left Matt behind? It doesn't seem to me like there are enough files in the world to erase the pain you're feeling."

Chemistry doesn't know how to respond. Inspiration is not wrong. Her silence is enough for Inspiration's anger to boil up again. "I hope this is a bad dream I wake up from very soon!" She storms away, leaving Chemistry alone with her thoughts.

Chemistry – *Jessica Sitomer*

In a garden spa, Mother Nature reclines gracefully on a chaise lounge, her tranquil demeanor unaffected as a Waxer meticulously removes a strip of hair from her legs and a Manicurist attentively polishes her nails. Chemistry paces the room restlessly. She is grappling with inner turmoil.

"Well?" Chemistry demands, impatience echoing in her voice.

With an air of unflappable calm, Mother Nature replies, "Even if I knew, I couldn't tell you."

Frustration laces Chemistry's voice as she persists, "But if he wasn't my soulmate, maybe Matt is."

The waxer performs her task precisely, ripping off another strip of hair while Mother Nature remains composed. Calm and collected, she instructs the waxer, "You missed a spot."

Desperation creeps into Chemistry's tone as she implores, "I am trying to make the most important decision of my existence. Can you stop primping yourself for one minute and help me?"

"No, I can't," Mother Nature responds. "The decision is yours to make. There's no formula to figure out. He may be your soulmate. He may not be. Not my department." Chemistry growls. Mother Nature tests her, "There's no formula for this. It's messy, it's painful, and it's uncertain. But that's love."

Chemistry's heart sinks. She's used to certainty, calculated decisions, and knowing the outcome before she even starts. Now, standing on the precipice of something unknown, she feels exposed. Raw.

This question haunts Chemistry. "But if I'm wrong?" she murmurs, her voice filled with doubt. "I've given up eternity and everything I've worked for."

"True," Mother Nature concedes. "But what if you're right?" Mother Nature's voice softens. "You've spent your existence crafting love for others. But do you love him enough to risk it? To find out if this…this thing you've built with him can last?"

Chemistry closes her eyes, her mind racing. She knows how much she's given up for control, how hard she's worked to avoid the chaos that love brings. But now, for the first time, she wonders if maybe the risk is worth it. Maybe being with Matt is worth losing everything else.

"I don't know," she whispers, her voice trembling with the weight of her uncertainty. "But even if I am right," Chemistry thinks out loud, "What I do here is important. I coordinate every match, opening the possibility to love... like the Topels." She sits next to Mother Nature, "You should have seen them," she chuckles, "Bickering and teasing each other in an easy pattern. They are so intertwined in the very best way."

"There's the girl I remember," Mother Nature says.

Chemistry sits quietly, reflecting. "I suppose I got a bit jaded, lost my way, treated them like 'files'-_"

Mother Nature interrupts, "You suppose?"

Chemistry changes the subject, "Inspiration doesn't get it."

"She will."

"How can I make her understand when I selfishly want to throw this all away and return to him?"

"Your actions will teach her everything she needs to know. Go back to work." Mother Nature shifts positions, "I'm about to be waxed in a place you don't want to see."

Chemistry grimaces as she jumps to her feet and out of the spa.

Chemistry – *Jessica Sitomer*

Chapter 20

Matt's Ghost Restaurant has come a long way. Now, a sleek, high-tech operation is bustling with precision. The room is vast, filled with gleaming stainless-steel appliances that line the walls in perfectly organized stations. The overhead lighting casts a bright, cool glow, highlighting the immaculate cleanliness of the workspace. The chefs, all dressed in matching white shirts, blue-striped aprons, and caps, move methodically between stations, their movements synchronized like a well-rehearsed ballet. Each is intensely focused on their tasks—chopping, stirring, plating—against the backdrop of the softly whirring machinery.

Digital screens, embedded high on the walls above each station, display real-time orders with precise timers ticking down. The screens show each dish's status—whether it's in prep, cooking, or ready for packaging. The phrase "IT'S JUST CHEMISTRY" glows in neon, adding a touch of branding to the space.

In the center, a long island serves as a prep station, covered in neatly arranged boxes of fresh ingredients—herbs, vegetables, and sauces, ready for assembly. Packaged meals sit in neatly stacked containers, waiting to be whisked away for delivery, a testament to the efficiency and output of this culinary assembly line. The air blends the savory, mouth-watering scents of various dishes being prepared simultaneously.

Around the kitchen, stacks of branded boxes with a bubbling test tube logo and the words 'It's Just...' are piled, ready for dispatch. The absence of a dining area or customers keeps the atmosphere focused and business-like, with the clear intent that this kitchen is all about high-volume, fast-paced production, churning out gourmet meals for remote consumers. It's a futuristic food hub where technology and culinary expertise collide, creating a seamless flow of meals without any of the traditional restaurant trappings.

In the far corner, separated from the bustling prep stations, stands an elegant tasting table, starkly contrasting the industrial efficiency surrounding it. The table is long and crafted from polished dark wood, its surface gleaming under the soft, amber lighting that drops from above. Set for ten guests, each place is meticulously arranged with pristine white plates, polished silver cutlery, and crystal glasses that catch the light, casting delicate reflections across the table.

The chairs are modern yet comfortable, upholstered in dark leather, inviting guests to settle in and enjoy a private, exclusive dining experience amidst the production bustle. In the center of the table, a low arrangement of fresh herbs and succulents adds a touch of natural elegance, their fragrant greenery subtly complementing the aromas wafting from the kitchen. Small, sleek candles flicker beside them, casting a warm, intimate glow over the space.

Behind the table, a large glass partition provides an unobstructed view of the kitchen in action. Guests can watch the chefs, adding a theatrical element to the dining experience. The air here feels calmer and more refined, as though time slows down in this corner. Plates of food are brought out in an orderly sequence. Each dish is an artful presentation of vibrant colors and precise garnishes, allowing the guests to taste and savor the fruits of the kitchen's labor while still feeling connected to the high-energy atmosphere around them.

Seated at the table, sampling Matt's latest creations, are Misty, Eli, Mr. and Mrs. Topel, and three couples from Matt's building, all sworn to secrecy. Before each guest, a dish is placed featuring a few brioche chips and small piped clouds of cheddar foam alongside them. Onion jam spheres delicately top the foam. They are garnished with microgreens and edible flowers for color and freshness, with a side of potato curls piled high in a minimalist, angular dish sprinkled with Parmesan dust generously over the top. Dollops of garlic espuma surround the plate for dipping.

"This is my Deconstructed Grilled Cheese with Cheese Foam, Brioche Chips, and Onion Jam Spheres, inspired by Mr. & Mrs. Topel," Matt says, "Please enjoy."

When the diners take a bite, they get the light foam, the crispy bread, and the burst of sweet onion jam, deconstructing the grilled cheese experience into distinct, interactive components.

Mr. Topel leans over to his wife and whispers, "This is not a grilled cheese sandwich."

"Oh, just eat it. It's delish!" Mrs. Topel instructs.

Chemistry – *Jessica Sitomer*

Matt watches the interaction and chuckles at what he can only imagine is a complaint. "Don't worry, Mr. Topel. You are invited to the Brownstone anytime for classic grilled cheese and curly fries."

"Oh, thank goodness!" Mr. Topel exclaims and pushes his dish away. Without thinking about etiquette, Eli reaches over and finishes off the plate.

The plates are taken away, and desserts are served, but before anyone can dig in, the social media manager pushes her way in to organize the perfect photo and a quick reel.

"This! This is our teaser for tomorrow," she shows Matt.

"Give them a chance to tell me if it belongs on the menu," he says as he turns to introduce the dish, only to find ten stuffed mouths with heads nodding 'yes' in unison.

"Listen up, you all have been coming for two weeks now, and I need you to help me narrow it down. Everything can't be on the menu," Matt reminds them. He pulls out surveys listing the starters, salads, soups, main courses, and desserts they've tried. "All you have to do is rate them. One is the best, then two for your second favorite, and go down the list until you've numbered them all. If there is a dish you don't remember, put an X next to

Chemistry – *Jessica Sitomer*

it. I don't want anything on the menu that's not memorable."

The task daunts the guests until they notice Misty putting the number one next to everything.

"Honey?" Eli says, "That's not going to help Matt."

"Well, this is impossible!" Misty cries. "It's like asking me to list my dogs in order of favorites. Each one is unique and wonderful and, in this case, delicious!"

Eli consoles her as the rest get to work on their surveys.

The lab is back to capacity. Everything is working smoothly, and everyone is back at their stations. Chemistry enters and walks to the shelves of jars. She checks the hummingbird section. Every jar is in place. Then, the waterfalls, the same thing. And finally, the rose petals, but everything is exactly as she'd left it.

"What are you looking for?" Inspiration asks, startling Chemistry.

Chemistry – *Jessica Sitomer*

"Just checking inventory..." she trails off with a sigh.

"Every day, you check the same inventory. Hummingbirds, waterfalls, and rose petals. Then you look disappointed," Inspirations says. "Tough case? I can help."

Chemistry considers her words carefully, "Not a case... I'm testing possibilities."

"Whatever you say," Inspiration replies and returns to her station.

Chemistry wanders over to the furthest station and finds Knowledge. He turns sparkle dust into numbers and then captures them in jars. Chemistry lurks around him, her presence annoying him.

"Just tell me what you want already. You've been looking over my shoulder for days, and you know I never make mistakes," he says.

"I don't want anything. You're doing a great job," she compliments.

He slams a beaker on his station, "That's it! You have never complimented me. Something is fishy, suspicious, dubious, and uncertain... and I can't work like this!"

"Shhhhhh!" Chemistry insists, putting her hand over his mouth and pulling him out of everyone's sight. "Has any prodigy ever been in a file?"

Chemistry – *Jessica Sitomer*

"What do you mean?" his eyes squint as he tries to understand her question.

"I know it hasn't happened since I've been here, but are there any records from before where perhaps one of us showed up in a department file?"

"Our department file?" he asks.

"Yes."

"To be set up with someone in Eternity?" his confusion growing.

"No."

Panic swells in his face, "To be matched with a mortal?!"

She covers his mouth again and nods 'yes' as he stares at her, stifled, and returns her nod with a 'no.' She removes her hand.

"You've read every book 18 times except Pleades' book that you've read nineteen—"

"Twenty, and I just read the new one by Sophie Kinsella. She's funny, quick humor!"

"Right, anyway, are there any records outside the library that may have information?"

"About immortal and mortal matches?" he asks.

"Yes."

"A match between someone dead and someone alive?" he digs.

"Exactly."

"About someone from Eternity matching with someone on Earth?"

"Yes! Yes! Yes!" Chemistry insists.

"No," he tells her, "But that would make a great Sophie Kinsella book."

Chemistry trudges away, still battling the risks and gains in her head. She steps into the center of the lab, assessing the productivity and weighing her options.

"Everybody listen up!" Her voice echoes through the lab. "I need help." There's a widespread gasp, "From all of you." She turns off the "out of order" sign and presses the elevator button. It opens.

"Follow me!" She commands determination radiating from her every word.

Lust shrugs and yells, "Let's go!"

Everyone stops what they're doing and follows Chemistry into the elevator, except for Inspiration, who ignores the order and returns to work, muttering, "Someone's gotta keep this place running."

Chemistry – *Jessica Sitomer*

Back on the Upper West Side, Chemistry dashes down a busy street, her eyes scanning for any sign of Matt. Suddenly, she spots Eli sitting on a mailbox.

Eli calmly states, "You're too late. He's getting married."

Breathlessly, Chemistry exclaims, "What?"

Eli points towards a turquoise church in the distance. Empathy, holding a cupcake, offers it to Chemistry, "Oh Honey, I'm so sorry."

Chemistry slams the cupcake to the ground and then bolts down the street toward the church.

Chemistry bursts through the church doors, inadvertently colliding with Humor, who's conversing with a Priest holding a tennis racket.

Panicked, she asks, "The wedding? Is it over?"

Humor chuckles softly, replying, "It never began. Matt called it off. Kidding! No, I'm not... that was just mean."

Surprised and relieved, Chemistry inquires, "He did? Where is he?"

Humor contemplates momentarily before responding, "I think he took the Paris tickets."

Without wasting a moment, Chemistry kisses Humor on the cheek and rushes out of the church.

Chemistry lurches into the traffic, frantically waving down a cab. Lust pulls over in a cab, his inappropriate charm oozing.

Chemistry instructs, "The airport!"

Lust, with a sly grin, replies, "Which one, hot legs?"

Chemistry winces, "The one where the Parisian women go."

Lust revs up the cab and speeds through a purple traffic light but collides with a car that jumps the green signal.

The ensuing traffic chaos brings everything to a halt. Chemistry leaps out of the cab and starts climbing over the halted cars until she reaches a free one.

She yanks open the door, only to find Knowledge behind the wheel. Firmly, she commands, "Slide over!"

Skeptical, Knowledge retorts, "Is this a carjacking?"

Impatiently, Chemistry asks, "Do you have a license?"

With an eye roll, Knowledge complies and slides over, allowing Chemistry to take the driver's seat.

She accelerates, weaving through the congested traffic.

Chemistry speeds through the nearly empty airport terminals.

Desperately, Chemistry asks, "Which airline goes to Paris?"

Knowledge, shaken, looks pale. He stammers, "I've memorized the flight numbers and departure times of all airlines that go to Paris according to season and concluded that if I eliminate the—"

Chemistry silences him by placing her hand over his mouth.

She says, "I've got a plane to stop!"

Knowledge points to an approaching terminal. She screeches to a stop.

Chemistry races through the terminal, bypassing Confidence to reach the Boarding Agent, idly petting a cat.

Breathless, she demands, "Where's the next plane leaving for Paris?"

Confidence chimes in, "Ooo! I know! I know!"

Confidence points outside to a plane on the tarmac.

Chemistry – *Jessica Sitomer*

With a sense of urgency, she exclaims, "Oh no!" She pushes her way through the bystanders, knocking and shoving them aside, gasping for breath.

Confidence shouts after her, "You go, girl!"

Chemistry reaches the window, but it's too late. She bows in defeat as the plane takes off down the runway.

She glances up, and her heart skips a beat. Matt stands on the tarmac. She bangs on the glass and screams his name. By chance, he looks up and sees her. Their eyes lock, and he starts to run towards her.

Chemistry's expression changes from joy to agony as she watches Matt get hit by a luggage cart and knocked unconscious.

Chemistry sits by Matt's hospital bed. Style, dressed in scrubs, reviews the chart. Matt lies unconscious, his monitor beeping steadily.

Style remarks as she exits, "No tears now. Your mascara will run."

Matt opens his eyes, unnoticed by Chemistry, staring out the window. She talks to him and admits to herself, "I was having second thoughts, you know, the day I left you. I was scared." Chemistry admits, her voice trembling as she sits on Matt's bed. "I was scared of loving you, of losing you. I've lost before, and it killed me. I didn't want to feel that again. So, I left. I thought it would protect me, but it only made the pain worse." She reached down the bed and gently brushed her fingers across his hand. "I've been running for so long, hiding behind my work and logic because it felt safe. But with you... I don't want safe. I want real. And that terrifies me more than anything. I mean, you have no idea when you said my name..." Her voice catches, "But then I saw you with that woman. I just knew you connected, so I... I kept going."

Matt coughs, drawing her attention. She jumps off the bed, her heart pounding, hoping for some sign that everything is not as wrong as it seems. Maybe he'll say something... something that will make this all worth it.

Gently, he says, "I'm glad you did."

The words land like a slap. Her breath catches in her throat, and a sharp sting of hurt flashes across her chest. She swallows, trying to suppress the rising tide of emotion, her throat tightening. She takes a step back, feeling the world shift beneath her feet, but outwardly, she tries to remain composed. Her

Chemistry – *Jessica Sitomer*

mind scrambles to make sense of it. He doesn't want me.

She takes the blow, every fiber of her being screaming to stay, to fight for what's between them. But her legs move on their own, turning to leave like she's trying to escape the hurt that's settling deep in her bones. The door looms ahead, the distance between them growing with each step. I shouldn't have let myself feel this.

As she reaches for the handle, Matt's voice breaks through the silence, "If you hadn't, I wouldn't have learned that I'd rather be alone than with anyone but you."

Chemistry stops and turns, her eyes filled with hope. Encouraged, she asks, "Really?"

She sits down on the bed next to him. Tentatively, she inquires, "So, if I had just shown up at your door—"

He pulls her closer and tenderly kisses her. His heart rate monitor speeds up. Beep, beep, beep... until it becomes his blaring alarm clock.

Matt wakes up from the dream in a sweat. He sits up hopeful, and then reality sinks in. He lays back down, defeated, and turns off the alarm.

Chemistry – *Jessica Sitomer*

"Alexa set a timer for fifteen minutes," Matt says as he sits up, staring at the ceiling while his heart rate slows. He runs a hand through his hair, feeling the ghost of Chemistry's presence. The room feels empty, but his thoughts linger on her words. The world outside his window is just beginning to wake up, but inside, his thoughts are spinning with possibilities and regrets.

Chemistry and her team stand in the white room. No one dares to move or push the elevator button. They stare at Chemistry, waiting for directions, but none come.

A bead of sweat trickles down Humor's brow. He looks like he's going to burst.

"Just say it," Lust sighs.

"What do you call seven people in an elevator?" Humor blurts out.

"Not now," Empathy insists and touches his shoulder.

Chemistry pushes the elevator door. It opens, and she beelines out of the lab. Everyone else, unsure of what just happened, returns to their stations.

Inspiration sizes up the room, then asks, "What happened?"

Chemistry – *Jessica Sitomer*

"No eye deer," Humor answers, and they all return to work.

Chemistry – *Jessica Sitomer*

Chapter 21

Chemistry sits at her desk. Her office feels colder than before, more distant, more suffocating. The familiar tools of her trade surround her, but they offer no comfort now. She stares at the files, trying to force herself to work, to distract herself from the lingering ache in her chest. But it's no use. The dream still clings to her—Matt's voice, his touch, the way he looked at her as if he was reaching for something real, something they both wanted.

Her hands shake as she picks up a file but can't focus. Not now. Not after what she's seen, what he said, what she's felt. It's too much, too overwhelming. She puts her head in her hands, the weight of her emotions finally breaking through. Her chest heaves with sobs as she curls in on herself. I didn't think knowing would hurt this much. For the first time in centuries, Chemistry lets herself feel her emotions, grief, longing, love, all of

Chemistry – *Jessica Sitomer*

it crashing down on her like a wave she can't control.

In the hospitality lobby, Chemistry peers out the window at the diamond-shaped mirrors in the waterfall. She is lost in a memory from long ago. She sees herself in a bed covered in a patchwork comforter. The shade on the window is drawn, permitting the slightest of light around its edges. In the memory, she is clutching her chest and trying to cry out but is unable to breathe. She silently screams and then gasps for air.

Tears prick at Chemistry's eyes. Even after 400 years, the pain of her loss causes a stabbing in her heart. She looks away, then back, hoping for a memory of her with Matt, but those memories don't count. That was work.

Inspiration walks up behind her, "What do you see?" she asks, catching Chemistry off guard, "is it your soulmate?"

Chemistry shrugs her shoulders because she doesn't know.

Chemistry – *Jessica Sitomer*

"I thought you went down. I saw you enter the elevator with the team and figured you chose Matt. But then the buttons went up instead of down."

Chemistry stares at the memory in the mirror of herself curled up in a ball, rocking from side to side in grief.

"There is so much pain on the other side of love," Chemistry says, "I went into Matt's dream to see if I risked it all for him if he'd take me back."

"And?" asks Inspiration.

"He did," Chemistry replies. The diamond mirror shimmers as Chemistry uncurls herself drags herself to a toilet and wraps herself around it. Watching herself makes Chemistry feel the nausea of that day when she lost her love.

Inspiration asks, "So, what are you waiting for?"

Inspiration's question echoes in Chemistry's mind. What is she waiting for? She stands still, the memory of Matt lingering in her thoughts. Every part of her has been trained to see emotions as variables in a grand equation. But Matt is the variable she can't solve, the unknown factor that threw off her careful calculations. She feared opening herself to a world beyond formulas and perfect matches.

Chemistry – *Jessica Sitomer*

Chemistry speaks her fear out loud, "It was a dream, Inspiration."

Inspiration chuckles. "You're waiting for a guarantee."

Chemistry doesn't know how to explain to this child without being condescending that she is safe here. Here, she is helpful and has a purpose—a single purpose—one that, until Matt Durand, had never disappointed her, never wavered her emotions. How complicated life would be down there.

"I guess you'll stay here and mentor me," Inspiration says, "Matt was just a file. A really cute file."

"No," Chemistry teases, "You're cute." Chemistry looks back at the mirrors as the light passes, and they disappear until tomorrow, "He is handsome, kind, funny, and boy, can he cook."

"I thought you don't like food."

Chemistry is exasperated, "I never said I didn't like food! Why does everyone keep saying that? We don't need food here."

"Welp, back to work then." Inspiration starts to walk, then calls to Chemistry, "You coming?"

Chemistry watches Inspiration walk away, the words of their conversation still echoing in her mind. She exhales slowly, her heart heavy with the weight of their exchange. Maybe she's right. The thought settles in but feels uncomfortable, like a puzzle piece that doesn't quite fit.

Chemistry paces, her mind spinning with everything that was said. She pauses by the window, her eyes scanning the enchanted landscape. She presses a hand to the cool glass, feeling the heaviness of her decisions press down on her. What am I doing? The question lingers in her mind, but she doesn't have an answer. Not yet. With one last look, she turns away from the window and walks back toward the lab. There's work to do, but she'll return to this later.

Chemistry – *Jessica Sitomer*

Chapter 22

Matt's clock flashes to 8:47 a.m. Alexa announces, "Your 15-minute timer is done. Do you want me to extend it—"

"Alexa off!" Matt commands, sits up, settles himself, and disappears into the bathroom. As the shower water is turned on, Lola goes to his closet, takes out a right shoe, and walks to Matt's chair, where his suit is set out for the day. On the floor is the matching left shoe. She drops it as the water in the shower stops. Matt comes out of the bathroom with his towel wrapped around him and grabs the suit.

Lola sits by the front door and shoots up when she sees Matt dressed and walking toward her.

"Give Daddy a kiss." He bends down so she can give him a sloppy kiss, unlocks the door, and opens it. To his surprise, Chemistry stands there with coffee and a croissant. For a moment, the world

Chemistry – *Jessica Sitomer*

outside Matt's door falls away. It is just the two of them standing there, eyes locked. Chemistry feels her heart skip, a sudden flood of emotions overwhelming her. This is the moment she has feared and hoped for in equal measure.

Matt stands in the doorway, frozen for a moment. Chemistry stands there, looking as out of place as she did the first time they met, yet... she belongs. Here. With him. A thousand questions race through his mind—why is she back? Is this real? He blinks, trying to make sense of it, his heart racing. He opens his mouth, but no words come. Chemistry shifts awkwardly, offering a hesitant smile as she holds the coffee.

She breaks the silence, "I guess I can't sneak in anymore."

Matt doesn't speak, but his gaze softens, silent questions erupting in his mind. Did she really come back? Is she here for me? And in that brief pause, neither of them move, unsure how to begin again.

Chemistry speaks out of nervousness, "Because, normally, I let myself in, but you got the door fixed." She waits for another moment, but Matt still can't speak. "Frog in your throat?" she hopes.

Suddenly, an excited Lola barrels right into Chemistry, who spills her coffee.

Chemistry – *Jessica Sitomer*

"Ouch!" she shouts as it burns her arm and jumps, causing her to slip on the coffee pooled on the floor and fall right into Matt's arms in a perfect movie star dip. She still has the croissant and the remainder of the coffee in her hands. She examines the burn on her arm with wonder.

Matt smiles, his voice soft as he says, "You're always falling at my feet." But this time, there was something more in his eyes, a tenderness she hadn't seen before. The warmth of his body against hers feels like coming home, and for a moment, the world narrows to just the two of them.

"And you always catch me," she whispers, her voice barely audible, but it carries the weight of everything she's been holding back. There's a quiet pause as their eyes meet, and in that moment. Matt's gaze softens, his thumb brushing gently against her cheek, wiping away the tear she didn't even realize had fallen. This is real. She can feel it, and she lets herself believe it for the first time.

In the lab, everyone is working as usual, so when Mother Nature comes in, it creates quite a stir.

Chemistry – *Jessica Sitomer*

She walks straight to Inspiration and asks, "How was your first assignment?"

"Perfectly orchestrated." Inspiration replies as she drops a BLUE SOULMATE FILE on a lab table. It reads ANA DE GOURNAY. "Poof!"

Mother Nature hands her a box with a bow. Inspiration tears into it. She pulls out a new lab coat with the name Chemistry on the pocket. Inspiration tries it on. It's a perfect fit.

The team cheers for her until Humor interrupts, "Am I going to get any credit for the banana peel?"

"You all get credit for a job well done," Mother Nature announces, "But you all know how much she did around here."

Knowledge does some quick math, "This could back us up for the next twenty years!"

"Or..." Mother Nature leads them. They all look at each other, wanting to be the one with the correct answer, but even Knowledge is stumped. "You have someone on the ground now who knows how this works. She can still be an asset."

"Hold on," Inspiration interrupts, "She gave all this up, but she still remembers everything?"

"Of course she does," Mother Nature explains, "She still needs all of her past lessons to make this work with Matt."

Chemistry – *Jessica Sitomer*

"Suddenly, this got insanely complicated," Inspiration says.

"Nonsense!" Confidence cheers, "We got this!"

Besides Inspiration, the team instinctively knows what to do as they go to their stations and make their lists.

Matt lifts Chemistry from their movie star dip. She reaches for his face and kisses him again. Reluctantly pulling himself away, he says, "I would love to do this all day, but I've got to get to work."

Chemistry looks disappointed as he's off to work again. He notes her expression and adds, "It'll be different this time. I promise. I have so much to tell you. Will you stay here with Lola until I get back?" Chemistry nods in agreement. "Thank you. There's a spare key in the drawer next to the fridge in case you want to go out." He kisses her again and leaves. Halfway down the hallway, he stops and asks, "What's your phone number?"

Chemistry's mind goes blank.

"I'll get it later," Matt assures her, "Not letting you slip away again."

Now what? She wonders. She sits on the couch and looks at her hands, examining her fingers. I don't feel any different. Not sure what I expected.

Chemistry – *Jessica Sitomer*

She looks at Lola, "How do I get a phone number?" Uncertainty creeps in. She takes a deep breath and suggests to Lola, "Walk?" Lola chases her tail in excitement and runs to fetch her leash. Chemistry walks to the drawer to retrieve the key. Opening it, she sees the Polaroid photo Humor had taken of them at Six Flags. She breathes deeply again, a calm washing over her.

Central Park looks clean and glorious, which is a vast difference from how Chemistry left it. As she and Lola walk, she hears a familiar voice.

"What made you give it all up?"

She turns to see Inspiration sitting on a bench, her Gucci sneakers dangling in the air just short of reaching the ground.

"I see Style is having her way with you," Chemistry smiles at the sneakers, then joins Inspiration on the bench. Inspiration pats Lola on the head as the dog sniffs the young girl and settles on the ground.

Chemistry considers Inspiration's question. "Up there, I don't get experiences. Everything is certain. There's no fear, no love, no joy—"

"Tell that to Confidence..." They both laugh.

Chemistry corrects her, "Ahh, you see, that's all it is- confidence. She's not joyful. Everyone has their job with the guarantee of an eternity with purpose but no pain."

"But you were so afraid of the pain," Inspiration insists.

"Yeah, but pain is part of the experiences. For over 400 years, I felt nothing until I thought I would be fired. That was my only moment of uncertainty, so I came down here to protect that certainty, and I was failing at every turn. It was frustrating and scary and maddening and so sweet and loving and happy... which was all part of your plan. He's my soulmate, right?"

"Can't tell you that," Inspiration zips her lips.

"But he is," Chemistry insists.

"Can't say."

Chemistry, feeling a bit uneasy, "I mean, I didn't give it all up to be hit by a bus tomorrow, right?"

Inspiration changes the subject, "If we don't feel things up there, then why do I feel so fulfilled by you?"

Chemistry – *Jessica Sitomer*

"Because you're down here... watch out, there may be a blue file up there right now with your name on it. Because there was a blue file with mine, right?"

"I'm proud of you," Inspiration grins.

They sit quietly for a moment.

"That would sound so much more meaningful if you weren't 12."

"I'm an old soul," Inspiration says.

Chemistry laughs, "That's why you were chosen."

Now it's Inspiration's turn to be confused, "I thought I was chosen-"

"To be Chemistry," Chemistry interrupts, "They promoted you, right?"

Inspiration smiles.

"I figured," Chemistry says, "I started as Inspiration, too." Inspiration's eyes widen at the new information. "Of course, I had a lot more time with my predecessor. You'll need my help for as long as I'm alive-- the biggest problem is Lust."

Inspiration retorts, "I think the biggest problem is that a staff who respects you is feeling a little lost and uncertain despite being 'up there,' so, yes, I will need your help. We all will."

"Hmmm, you need me," Chemistry's wheels are turning.

"Yes," Inspiration confirms.

"That's good because I need your help, too. I don't have clothes, money, or a phone number!" Inspiration hands her the Prada tote bag. Chemistry beams with excitement. "No! The magic bag?"

"It's not magic. No more pulling out huge sums of money. You will find photos of your entire life and family history there." Chemistry reaches in, but Inspiration slaps her hand away and continues, "Some starter money, a phone, and an idea for a business."

"A business?" Chemistry asks.

"To make money... and to help us." Inspiration hands Chemistry a thick manilla envelope. "You are officially Chemmie now. Chemmie Yanruoged."

"Yan, what now?" Chemmie asks.

"Humor thought it would be funny if your last name were your actual last name spelled backward. We only agreed because we knew it wouldn't be long until it changes to Durand."

Chemmie reaches into the envelope and pulls out a birth certificate, social security number, doctor reports, voting records, and photos spanning the life of a thirty-something.

"How did you?" Chemmie asks with a confused expression

"You think AI technology is good down here? You should see what the tech department has planned for the future," Inspiration explains.

"So, this is me?" Chemmie says, looking at a photo of her with her actual parents in modern-day clothes.

"Yup! There are three notebooks filled with your life story and current circumstances.

"Wow," Chemmie whispers, reading through one of the notebooks, "This is so detailed."

"Everybody put their contributions in. Lust's had to be toned down, and my firsthand experience in the modern world takes up the bulk of it." Chemmie pulls out the latest iPhone. "Knowledge apologizes that he couldn't give you back the 'cool one,' but your phone number is here." Inspiration shows her where to find her number. Off Chemmie's baffled expression, she says, "There's a place called the Apple Store. Go there and ask to speak to a Genius."

Chemistry marvels at everything her staff has put together for her. "How can I ever thank you?" Chemmie asks.

Chemistry – *Jessica Sitomer*

"I'm glad you asked," Inspiration says, pulling a file out of the bag.

Chemmie looks through the file and stops on a logo for an edible essential oils company. "What's this?"

Inspiration smiles and notices the park is becoming more active, with people on their morning runs and setting up for breakfast picnics. "Read it. Everything will make sense. I've gotta go," Inspiration says. And you know it's too risky for me to come back, so read up, and the rest of the team will be down when we need you." She hugs Chemistry, pulls the hood from her sweatshirt over her head, and walks away.

Chemmie walks into the brownstone with Lola when she hears, "What?! How?! I must be seeing things!"

Lola runs toward Misty, and Chemmie runs right behind her, allowing Misty to embrace her in a bear hug. Misty pulls back to look her over and calls into her apartment, "Eli! Get out here. You're not going to believe who's back!"

Chemistry – *Jessica Sitomer*

"Eli's here?" Chemmie asks.

"He moved in a few months ago," Misty says with glee, then her expression changes, "But don't worry, I've got a cot that I think you will find very familiar. Now, get in here. You've got a lot of explaining to do." As she pushes Chemmie into the apartment, she asks, "First, are you a Princess?"

Eli, Misty, Chemmie, and Matt feast on pizza at dinner. Matt jokes to Chemmie, "Do you still have your food coloring?"

"I have something better." Chemmie pulls out three small bottles and places a green, blue, and orange drop on the side of Matt's plate. "Taste," she encourages him.

Matt looks at the bottles suspiciously, then dips his pinky into the green drop and brings it to his tongue. "Rosemary," he says. Chemmie nods. He tastes the blue. "Blueberry," he nods as if blatant, then before tasting the orange drop, he says, "Let me guess, "Orange." His eyes widen as he tries the flavor, "Wow, saffron."

"I've started a business," Chemmie shares, "Edible essential oils. They can be added to drinks and food. I'll start in the US, but eventually, I'll ship them worldwide."

Chemistry – *Jessica Sitomer*

Matt cautiously asks, "What makes them different from all the other brands?"

Chemmie reaches into her bag and pulls out three brochures, handing one to each. They read: Introducing our new line of Edible Essential Oils—crafted for people who care about their health and the planet! Our oils are all-natural, GMO-free, and made with a commitment to sustainability. Whether you're enhancing a dish or seeking the wellness benefits of essential oils, you can trust that every drop is pure, clean, and eco-friendly. Enjoy flavors that nourish both body and soul while making choices that are good for the environment. You don't have to compromise with these oils—taste and wellness come naturally!

Matt looks worried, "I'm happy for you, truly, and don't want to discourage you, but this doesn't scream 'unique.'"

"Oh, they are," Chemmie smiles. "I have exclusive access to an exceptional group of scientists who developed these just for me." The three of them look at her with concern. She responds with a laugh, "Don't worry. It's been a fun project for me, and I have nothing to lose, but I'm pretty confident it will be exactly what this world needs."

Chemistry – *Jessica Sitomer*

"Well then, I support you!" Misty cheers.

Eli agrees, "We all do! Right Matt?"

Matt treads carefully, "I support you. I'll even have my team run some tests, and if they approve—"

Chemmie cuts him off, "I can use them in the drinks?"

Matt's face lights up, "Are you offering to bartend?"

"I would be thrilled to," Chemmie says and kisses him.

The dogs crowd around them, playing and fighting over toys. Misty throws Lola a piece of carrot from her veggie pizza.

Chapter 23

Police manage an enormous crowd that lines the street outside the ghost restaurant that has become the buzz of Manhattan. Reporters stand in a roped-off area right in front of the door. Cameras start flashing, and microphones shove forward as the door opens. Eli walks out with two vegetable baskets filled with heart-shaped cookie puffs with paper sticking out. The reporters groan with disappointment at his lack of recognition. As he begins handing out the cookies, the three Chefs from Chef's Delight also walk out with baskets of cookies. The reporters go crazy snapping photos and calling out questions. The Chef's Delight host walks out with a microphone and steps up to a podium, causing more media and crowd frenzy.

"Great day, everyone! I'm Tatum Ahloof from Chef's Delight." The crowd goes wild. "Today, rather than a beautiful poem, the paper in your cookie has the restaurant's name on it." As murmurs come from the crowd, Tatum pulls the brown paper off the restaurant's glass window, revealing its name: Chemistry.

"Who thinks they guessed the Chef?" she asks. "Anyone getting free meals for life?" The crowd goes wild.

Then they start chanting, "Joshua! Joshua! Joshua!"

Tatum uses the mic to quiet everyone down. Then she says, "Okay, okay, let's see if you are right. Please allow me to introduce the Chef of Chemistry, Chef Matt Durand."

Matt walks out of the door, and there's confusion in the crowd as he waves, thanks Tatum, and takes the mic. "Thank you for all your support over the last year. This restaurant has been a labor of love and redemption. I know you are going to love the food--"

A reporter cuts him off, "Matt, weren't you a business partner at Bacchus?"

"Among other things," Matt answers, only to be thwarted by other questions.

"Matt, how come your food tastes exactly like Joshua's?" The crowd roars with anger. Matt is forced to yell into the microphone as Chemmie walks out of the restaurant and squeezes his hand.

Chemistry – *Jessica Sitomer*

Matt continues, "It doesn't taste anything like Joshua's. It tastes exactly like mine." More reporters yell questions as the crowd boos and jeers. Chemmie takes the mic.

"Perhaps the question you should ask is, what does Joshua's food taste like? Everything at his restaurant is someone else's dish. Really, the only people who know what his food tastes like are these three world-renowned Chefs."

The three Chefs from the reality show step onto the podium and get bombarded with questions. Matt and Chemmie slip back into the restaurant. She starts to kiss him and slips off his suit jacket.

"What are you doing?" Matt laughs.

"It'll be at least another 30 minutes until they've made sense of all this and are ready to meet "The Chef," so what do you say we christen the place."

"I say I want to keep my A rating," he kisses her back as he pulls his suit jacket back on.

Suddenly, they hear chanting from outside, "Matt! Matt! Matt! Matt!"

"Seems they're even quicker than we gave them credit for," Matt says, taking her hand.

"No," she pulls back. Go take your moment." He smiles at her and then exits the door to roaring cheers.

Chemistry – *Jessica Sitomer*

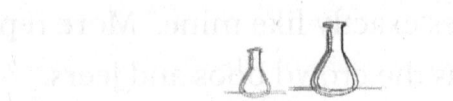

The restaurant is filled, and everything about it is perfect. Chemmie is twirling colorful drinks at the bar. Clapping is heard as Matt walks out of the kitchen to greet his guests. He holds two plates of vegan grilled cheese and curly fries in his hand. He walks through the tables and places them before Mr. and Mrs. Topel.

"Is the place always this packed, Matt?" Mr. Topel asks.

"Well, it is Saturday night," Matt laughs.

There's a scuffle at the hostess stand when Chemmie sees Joshua arguing with the hostess. She leaves the bar to assist.

The hostess looks frazzled, "Chemmie, I told him we're completely booked."

"She's right, Josh," Chemmie enunciates his name as the press no longer refers to him as Joshua. "For the next year."

"You are poison," Josh seethes.

"You should go," Chemmie insists, "Besides your embarrassment, we wouldn't want to tarnish our

Matt continues, "It doesn't taste anything like Joshua's. It tastes exactly like mine." More reporters yell questions as the crowd boos and jeers. Chemmie takes the mic.

"Perhaps the question you should ask is, what does Joshua's food taste like? Everything at his restaurant is someone else's dish. Really, the only people who know what his food tastes like are these three world-renowned Chefs."

The three Chefs from the reality show step onto the podium and get bombarded with questions. Matt and Chemmie slip back into the restaurant. She starts to kiss him and slips off his suit jacket.

"What are you doing?" Matt laughs.

"It'll be at least another 30 minutes until they've made sense of all this and are ready to meet "The Chef," so what do you say we christen the place."

"I say I want to keep my A rating," he kisses her back as he pulls his suit jacket back on.

Suddenly, they hear chanting from outside, "Matt! Matt! Matt! Matt!"

"Seems they're even quicker than we gave them credit for," Matt says, taking her hand.

"No," she pulls back. Go take your moment." He smiles at her and then exits the door to roaring cheers.

Chemistry – *Jessica Sitomer*

The restaurant is filled, and everything about it is perfect. Chemmie is twirling colorful drinks at the bar. Clapping is heard as Matt walks out of the kitchen to greet his guests. He holds two plates of vegan grilled cheese and curly fries in his hand. He walks through the tables and places them before Mr. and Mrs. Topel.

"Is the place always this packed, Matt?" Mr. Topel asks.

"Well, it is Saturday night," Matt laughs.

There's a scuffle at the hostess stand when Chemmie sees Joshua arguing with the hostess. She leaves the bar to assist.

The hostess looks frazzled, "Chemmie, I told him we're completely booked."

"She's right, Josh," Chemmie enunciates his name as the press no longer refers to him as Joshua. "For the next year."

"You are poison," Josh seethes.

"You should go," Chemmie insists, "Besides your embarrassment, we wouldn't want to tarnish our stellar reputation with you as a guest. What if the Michelin people show up?"

"Like he'd ever get a star," Josh huffs.

"He doesn't want a star, never did. Just wants people to love his food." She turns and beams when she sees Matt chatting with the Topels. "And they do, and they love him too," she says, turning back, only to find the hostess relieved that Josh has left. As Chemmie returns to work, a caped couture-dressed woman speaks to the hostess, who points her to the bar.

When she sits down, she crosses her legs, revealing the red bottoms of her shoes. Chemmie spots her, smiles, and rushes over.

"Well," Chemmie says, "I haven't seen you since Eternity."

"If you miss me so much, you know where to find me," Style challenges.

"These days, I can't afford the free perfume spritz in a department store."

Unamused, Style places a file onto the bar and an oil on top. Chemmie does a quick inspection.

"Eww!" Chemmie winces, reading the label, "What did this guy do to you? I hope he likes Tequila. I have to drown this flavor."

"Can you help me or not?"

Chemistry – *Jessica Sitomer*

"Of course, I can help you. What's the urgency?" Chemmie asks, looking at the file and the photo. When she looks up at Style, out of the corner of her eye, her attention is drawn to a man, causing every woman's head to turn. "Oh, I see. No wonder you came down personally. He's wearing Tom Ford."

Style's eyes roll into her head, "Stop! You wouldn't know Tom Ford from Duke Cincinnati," she reprimands as she cautiously turns to check him out. Her head snaps back in confusion. "Girl! He is wearing Tom Ford!"

"You taught me well," Chemmie says as Style hides her face as he approaches, her brow tensed. Chemmie doesn't understand, "You look disappointed."

Style says, "I was expecting a Men's Wearhouse at best." She skims over the file again, "Maybe only three drops."

"Maybe half a drop," Chemmie teases.

"Three! I have to go." Style barely misses the man as she bolts out of the restaurant.

Matt joins Chemmie behind the bar and signals her to follow him into the kitchen. He is giddy.

"What's up?" she asks.

"We did it!"

Chemistry – *Jessica Sitomer*

"I know, you've been saying that every night since we opened." She kisses him and turns to go back out. He grabs her hand and twirls her back to him.

"I know, but I will never take this or you for granted. I want to be grateful every day." He kisses her.

"Okay," she pulls away. We are closed tomorrow. We can be grateful all morning and all afternoon." She tries to walk again, but he pulls her back.

"What about all night?" he jokes.

"We need time to rest for Monday," she jokes back.

"Fine, as long as we can do the helicopter thing again."

"Shhhhhh!" she warns with a smile.

Humor and Lust are watching through the cracked door in the back alley. "And she doesn't want me in here," Lust complains, "I taught her everything she knows."

"But did you teach her to pull a quarter out of your ear?" Humor says as he pulls a quarter out of Lust's ear. Lust swats him as he watches Chemmie and Matt kiss with a proud smile.

Chemistry – *Jessica Sitomer*

"I sincerely have no clue how you got this job," Lust tells Humor. They both sigh with smiles as Chemmie and Matt continue to kiss.

Chapter 24

Young Chemistry overlooks her team of scientists who drop her department's mixtures into contraptions that squeeze them into oil that drips into small glass bottles. The glass bottles are given to a new team in the department wearing familiar brown uniforms. The new squad forms an assembly line for packaging and labeling each oil bottle. The packages are put into a bigger box and addressed to Chemmie Durand, then dropped down a new delivery chute.

On the other side of the lab, Lust puts the finishing touch on his formula and drops a tiny peacock feather into a jar. A scientist comes over to collect it, but Lust shields it like a child in danger.

"Move on," he orders the scientist, "I'm doing this the old-fashioned way." Lust puts the jar in his lab coat pocket and heads to the massive elevator, pressing the up button.

Chemistry – *Jessica Sitomer*

The thump of files falling from the chute catches Young Chemistry's attention. A slight crinkle on her forehead appears as she walks toward them and picks up her pace. Confidence, always the first to the files, beats her there and greets her with a pained expression and a red file in hand. A hush fills the air as Young Chemistry reads it.

"Style... you have a problem."

About the Author

Jessica started as a screenwriter in the Romantic Comedy world, so she's basically spent years crafting swoon-worthy moments and awkward meet-cutes. She's also the author of three Amazon best-selling business books (Make Shift Happen, You Got This!, and Retreat Riches), proving she can do more than just write about love—she can help you boss up, too. Now, she's

Chemistry – *Jessica Sitomer*

thrilled to bring her rom-com magic to the world of fiction with Chemistry, adapted from her own screenplay. When she's not writing, you'll find her adventuring—whether it's hiking, kayaking, or wrangling her Australian Labradoodle. Single at the publishing of this book, but open to Chemistry doing her magic…

Chemistry – *Jessica Sitomer*

Book club discussion questions for Chemistry

Chemistry's Journey: How does Chemistry's emotional growth evolve throughout the novel? How does her struggle with vulnerability impact her decisions, especially in her relationship with Matt?

Matt's Role: Matt is often reactive rather than proactive in the story. How does this affect his role as a co-lead? What do you think of his progression by the end of the novel?

The Role of Humor: The book balances humor with more profound emotional moments. Do you think the humor enhances or detracts from the emotional weight of the story?

Mother Nature's Influence: How does Mother Nature's character influence Chemistry's decisions, especially as she grapples with her mission and feelings for Matt? Does Mother Nature serve as a mentor, antagonist, or something else?

Themes of Love and Time: Chemistry has had centuries to reflect on love, yet finds herself conflicted when faced with her feelings for Matt. How does the

Chemistry – *Jessica Sitomer*

theme of time impact the story and Chemistry's perception of love and relationships?

Matt's Kitchen Confrontation: The dynamic between Matt and Joshua in the kitchen is a pivotal part of the story. How does this confrontation reflect Matt's internal struggle between love and ambition? Do you agree with how Matt handled the situation?

Chemistry's Mission: Throughout the novel, Chemistry guides Matt to a deeper understanding of himself. Do you think Chemistry ultimately fulfills her mission? What does her final decision say about her character?

The Importance of Secondary Characters: Inspiration, Lust, and Eli add unique flavors to the story. How do these characters contribute to the overall themes of the novel? Could the story work without them, or do they serve a greater purpose?

The Balance Between Destiny and Choice: The novel plays with the idea of destiny—Chemistry is supposed to guide Matt, but both face many choices. Do you believe in the concept of destiny as it's portrayed in the novel, or do the characters have more control over their fates?

The Ending: Without revealing too much, how did you feel about the final resolution of the novel?

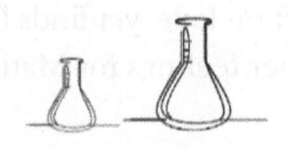